Prior to taking the decision to write full time, Sheila O'Flanagan pursued a very successful career in banking, becoming Ireland's first woman Chief Dealer. She writes a weekly column for the *Irish Times* and in her spare time plays badminton at competition level.

0130272 155

Destinations

Sheila O'Flanagan

headline

'Charlie's Dress' was first published in *Woman's Day*,
Australia in January 2003.
'A Good Sense of Humour' was first published in the
Sunday Express in May 2002.

First published in Great Britain in 2003 by
HEADLINE BOOK PUBLISHING

10 9 8 7 6 5 4 3 2 1

ISBN 0 7553 0761 5

Typeset in Galliard by Palimpsest Book Production Limited,
Polmont, Stirlingshire
Printed and bound in Great Britain by
Clays Ltd, St Ives plc

HEADLINE BOOK PUBLISHING
A division of Hodder Headline
338 Euston Road
London NW1 3BH

www.headline.co.uk
www.hodderheadline.com

Acknowledgements

Thanks to everyone at Hodder Headline Ireland:

Breda Purdue, who made me do it
Ciara Considine for her conscientious editing
Ruth Shern and Heidi Murphy for everything else

And, as always, to my family, who keep on supporting me!

Author's Note

From the moment the Dart system became part of Dublin I dreamed about writing a collection of short stories centred around it. In my imagination there were so many different tales to tell – and I wanted to be the person who brought those fictional stories to life. It's taken a long time but I do hope I've succeeded and that you enjoy reading them, no matter where you are.

Contents

SATURDAY AT TWELVE

KILLINEY

He sold the car because it was an unnecessary expense. He'd thought about getting rid of it before but knew it wouldn't look good. People in his position always had cars no matter how ridiculous the traffic was or how much longer it took them to get to work. But getting to work wasn't a problem now that he was living in a basement flat which was only a ten-minute walk away. There was, he thought, a lot to be said for the concept of living within walking distance of the office instead of having to endure the early morning commute through south Dublin traffic, guiltily listening to 98FM when he felt he should really be listening to the business news on Radio 4.

The only difficulty in being without the car was days like today. He was hoping that there wouldn't be too many days like today, that things could get sorted out and that eventually everything would be back to normal, but right now it was all a bit of a strain. He walked along the carriage to the doors so that he would be ready to get off the Dart as soon as it pulled into Killiney station. Until a few months ago he'd only known that the station existed; he'd never even dreamed of getting the Dart anywhere. Now he was getting used to it although the variety of people who got on it never ceased to amaze him. Previously he would have considered them losers. He'd have thought of them as people lower down the pecking order than him: office dogsbodies, temps, PAs, people who had to get the train because they didn't have decent cars. He hadn't realised that Dublin had changed so that more and more men like himself – men dressed in tailored suits, wearing shirts with cufflinks and carrying briefcases – actually used the train. Maybe they were more like him than he thought. He smiled wryly at the idea. They weren't on the train today, of course, since it was Saturday. Presumably they were at home in their five-bedroomed houses with family rooms, big kitchens and conservatories. Five-bedroomed houses like his.

The house was exactly a mile away from the station. He didn't mind the walk, not on a day like today, with the sun shining from a clear blue sky and the gentle south-westerly breeze which rustled through the trees and sent the occasional early-autumn leaves skidding along the pavement.

They'd chosen their home with care. It was a modern house in a prosperous suburb; a small development off the main road so that it was safe for children. Located close to

2

the school and not too far from a small row of shops – although, as he often said to Helena afterwards, what difference did being near the local shops make when she bought everything in an incredibly expensive Friday afternoon foray into the supermarket? Handy for essentials, she'd replied. Milk or the papers or anything like that. But as far as he knew she never went to the local shops, instead she drove to Dún Laoghaire or Blackrock and loaded up her 4x4 with enough groceries to keep them going for months. She did this every week. On the same trip she usually got her hair done – sometimes just washed and blow-dried, other days trimmed and, once a month, highlighted, refreshing the golden glints that softened her natural fairness and added life to her shoulder-length locks.

He was always turned on after her visits to the hairdresser. He didn't know why. There were lots of other things about her that turned him on – her lithe figure which she kept in shape by a rigorous diet and three-times-a-week visits to the gym; her pouting lips which always made him want to kiss them; her habit of rubbing the base of her throat when she was worried – whenever she did this he would put his arms around her and rub her throat himself, his fingers then sliding very gently downwards to the swell of her breasts.

Even thinking about it turned him on. He stopped thinking about it and crossed the road.

The maroon and silver 4x4 was parked in the neatly

cobbled driveway. The midday sun reflected brightly off its freshly polished surface. She always kept it looking as though she'd just driven it from the showrooms. She was unlike many women, he realised, in not turning the interior of her vehicle into an extension of the house, filled with toys and tissues and discarded sweet wrappings. As far as Helena was concerned, the car was for getting around in. Not for bringing everything with them.

He rang the doorbell, heard the chime echo through the house and the sound of Helena's high heels tapping on the solid oak floor, which they'd had put down when they moved in.

She opened the door. 'You're early.'

'Nice to see you too,' he said. 'I'm five minutes early.'

'She's out the back.'

Helena's eyes were flint grey. There was no warmth in them, there hadn't been any warmth in them for the past four months. It bugged the hell out of him. She'd had a right to be angry but she didn't have any right to keep on being angry, to keep on punishing him for something that had been nothing more than a mistake. Everyone made mistakes. He was sure she'd made her fair share of them except, of course, nobody knew about them. She kept hers quiet. It had been different with him.

'Daddy!' A small blonde whirlwind burst into the room and dived into his arms. He picked up the little girl and held her close to him, taking in her powdery scent, the freshness

4

of her newly washed hair, the plumpness of her skin.

'How's my favourite girl?' he asked.

'Starving,' she told him seriously. 'Mum wouldn't allow me to have anything to eat. She said you were taking me to lunch.'

'I guess she was right,' he told her.

'There's a new burger place opened at the top of the main road,' Helena told him. 'I booked it for you because it's crazy on Saturdays. They have colouring sheets for the kids and that sort of thing. She's been begging me to go again since I took her there last month. I thought it would be convenient for you.'

He clenched his teeth and then smiled at her. 'Thank you.'

'Get your coat, Dana,' she told the little girl.

'I don't need a coat,' replied their daughter mutinously.

'You do,' said Helena. 'It's cold outside. Tell her, Greg.'

He looked at both of them. 'It's cold,' he said.

'Oh, OK.' Dana clambered down from his arms and went to get her coat.

His eyes flickered around the kitchen. 'New portable TV?'

'The other one blew up,' Helena told him curtly. 'It wasn't expensive.'

'No,' he said. 'Mine only cost about €200. Mind you, it's smaller than that.'

She said nothing but began to fold clothes from the big laundry basket in the corner of the room.

'It was a mistake,' he said into her silence. 'I told you it was a mistake.'

She continued to fold the clothes.

'For God's sake, Helena, can't you just accept that? For the sake of Dana?'

She turned to look at him, a bright pink T-shirt in her hands. 'Don't ever say that again,' she hissed. 'Don't try and make me feel bad about you because of our daughter. Just don't.'

'But—'

'We've been through it all, Greg. I don't want to go through it all again. And if you continue to harass me every time you call by then I'm going to ask them to stop you coming at all.'

'You are such a bitch.' His voice was low.

'I'm not,' she told him. 'I wasn't the one to fuck up our marriage.'

'It doesn't have to be like this,' he said. 'We can make it right again.'

'I never made it wrong,' she said fiercely. 'So it's got nothing to do with me.'

'I miss you,' he said. 'I really do.'

'I don't care,' said Helena.

Dana rushed back into the kitchen, the buttons on her coat done up the wrong way. Helena leaned down and re-buttoned it for her, then ruffled her hair and told her to be good.

'What's the place called?' asked Greg.

'Heavenly Hams.' Helena shrugged. 'Sounds awful, I know. But she'll love it.'

He walked hand-in-hand with his daughter who kept up a flow of chatter the whole time about the things that she'd done during the week: the friends that she'd made, the friends that weren't friends any more, the unfairness of her teacher for giving them ten new spellings to learn over the weekend. Hard spellings, Dana told him. Big words.

'What words?' he asked, and his heart contracted as she wrinkled up her nose in an exact replica of Helena when she was concentrating.

'Bump,' she told him. 'Frost. Head. Pant. Kitten. Sniff. Wizard.'

'Do you want to do them for me?' he asked.

She shook her head. 'I don't know them all yet. Except Wizard.'

He frowned. 'Isn't that a hard one?'

She grinned. 'I know it from Harry Potter, Daddy.'

'Of course,' he said. 'Good old Harry Potter.'

He remembered reading it to her, a chapter every night before bedtime. He'd thought it would frighten her and sometimes she pulled the sheet up over her nose as she squirmed uneasily beneath the covers, but she always made him go on and she never minded going to sleep afterwards.

'Bad magic can't happen here,' she told him confidently. 'It's only in other places.'

They reached the restaurant – it was already crowded with children and tense-looking parents, a babel of noise and music and activity. He could feel a headache begin to take hold.

A waitress, dressed in bright red shorts and a yellow T-shirt and wearing roller skates, led them to their table. She gave Dana a sheet of colouring paper and a bowl full of crayons.

'What would you like to drink?' she asked.

'Do you serve beer?' asked Greg.

The waitress nodded.

'Beer for me,' he told her. 'What about you, Dana?'

'Coke,' said his daughter absently as she selected a blue crayon and began colouring.

'I'll be back for your food order.' The waitress skated in the direction of the kitchen.

'What do you want to eat?' he asked.

'I want the burger with the cheesy sauce and the spicy chips,' said Dana. 'I don't want any onion because I don't like it. And I want the burger well-done.'

He was glad that she knew what she wanted, astonished at her confidence. He was sure that as a child brought into any restaurant he would have been in agonies of indecision, wondering whether he was allowed to have what he really wanted, concerned that perhaps he was asking for the wrong thing.

He gave the order to the permanently smiling waitress, choosing a plain burger for himself. He looked around him again. Mostly families. Trying to keep their kids under some control but with varying degrees of success. Some mothers on their own dealing with small armies of children. He saw two other lone fathers. Their children were sitting at the table, like Dana, colouring furiously.

This wasn't the way it was supposed to be. This wasn't how things were meant to turn out. She blamed him for it all and he supposed that he had to take it but it wasn't fair. It really wasn't. Surely there was room for forgiveness somewhere? He watched the other father talk to his son and wondered if it was the same with him. If he'd had to leave the family home too? If he was spending most of his money on damn solicitors, knowing that he was still going to end up the wrong side of it? He wondered had the other father been as stupid as him. He wanted to ask but he knew that he wouldn't.

Their food arrived and Dana ate her way through the burger and chips. She was a slow, deliberate eater. He'd finished his long before her but even though her chips were now cold she continued to eat them, dipping each one into the bright-red tomato sauce before popping it into her mouth.

A few months ago he would have been on the golf course every Saturday. That was how he spent his Saturday mornings before the split. Himself, Jim Pallister, Noel O'Gorman and Mick Hogan had been an established fourball, teeing off at eight-thirty, getting back to the clubhouse in time for a steak sandwich and the start of the football. He'd get home mid-afternoon and beg Dana not to jump on him, that he was tired, and Helena would lift the little girl off his shoulders where she'd wrapped herself and tell her that Daddy would play with her later.

He was the one who'd fucked it all up. Helena was right about that. Only he hadn't meant to. It wasn't as though he'd intended to do what he'd done. It had been a mistake. He told her over and over again how sorry he was.

It was at the office Christmas party, of course. There was a free bar and everyone taking full advantage of it. In-house catering, good food, though more people were interested in the drink. He'd drunk far too much himself. He always did at the office Christmas parties. It was how he'd met Helena in the first place.

But at this party, eight years after he'd kissed Helena in the lift on the way to the ground floor, it was Kimberley he met. Kimberley from Accounts, twenty-two years old, raven-haired, blue-eyed – the hottest property in the company. He'd been flattered that she'd danced with him to the totally terrible play-list of DJ Ricky Rollinson (also from Accounts and usually known as Richard). He'd been stunned when she was the one to kiss him, a promising, probing kiss that had fired through him, making him pull her towards him, his hands sliding down her back. And she'd giggled then and said 'not here' and the next thing he knew they were in his office and he was having sex with her even though he'd never looked at another woman (well, looked, but that was all) since he'd married Helena.

It had been fast and frantic and absolutely fantastic.

Afterwards he'd felt guilty and he'd worried that Kimberley might have thought there was more to it, that he cared about her. And then he panicked a little bit because he wondered what would happen if she got pregnant.

He needn't have worried about any of those things. Kimberley wasn't interested in him and Kimberley couldn't be pregnant. What he should have worried about he hadn't known about – Liam O'Reilly and his digital camera. Greg and Kimberley had been putting on a show for half the office because he hadn't realised that the blinds on one of the glass walls had been open. Liam had spotted that and had taken their photo with the digital camera.

It wasn't the most compromising photo Liam could have taken. But it was bad enough. Liam had e-mailed it to a few of the blokes in the office, who hadn't wasted any time letting Greg know. The lads had had a good giggle and, after a few weeks, Greg had pushed it to the back of his mind, hoping that it was yesterday's joke.

Only someone (he didn't know who and not knowing was killing him) had printed a copy and sent it to Helena. Who, understandably, had gone ballistic. Who hadn't accepted his 'I was drunk and it didn't mean anything'

11

excuse. Who didn't want to believe him when he told her that it would never happen again. Who didn't understand that just because he'd had sex with a girl from the office at the Christmas party, it didn't mean that his marriage wasn't the most important thing in the world to him. Helena had told him to leave, he'd refused, there'd been under-their-breath screaming matches held when Dana was in bed asleep in which Helena had called him a traitorous, unfaithful bastard and where he'd pleaded with her to realise that the Kimberley thing was meaningless, nothing, and that she had, in fact, left the company a few weeks earlier.

Helena ranted that he didn't understand, that he couldn't go around having casual sex with women and expect her to put up with it. And he'd tried to explain that it was a once-off and that it had happened because of circumstances and it would never ever happen again.

She'd asked whether or not those circumstances could happen again – whether or not he could get drunk at a party and if so whether or not he'd regard any woman as fair game and he'd begged her to believe that he wouldn't. And then she'd said that she didn't trust him any more and she wanted him to leave.

He'd left, eventually, because he couldn't take it any more even though his own solicitor advised him to stay. Next thing he knew there were maintenance orders being slapped on him and vicious letters from her solicitor. He couldn't quite believe the fact that she wasn't going to forgive him, that she wanted to set out a schedule for him to visit Dana, and that suddenly he was a stranger in his own home. He was the one paying the mortgage, he was the one providing for them, but he was the one living in the basement flat ten minutes away from the office and he was the one without the car because he needed the money for his own legal expenses.

Everyone was on Helena's side. He was the bastard. He'd made the fatal mistake.

'I want to go now, Daddy.' Dana's words brought him out of his troubled thoughts.

'Sure.' He paid the bill and they left the restaurant, her hand tucked into his again.

'Mum says you're not coming home,' Dana told him as they walked down the road again.

'It's difficult,' he said.

'I said I wanted you to come home.'

'I'd like to be there,' said Greg. 'But I can't at the moment.'

'I don't like it that you're not.'

He wanted to cry when she said that. Helena didn't know how bad he felt. She was wallowing in her self-righteous indignation and her own hurt and he knew she'd a right to feel like that but, goddamn it, he was sorry, wasn't he? He knew it had been wrong. If he could change things he would. He hadn't wanted it to turn out like this.

Back at the house, Dana wrapped her arms around him and asked him not to go. He looked over her head at Helena's expressionless face.

'For her sake?' he mouthed. 'I love you.'

'Daddy's got to go now,' said Helena shortly as she prised Dana's fingers loose. 'He'll be back soon.'

'I want him to stay,' she wailed.

'Another time,' said Greg.

Helena shook her head.

'Can't you just . . .' he looked at her pleadingly as Dana ran upstairs.

'I know it's different for men,' said Helena. 'I know you don't think that it was such an awful thing. But to me it was. And I can't live with you any more.'

'But you can take my money,' he said harshly. 'You can stay in this house and you can have all the things that I work for.'

'You should've thought of that before you shagged the bitch,' hissed Helena.

'I love you,' he said. 'I always have and I always will.'

'But I don't love you,' said Helena simply. 'Not any more.'

He walked back to the Dart station and waited on the platform. The breeze was stronger now, skimming papers along the tracks. This wasn't how it should turn out, he thought despairingly as he watched the train approach.

This wasn't the life he thought he was going to lead. But somehow it had all gone wrong and now he was getting the train again, going home to somewhere that would never be home and leaving the things he cared about behind. Until next Saturday. At twelve.

CHARLIE'S DRESS

DALKEY

I'm not a fashion victim. I'm not even a fashion bystander. I can't tell my Dolce & Gabbana from my Prada or my Ralph Lauren from my Donna Karan. I don't know what their little designer signature touches are because I buy most of my clothes from high-street stores and once they look good I'm happy. I do have a vague notion of Versace, mind you, because of Liz Hurley and the safety pin dress. I remember seeing the pictures splashed all over the newspapers and I looked at Charlie and asked her what on earth all the fuss was about, the bloody dress was awful.

'It's a fashion statement,' said Charlie, who knows as much about fashion statements as Liz. She's been making them herself ever since the day she hitched her St Gabriel's navy-blue skirt up high on her waist and showed more thigh than the nuns ever intended them to show. Unlike me, Charlie knows her labels. She knows her make-up. She's good at that kind of thing.

I've known her ever since we met in our first year at St Gabriel's and despite a lot of things, we hit it off. Don't panic. This is not a story about a gorgeous-looking girl who hangs around with an ugly girl and tries to rob her kind, caring boyfriend. Unfortunately, I don't have a kind, caring boyfriend. But even if I had, Charlie wouldn't try to rob him. She is, and always will be, gorgeous. She's tall and slender and she has a certain style about her which I'll never have. But she's never tried to rob any of my boyfriends. Anyway, I'm not ugly! I'm OK, nothing spectacular – although when I'm bothered to slap on the foundation I can look quite good. But most of the time I don't worry about make-up, I'm just not into all that sort of stuff.

The reason Charlie and I have been friends for so long is that we both share similar tastes – books, music and creating things. With Charlie, naturally, it's clothes. With me it's ad campaigns. I regret to say that I work in that whole advertising, media, PR world. Everyone thinks it's nothing but parties and drinks and glamorous nights out and, of course, it can be. But I try not to bother because, in truth, I hate that part of it. I like coming up with the ideas and the slogans and I like making the pitch. But I don't like the palaver that goes on afterwards where everyone pops bottles of champagne and congratulates themselves on another breakthrough ad for cornflakes. I prefer nights in with a glass of wine and a book because – well, meeting people is so damn difficult, isn't it? And I meet them when they're at their worst – usually having had a few drinks, always trying to impress and cracking very unfunny jokes. And that's just the women. I've never, ever met an interesting guy at one of these parties. Not the sort of guy I'd want to go out with at any rate.

Charlie has lots of boyfriends because she can't help but attract men and sometimes we double date, which is a bit of a laugh. But she hasn't found anyone serious yet and she's not rushing. The drawback to working in fashion, of course, is that she meets lots and lots of absolutely wonderful men, all of whom are gay. I thought it was a cliché to think that gay men populated the fashion world, but – at least in Charlie's world – it's not.

So neither of us really have the opportunities that you'd expect to meet men, which means that both of us spend more time in the house that we share than two single girls aged twenty-eight should.

And just in case you think you've got to grips with us, this is not a story about two lesbian girls denying their sexuality. We're not lesbians. Charlie has been called by her abbreviated name ever since she was a child and I don't know why they christened her Charlotte at all. So it's not some girl-wanting-to-be-a-man thing with her. And my name's Kirsty which, as far as I know, doesn't have any lesbian connotations and, if it has, they've passed me by.

No, this story is about the night I had to go to a glamorous and glitzy PR event and didn't have a thing to wear.

Mostly I manage to avoid the PR events and, because everyone else loves them (or pretends to, we're talking about the whole marketing thing after all) it doesn't usually matter that I don't show up. But I was warned to come to this because it was for one of our biggest clients and the whole firm was going to the latest must-be-seen-in restaurant for drinks and dinner.

I stood in front of my wardrobe and looked at the meagre selection of clothes dangling limply from the hangers and wondered why it was that everything I possessed was either cream or sludge green, or blue jeans. I had plenty of clothes for a night in the pub, but not for must-be-seen-in restaurants where what you wear is much more important than what you eat.

'What's the occasion?' Charlie asked as she lay sprawled across my bed.

'PR dinner for a new watch promotion,' I said gloomily.

'What about your cream knit?' she suggested. 'That's nice and safe.'

'This.' I held the dress out to her. I'd worn it the last time I'd been dragged out to dinner. It still had a splash of tomato sauce on the front.

'Oh, Kirsty, you're such a slob,' wailed Charlie. 'How could you just shove that back in your wardrobe like that.'

'Sorry,' I said.

'Do you have to get dressed up?' she asked.

'Des told me that he'd fire me if I turned up in jeans,' I told her. 'And he probably would.'

'I thought you had a few dresses that you kept for special occasions.' Charlie frowned. 'What about the red one I made for you?'

'I split it,' I told her. 'I was going through my fat phase at the time, remember?'

'You are useless!' She got up and rummaged through my wardrobe. I thought that she'd pick out something and mutter about accessories and the like and would be able to turn me into someone lovely by carefully draping a scarf around my neck. But she didn't.

'You're right,' she said. 'You have nothing to wear! You need to clear out this junk, Kirsty, and buy a whole new wardrobe. Look at this!' She held up a short black leather skirt. 'The last time you wore this you were about twenty!'

'It's leather,' I said. 'I didn't like to throw it out.'

She sat on the end of my bed and scratched her head. 'Do you want to be experimental?'

'No,' I said firmly.

'Not radically experimental,' she reassured me. 'Just – different.'

'How different?'

'I've been working on a sexy little number . . .' She eyed me speculatively. 'You're way too fat for it in its creative incarnation, of course, because obviously you should be a size six to wear my clothes. But I could do a bit of rejigging . . .'

'For God's sake, Charlie, I have to be in the restaurant in an hour,' I said. 'I can't hang around here for you to run up a dress for me.'

'Wait here,' she replied.

She can do this sort of thing. I don't know how. I can hardly thread a needle. Next thing I knew I was being pinned into a hanky.

'I am not going out in this,' I told her. 'It barely covers my bum.'

'But it doesn't look big in it,' she said innocently. 'Come on, Kirsty. You look fabulous.'

Actually, it didn't look bad at all. But there was so little of it. It was cut away at the neck and slit up the side and it was short to begin with . . . you get the drift. I began to wonder whether or not Charlie wasn't the sort of gorgeous friend who'd deliberately send you out looking terrible after all. But, as I said, I didn't look terrible. I looked kind of sexy.

'It's still too short,' I protested. 'And you can almost see my nipples.'

'If I was Westwood you *would* see your nipples,' Charlie told me. 'Nipples are in, didn't you know. Or out, I suppose, is the better way of looking at it.'

'Charlie, if my boobs pop out of this dress I'll kill you,' I told her.

'They won't,' she said. 'I promise. And you look great.'

I eyed myself in the full-length mirror. I still wasn't certain.

'Please.' Suddenly her voice was serious. 'I'm hoping that someone will spot that dress, ask you who designed it and come knocking at my door.'

'Really?'

She shrugged. 'I'm getting nowhere fast, Kirsty. I need to move on.'

What could I say? I wore the hanky to the PR event.

The new watch being launched was thin, stylish and very cutting-edge. There was a male and female version, both being worn by the celebs who were endorsing them and who were being paid mega-bucks for the privilege. I was standing close to the female celeb when the photos were being taken. I hoped someone got a good picture of Charlie's dress.

After a couple of hours of smiling until my cheeks were sore, I slipped outside. I shouldn't have, really, there was an icy wind whipping down the street and it was bloody freezing. The dress wasn't designed for keeping out the cold. A train slid into the nearby station and I looked at the passengers huddled into their heavy coats and woollen hats. I shivered and looked up as someone else walked out of the restaurant door.

It was the male celeb. He was tall, dark and impossibly handsome with a chiselled jawline. He looked great when he held his wrist up in a pose to show off the watch.

'Hello,' he said.

'Hi.'

'I've been looking for you,' he told me.

23

'Really?'

'Absolutely. I've never seen anyone like you in my life before.'

'I'm sure you have,' I said. I couldn't make up my mind about him. Was he really trying to chat me up?

'You have legs that belong to an angel,' he said. 'I've been watching them all night.'

Not difficult, I thought. Charlie's dress was designed to allow for plenty of leg-watching opportunities.

'Thanks.' I wasn't sure what I was supposed to say.

He came closer to me. He was reasonably drunk, not completely and utterly drunk (well, it would have been too depressing to be picked up by a totally pissed celeb), but the champagne had flowed pretty freely and he hadn't said no to any of it.

'I think I love you,' he said and lunged at me.

It was all over in a matter of seconds. I side-stepped. He grabbed me. I lurched. He pulled. The dress tore. My boob popped out. And then lots and lots of flashlights burst into action because the reporters had followed the celeb outside.

'I wish they'd got more of the dress.' Charlie looked at the photos in the tabloids. 'I mean, it's a great pic of your boobs, Kirsty, no question, but it would've been nice if they'd got the style of the dress.'

'By the time he'd finished there was no style to the

dress,' I told her. 'God, it was a nightmare.'

'Come on!' She grinned. 'It must be fun to have your face splashed all over the papers.'

'It's not my face!'

She laughed. 'I suppose not.'

My phone rang.

'No comment,' I said tersely. I couldn't believe that I was being phoned and door-stepped by journalists. Honestly, it was a non-story. Sort of. I unplugged the phone.

My mobile rang and I nearly jumped off the seat.

'You have to hand it to them,' said Charlie, 'they're persistent.'

'No bloody comment,' I said before the hack spoke. 'I've absolutely no comment.'

'That's fine,' he said. 'I don't want a comment. I just want to know if I can collect my jacket.'

'Sorry?'

'My jacket,' he said patiently. 'I gave it to you last night.'

'Oh, God. I forgot.'

He'd been very nice, whoever he was. When the hubbub had died down outside the restaurant he'd given me his jacket which I'd fastened over my topless form. I'd thanked him profusely and told him to call. My mobile number was on the card I'd given him.

'It's a little bit manic here at the moment,' I told him. 'D'you think you could wait until tomorrow?'

'I don't mind manic,' he said.

'I do. What do you look like?' I was suddenly suspicious. I couldn't actually remember what the bloke who'd given me his jacket looked like but I wouldn't have put it past one of the journalists to pretend to be him simply to get a photo of me. Or, as they really wanted, of my left boob again.

'Average,' he said.

'Do you really need this jacket tonight?' I asked.

'Nope,' he said. 'But I thought I'd strike while the iron was hot.'

'Strike what?'

'Look, you're bound to be feeling vulnerable and under pressure today,' he told me. 'So I thought it'd be a good opportunity to ask you out.'

'Are you mad?'

'Just a little.'

'Are you a journalist?'

'No!' He sounded horrified. 'I'm a photographer.'

'Well, piss off then!' I hit the 'end' button on the mobile and switched it off as Charlie dissolved into laughter.

Charlie's dress lay stretched on the bed. I shouldn't have worn it, I'd known it wasn't me. But it had done one of us a favour. A designer in the city had phoned Charlie on her mobile and asked her if it was her work. He'd recognised the style, he said. He thought they might be able to come to some arrangement.

'It'll probably be a disaster,' said Charlie. 'But I'm going to meet him anyway.' She grinned. 'You've done for me what Liz did for Versace after all!'

'You've done for me what Versace did for Liz,' I told her. 'That last call was from a newspaper wanting to know if I'd model topless for them.'

'You need to get an agent,' she told me. 'Milk it for all it's worth.'

'Whatever possessed that guy?' I asked. 'He's supposed to be going out with some blonde-haired, brown-limbed nymphet from Beverley Hills.'

'Couldn't resist your Celtic charms,' said Charlie. 'Or your left boob.'

By midnight I felt as though I could plug in the phone and switch my mobile back on again. It didn't ring straight away, but up popped 20 messages. One of them was from my boss. There was some question about my long-term future with the PR company. Why wasn't I surprised?

Ten of them were from the photographer who'd lent me his jacket.

'I don't want to take your photo for the paper,' he said. 'I just want my jacket back. Please call me.'

Who does he think he's kidding, I thought. It was bad enough that my mother had seen my picture and was now saying prayers to all the saints in heaven to preserve me from a variety of different sins.

The phone buzzed and I almost dropped it.

'Thank goodness you're finally answering it,' he said. 'I'm going demented here. I need my jacket.'

'Buy yourself another one,' I told him. 'Send me the bill.'

'I need that one,' he said urgently. 'I really do.'

'Why?'

'Because,' he said, 'there's a film in the pocket which has explosive pics of the celeb.'

'I rather think he's already been in some explosive pics,' I said.

'These are even better,' the photographer told me.

'Don't you think that he's been somewhat over-exposed?' I asked.

He laughed. 'Of course he has. But the papers are crying out for more. They're crying out for more of you too. Actually, they probably want more of you than they do of him. But when I sell these . . .'

'Are you bribing me?' I asked.

'Don't be silly,' he said.

I walked into my room and put my hand into the jacket pocket. There was a roll of film there.

'OK,' I said, although I wasn't sure about this. 'But if you dare take a photo of me my lesbian housemate will beat the crap out of you.'

'I beg your pardon?' Both he and Charlie spoke at the same time. 'You heard me,' I said as I made nonsensical gestures to Charlie and gave him our address.

'What was all that about?' she asked.

'The photographer who lent me the jacket.' I explained the situation to her.

'And the lesbian thing?'

'I thought it'd make me less interesting.'

'God almighty, Kirsty. And you work in PR?'

The photographer was rather good-looking in an old-fashioned kind of way. He didn't have a camera with him and so I let him into the house while I got the jacket.

'It's such a shame,' he said as I handed it to him.

'What?' I asked.

'That you're a lesbian.' He sighed. 'Such a waste.'

'She's not a lesbian,' said Charlie. 'Neither am I. She's just a particularly terrible PR person.'

'Why did she say she was a lesbian?' He looked at me. 'Why?'

'I didn't think you'd bother with photos if you thought I was a lesbian,' I told him. 'And I was right.'

'Don't be so sure about that.' He grinned and I thought that he was actually very good-looking. And not in quite as old-fashioned a way as I'd first decided. 'I could have a hidden camera sewn into my top button. Or in my glasses. Or just about anywhere.'

'And have you?' I asked in horror.

'No!' He looked at me. 'What do you take me for? The screen persona of the celeb?'

I giggled. 'Maybe not.' Then I handed him the jacket.

'Thanks for covering me up last night,' I said. 'And sorry I was a bit abrupt earlier.'

'That's OK,' he told me. Our eyes met. It was one of those things. We kept looking at each other.

'I have a confession to make,' he said.

'Oh, no!' I sighed. 'So where is the hidden camera?'

'No hidden camera, I promise. Just – no other photos of the celeb either.' He put his hand into his pocket and took out the roll of film. 'Not used,' he told me. I felt myself flush with embarrassment.

'Then why this mad rush to get the jacket?' I demanded.

'Don't be so thick,' said Charlie who was sprawled on the sofa. 'He fancies you, Kirsty.'

'Do you?' I asked.

'How could I not?' He looked at me helplessly. 'You're a stunning girl who clocked the celeb on the side of the jaw while he ripped off her dress. You've got legs to your armpits and a chest to die for. And you're smart too. I heard them talking about you. I wanted to ask you out before your encounter with Mr Hollywood but I didn't have the nerve. Afterwards, the jacket was the ideal ploy.'

'Are you serious?'

'Of course,' he said. 'I'm only here to try to date you.'

I looked at Charlie. She grinned at me. 'Kirsty, talk about killing hundreds of birds with the one stone! I get to meet a designer. You get fifteen minutes of fame. And a boyfriend.'

'And the sack,' I muttered.

'Surely not,' he said.

'Maybe,' I told him.

'Rubbish,' he said robustly. 'Nobody will have the nerve to sack you when I get my mate to write a great piece about you for Sunday's paper.'

'You're just like the rest,' I said forlornly. 'You just want a story too.'

'Hey, Kirsty, no.' He put his arm around me and I was stunned to find it comforting. 'If you don't want to, that's fine. I was just trying to help.'

'Were you?' I asked. He was actually incredibly nice, I thought. Really, really nice.

'Absolutely,' he said.

And he was. Really, really nice. He didn't take any photos of me and my 'story' didn't appear in the Sunday papers. A variety of stories appeared in the tabloids but only for a couple of days and then they were replaced with the news that Charlotte Sanderson had joined a major French fashion house. Charlotte, the papers told us, had designed the famous topless dress etc., etc.

So I kept it, because it was a lucky dress. I was promoted in work due to the fact that I'd kept my head in a crisis and because the watches had a blaze of publicity unlike anything they'd ever had before because, of course, we'd done a spin on the story which made everyone come out with glory: misunderstanding between me and the celeb; everyone friends; photo of me and the celeb, both wearing the new watches, taken by my new boyfriend – though I didn't wear the dress, I stuck to jeans. Somehow they were more me.

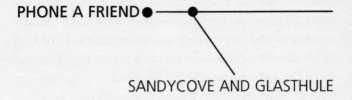

PHONE A FRIEND

SANDYCOVE AND GLASTHULE

I had a headache. The sort that the advertisers describe as a tense, nervous headache, where you know that it's the fact that your shoulders are knotted up which is making the pain start at the back of your neck before pounding at your temples. My shoulders had been knotted up for hours and my head was aching because it had been a terrible day, one where nothing I could do was right. First off, I was late for work: leaves on the line or some kind of pathetic railway excuse for the train not showing up. I clattered into the office knowing that it was going to be busy and then spilled the double-mocha coffee I'd grabbed on the way in all over the brochures I'd spent ages getting together the previous evening for a presentation my boss was giving in an hour's time. So it was back to the printer and the photocopier and the binder – by eleven my head was already splitting.

Christine, my boss, was less than sympathetic and

didn't accept the leaves-on-the-line excuse for my lateness. She blamed it on what she called my erratic, juvenile lifestyle of late nights and too much drink.
Sometimes she had a point when she ranted at me but
not today. The night before hadn't been a late night. It
should've been because I was supposed to be going out
with my boyfriend, Ian, but he'd phoned to say that he
was busy and he couldn't make it and he'd see me
tonight instead – maybe. Ian's phone call worried me. It
was the third time he'd been too busy to meet me in the
last month and I was getting the impression that he was
cooling off on things. I didn't really want him to cool
off on me. Ian is strikingly attractive, well-fancied by
every girl who sees him, and (the icing on the cake) he's
loaded. Not exactly personally loaded but his folks have
a huge house on Sorrento Road with its own gym, swimming pool and, I kid you not, full-time housekeeper. Ian
was a good catch and I didn't intend to let him go without a fight. Besides, I was crazy about him and it wasn't
just because of his looks and his money. It was because
we had good times together and our late nights were
usually very late and very exciting. The trouble was that
he also had a very exciting life when he wasn't with me.
He works in advertising and he's forever going to media
bashes at trendy places. Last night, besides being too
busy to call me, he'd also been photographed at the
opening of the latest hotspot nightclub with a gorgeous
ginger-haired girlette hanging out of him. The picture

had been in the *Independent*. When I asked about it he simply laughed and said that she was part of the package. I was afraid to ask what the rest of the package actually was.

Although I'd spoken to him already that morning, I'd tried ringing him again during the few moments of unfrenzied office activity later in the day, but I kept getting his voice-mail, and I didn't want to leave a message. I didn't wish to appear madly needy but I wanted him to know that where he was and what he was doing mattered to me. Because, as far as I was concerned, Ian Travers wasn't going to join my list of the ones who got away. His name wasn't going to appear after Les, John, David, Stephen, Alan, Michael, Stuart, Dermot, Declan . . . God, I thought miserably as I got onto the train to Sandycove, my track record was utterly abysmal.

I wondered why. It wasn't as though I kept picking out the same type of loser in a different body in some kind of co-dependent want-to-get-hurt type of relationship. You know the type of thing the self-help books accuse you of. They were all very different kinds of blokes; some were fun-loving party-types; some were more intellectual; and some (God help me) were sporty. Going out with Stuart had meant spending Saturday afternoons on the touchline watching him get covered in mud at the local rugby ground and wondering exactly how dangerous a sport it was – it seemed to me that the major skill was not in scoring a try but in being able to walk intact off the pitch afterwards. I think it was my inability to find any positives in the sport whatsoever that finished me and Stuart off even though he was actually a kind and decent sort of bloke.

Anyway, I was determined that my relationship with Ian would be different. And mostly it was, especially since he wasn't the sporty type either. But I didn't make the mistakes I'd made with Alan and Michael either. I wasn't too clingy or too possessive. I didn't moan at him about going to launches instead of having romantic meals for two. I never freaked out when he told me that he was working with models/actressess/whatevers. I trusted him. And I wanted to be with him. I wanted him to be The One.

A girl sat in the seat opposite me. We were lucky to have seats at all, it was six o'clock and the train was crowded. But sometimes you get lucky. I was kind of hoping that finding the seat was an omen for what would happen in the future. (I like omens and signs. I wouldn't say that I was superstitious exactly but if I see one magpie I look around frantically until I see another one. And I don't walk under ladders – well, something could fall down on you, couldn't it, so it's actually a superstition that makes perfect sense.) Anyway, I thought that finding a seat was telling me that I would find my place with Ian too. I wondered if the girl who'd squeezed into that last available space had any karmic thoughts about it herself.

She was pretty in a way that I could never be. Her curly, fair hair tumbled from beneath a denim baseball cap. She wore a shocking-pink jacket over a plain white T-shirt and her long legs were encased in the tightest jeans imaginable. I had a horrible, fleeting thought that she'd be more suitable for Ian and his media life than me. You see I'm a bit overweight, with short dark hair, and short stubby legs . . . I'm making myself sound totally unattractive and I know I'm not but sometimes, despite my good features like huge blue eyes and a kind of button-nose which loads of men think is cute, sometimes I just feel ugly. And looking at the Barbie clone opposite me made me feel very ugly indeed.

She was listening to a personal stereo. I've got a bit lost on the whole personal music bit and so I've no idea whether people's music is now on MP3 players or Walkmans or cassettes. But the funny thing about it is that no matter what system they're using and no matter what kind of music they're listening to, it all sounds exactly the same when you hear it echoing from their so-called personal headsets. A kind of thunka-thunka-thunka bass with a tinny treble overlaying it. I mean, it could be gangsta-rap or disco-diva stuff but the beat still sounds the same when you overhear it. I thought she was a bit disco-diva myself but that was just guessing. Regardless, the relentless tuneless sound was getting to me. I could feel my shoulders bunch up again and the headache take up another prominent spot at the back of my head.

I closed my eyes and tried to do some conscious breathing. My best friend Leanne and I had done a set of yoga classes earlier in the year and our instructor told us that whenever we were feeling stressed or tense we should try to breathe slowly and concentrate on the sound and the feel of our breathing as we allowed our bodies to relax. Great in theory, hopeless in practice, because I can't concentrate on the sound of my breath – all that happens is that I either fall asleep (if I'm doing it in a quiet place) or my mind wanders (if I'm trying to be calm under pressure). So though I tried the deep breathing now I remained conscious of the hissing music from the girl opposite.

I opened my eyes again. I was tempted to rip the earpieces out of her ears and stomp on them. After all, I'd had a bad day, my boyfriend and I weren't getting along as well as I wanted, I had a headache and her damn music wasn't allowing me to find a moment of peace and serenity on the Dart.

Then her phone rang. I have to admit that I got a kick out of the fact that her ringtone was Aqua's 'Barbie Girl'.

She switched off her personal music system, took out her earpieces and answered the phone. Her face lit up.

'Janine! How's it going?'

It was obviously going quite well. The girl opposite nodded as she listened to what her friend was saying even though the caller couldn't see her. (I suppose eventually we'll all have phones that you can wear on your wrist or something so that the people you're talking to can actually see you. Shouldn't take long now, I expect.)

'I can't.' The girl didn't sound totally sincere when she said this. 'I'd love to but I can't. I'm meeting Tom.' Her voice softened when she said Tom's name. Pretty much the same way my voice softened when I talked about Ian. So I guessed that Tom was the current boyfriend. Despite the myth of sisterhood, very few girls give up a date with their bloke to meet their mates. I wonder why that is when most men I know will happily head off with their mates instead of their girlfriends.

'Oh, bloody hell.' She sounded annoyed now. 'I'd love to have gone, really. But we're having dinner tonight. He's booked it and everything.'

More chatter from Janine, which made the girl smile.

'I don't know. I mean, Jan, I should know, shouldn't I?' She said this with a question in her voice but without conviction, a fact that Janine clearly picked up on.

'Well, if you're really in love with someone and they're in love with you then the whole engagement thing shouldn't really come as a surprise, should it? I mean, you'd have talked about it already, wouldn't you? And we haven't.'

So it was kind of serious with her Tom. Serious enough from her point of view to have been thinking about solitaire diamonds and floating white dresses. She extended her left hand and gazed at her fingers as she spoke.

'But I still feel bad about it,' she continued. 'I haven't seen you or the others in ages.'

They warn you about that, don't they? About not dropping your girlfriends when you have a man in your life. I remembered, guiltily, that I hadn't called Leanne in ages either. But that was because the last time we'd talked she'd lectured me about Ian, telling me that I was only with him because he was seriously gorgeous and seriously rich and that we had sweet FA in common. She was seriously jealous, of course.

'No,' said the girl opposite me. 'We didn't get to see it after all.'

She paused and listened before replying. 'We would have. He wanted to. He just wasn't able to. And next thing it was too late.'

I wondered what that was all about. I get really pissed off about people having conversations on their phones in public places but I can't help listening and getting involved. I wanted to know what Janine was saying to make the girl opposite frown.

'He sent me flowers the next day,' she told her. 'Roses. With a card saying, "To Cheryl with all my love".'

Cheryl. She looked a bit like a Cheryl, I supposed.

'He's not like that,' said Cheryl, her voice now tinged with anger. 'Honestly, Janine, you're getting it a bit out of proportion. And a few minutes ago you were asking me about getting engaged to him!'

True, I thought. Maybe Janine wasn't such a good friend. Maybe she was just trying to stir it up and maybe she was seriously jealous like Leanne with me. 'He's using you, Natalie,' she said. 'He wants someone around when he's stuck and he's out with other women whenever you're not there.' I was able to knock that one on the head fairly quickly. I was always there for him.

'I've got to go,' said Cheryl suddenly. 'I've another call coming in. I'll talk to you soon.'

There wasn't another call coming in to Cheryl's phone but she'd clearly got fed up with talking to Janine. I didn't blame her. After all, everyone bangs on about how great your friends are and how important their opinions might be and how, in the end, women support each other all the time, but the bottom line was that me and Cheryl both had jealous friends who didn't realise that the relationship we had with our boyfriends was just as important. Leanne wasn't going out with anyone at the moment and that, in my view, was why she was so het up about Ian. I'd bet any money that Janine didn't have a boyfriend either.

Then Cheryl's phone did ring again. This time she smiled as she answered it.

'Hello, darling.'

It was the wonderful Tom, I guessed. She was besotted with him. I could hear it in her voice.

'Oh, no, Tom – why?' She looked aghast. '. . . Yes, but, well I've just told Janine that I couldn't go out with them because I was going out with you and she said that they were going to ask Martina instead . . . A few minutes earlier . . .' She was looking at her left hand again. '. . . No, but

you told me you booked it so I didn't want to let you down
. . . of course I realise that you have to work but . . .'

I watched her face. This had happened before. I knew
it had. She had that kind of resigned expression that
means the excuse has already been used. And she's accept-
ing it even if she isn't very happy about it.

'It's not that,' she told Tom. 'It's just – well, this is
always happening.' She bit her lip and listened again. 'No,
I'm not going to ring Janine back . . . Because I already
told her I was going out with you . . . No. Oh, come on
Tom! Give me a break.'

That's something else that men don't understand.
Presumably if Cheryl had told Tom that she couldn't go
out with him he'd simply ring up his mates and happily
announce, 'Guess what, I'm free after all,' and head off to
the match or the pub or whatever with them even if he'd
told them five minutes earlier that he couldn't go. But
with women . . . I don't know. Maybe we think we're
losing face or something if we're supposed to be going
out with a guy and it gets called off. I mean, it's totally
stupid but that's the way it works.

Tom ended the conversation, Cheryl closed her little
snap-shut phone and gazed out of the train window at the
backs of the houses we hurtled past. And then I noticed a
tear tipping over the brim of her eye and rolling slowly
down her cheek.

I bit my lip. There was something sadly wrong with her
relationship if she was crying over this. I felt uncomfortable

at having listened, at having sneaked a look into her life. She wiped the tear away and turned back into the carriage, opening up her phone again. She hit speed-dial.

'Tom, hi.'

Maybe she was going to break up with him, I thought. Maybe she'd decided that being with the girls was more important after all.

'I'm sorry,' she said. 'I hung up on you.'

I hadn't noticed that. I'd assumed that after she'd said 'Give me a break' he'd said something else before they'd stopped talking because she hadn't closed the phone straight away. But apparently not, they'd ended on a sour note and now she was retrieving the situation.

'Yes, well it was a hard day,' she said. 'That bastard Moriarty went on and on at me.' She rubbed the bridge of her nose. 'I was looking forward to seeing you.' She winced at whatever he said and then responded with, 'I don't mean to be.'

He was calling her possessive. I knew. That was the rock on which Alan and I had perished and the same with Michael. And so the first time that Ian had suggested it to me I'd backed right off and now he thought that I really didn't care where he was or who he was with. As if.

'Oh, look, Tom – it doesn't matter. No, I can't go tomorrow evening. I have that interview, remember?' She listened to him again. 'No, with the computer company. I told you about it.'

I was rapidly going off Tom. He really didn't give a

toss about her, did he? He'd broken their date and now he was asking her to go somewhere with him when he knew she already had to be somewhere else. Surely he should remember her having an interview? That was important, wasn't it? A life-changing kind of thing.

'I will not wear my blue dress to the interview!' She sounded quite annoyed. 'I'm wearing my suit.'

She didn't actually look like the kind of girl who'd even own a suit, but then I have a horrible habit of making snap judgments about people and maybe she was really Office Barbie after all.

'Why don't you pick me up afterwards? I'll be finished by eight.'

He clearly asked her why she wasn't having the interview during working hours because she said, rather tersely, that it was impossible to get the time off and she'd already used a doctor's appointment and a visit to the dentist in the last few weeks. Obviously Cheryl was desperate to change jobs. I knew the feeling. I was thinking strongly about it myself after today's disaster.

'OK, it doesn't matter. I'll call you after it anyway to let you know how I got on.'

But he won't care, I thought suddenly. He doesn't care. He only cares about himself. I jumped as my own phone rang. It was Ian.

'Hi,' I said happily. 'How are you?'

'Guess what!' He sounded very pleased with himself.

'What?'

'I'm going to Milan.'

'Milan!' I was suitably impressed. 'When?'

'Tomorrow,' he said. 'Tanya was supposed to go but she's got a flu bug or something and can't so they're sending me instead.'

'That's great,' I said insincerely. 'For how long?'

'A whole week.'

'I'll miss you,' I told him.

'Oh well.' He laughed. 'All in the line of duty.'

'Yes. I'll see you tonight anyway,' I said. 'Give you a goodbye kiss. Maybe more if you're lucky.'

'Ah, well, Natalie, sorry about this but I can't make it tonight.'

I gritted my teeth. 'But you said yesterday that we'd go for a drink.'

'I know,' he told me. 'I can't though. Sorry.'

'So you broke a date with me last night and you're standing me up tonight and you're going to Milan tomorrow?' I kept my voice as light as possible but he could hear my anger all the same.

'Chill out, Nats,' he said. 'We don't have to be in each other's pockets all the time, do we?'

'No,' I said. I wanted to add that he just didn't seem to care any more but I didn't because that would make me sound pathetic.

'Anyway I'll bring you back a little something from Milan,' he promised.

'Prada?' I suggested.

He laughed. 'Do they do key rings?'

'Don't you dare bring me back a key ring,' I warned. 'A bag or a belt at least.'

'We'll see. Look, Nats, got to go. Talk soon.'

'Yeah,' I said. 'Talk soon.'

My phone wasn't a trendy little snap-shut one like Cheryl's. I simply hit the red key. Then I glanced up. She was looking at me and her gaze was speculative. Clearly Cheryl had been listening in to my conversation in the same way as I'd listened in to hers. Our eyes met. She shrugged. I smiled.

And then I did something I rarely do on the train. I spoke to her. A complete stranger. 'My boyfriend's going to Italy,' I said. 'Lucky him.'

'I couldn't help overhearing,' she said.

'He works in advertising,' I told her. 'It's his job.'

'Even luckier.'

'And if he brings me back something by Prada . . .' I smiled happily.

'If he comes back at all,' she said.

I stared at her and she looked embarrassed. 'Sorry.'

'He's going for a week,' I told her. 'That's all.'

'And you're not meeting him tonight.'

'Butt out,' I snapped angrily. 'If I want that kind of shit I can talk to any of my friends.'

I was really annoyed. How dare that girl listen in to my personal conversation and draw all the wrong con-clusions! OK, Ian was going away for a week. But he was going to bring home a present for me. Sure, he wasn't able to meet me tonight. But he probably had things to do. And fine, he'd broken our date the night before. He'd had his reasons. Work reasons, he'd told me. Something to do with having to be at IceCool all night. It wasn't anything like her boyfriend who clearly didn't give a shit about her and who kept her hanging on so pathetically that even her friends felt sorry for her. *I* felt sorry for her, for God's sake, and I was a complete stranger.

The train sped southwards around the curve of the bay. I'd be glad to get home. My headache was as bad as ever.

'I'm sorry,' she said again suddenly. 'I shouldn't have listened.'

'Doesn't matter,' I told her. 'I didn't think much of your boyfriend either.'

Her eyes filled with tears and I squirmed uncomfortably in the seat.

'Everyone says he's using me,' she said. 'But I love him. He's kind. Nobody sees that side of him because he's a bit silly when we're together with other people. But he's great really.'

'So's mine,' I said.

Both of us got off the train at Sandycove. I wondered if this was her usual commuting train. You tend to recognise the people who get the same train as you in the evening. I normally got the one a bit earlier.

'Looks like we're both at a bit of a loose end this evening,' I said suddenly. 'Fancy a drink?'

She looked surprised but said yes. So the next thing I knew we were sitting in the pub, two glasses of Miller on the table in front of us. And she was telling me all about Tom who worked in graphic design and who was such a pet really, although she didn't think he was the commitment kind. I told her all about my lovely, lovely Ian and wondered if he was the commitment kind either. And then we told each other, over another couple of Millers, that neither of us was really looking for commitment. But it was nice to know it was a possibility. Which it probably wasn't with Tom. Or with Ian.

'You know,' she said much later, 'I don't know if either of them are worth it.'

'I want Ian to be worth it,' I told her. 'I really do.'

'I want Tom to be worth it too. I had a messy break-up before. I don't want to go through it all again.'

She was quite a nice girl, was Cheryl. I liked her. I didn't want her to have a messy break up with Tom either.

'But you will break up with him?'

She looked at me miserably. 'He'll break up with me first.'

'And Ian will break up with me too.' I knew I was right. I kept making excuses for him but I was being naïve. Me and Ian weren't meant to be together. Just because I wanted something to happen didn't mean that it would.

'Give me your phone,' I said.

She looked at me in surprise but handed it over.

'Tom's number?'

'Speed-dial four,' she said.

I hit the button and waited until he answered. He sounded peevish, I thought.

'What is it, Cheryl?' he asked. 'I told you I was busy.' I wondered where exactly he was busy. It was ominously quiet in the background. Maybe he was working late or whatever excuse it was he'd given her but somehow I didn't think so.

'This isn't Cheryl,' I said. 'This is Natalie.'

'Natalie?' He sounded confused. 'But you're calling from Cheryl's phone.'

'Calling on Cheryl's behalf,' I said. 'Calling to tell you it's over.'

Cheryl looked at me in astonishment. She made a half-hearted attempt to retrieve the phone and then sat back again.

'Over?' said Tom.

'Yes,' I said. 'Cheryl realises that you and she don't have a long-term future together and on her behalf I'm saying that she's prepared to never see you again.'

'Hang on,' said Tom. 'Who the hell are you? I don't know any Natalie.'

'There's a lot of things about Cheryl you don't know,' I told him sweetly.

He spluttered and I closed the phone, cutting him off.

'Natalie!' Cheryl stared at me. 'I didn't want you to do that. And now he thinks . . .'

'Who cares what he thinks?' I demanded. 'Besides, you didn't try very hard to stop me.'

'No,' she said in wonderment. 'I didn't.'

I slid my phone across the table. 'Speed-dial three,' I told her.

Cheryl phoned Ian. I was a bit surprised he answered it at all because he had a habit of letting it ring until it was diverted to his voice-mail. But he picked up and she told him not to bother bringing back the present from Milan because it was OK, I'd wised up, it was over. And I rather think he spluttered a bit too as she cut him off.

'So that's that,' I told her. 'We're two single women again.'

'Yes.' She grinned. 'And tomorrow I'm going to do a brilliant interview and you're going to go for that promotion in work you were talking about and we're going to cop on to ourselves about men and not let ourselves get walked on any more.'

And guess what? That's how it turned out.

Well, almost. Cheryl didn't get the job but she was offered a different one which worked out even better than she'd hoped. She's still waiting for the right man to come along but she's having a great social life in the meantime. I spent three whole months cultivating a more mature image at work and at the end of it I was promoted. Then I was transferred to Human Resources. Where I met Larry. He's a decent bloke, Larry. He's doesn't play rugby, he likes me being possessive and when he had to go to a business meeting in London he brought me along for the weekend. Which was much better than Ian bringing back a fake Prada key ring from Milan, I thought.

I don't know whether or not we'll last the pace. But I hope so. I never take phone calls from him on the train.

RECYCLED LOVERS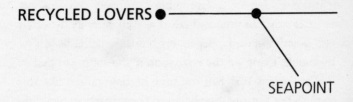

SEAPOINT

It had been Mark's idea to get the train. Carol had objected strenuously, she told him that she'd be just as happy to drive, that she rarely drank alcohol at these kind of things and that getting home across town would be a nightmare without the car. But Mark, supported by his best friend Tony and Tony's wife Finola, argued that it would be fun to get the Dart. He hardly ever got to travel on the rail system, he told her, and it would be an eco-friendly thing to do.

Carol stared at him in total amazement when he said this. Her husband was the kind of man who insisted on pointing out that it took more fuel to drive to the recycling depot than the miserable amount generated by the few bottles and jars that she brought, and that encouraging recycling was simply a sop to the environmentalists because it really made no difference whatsoever. Mark thought that until recycling became commercially more profitable than it was, it simply made people feel good rather than served any useful purpose. And he reckoned that the sudden use of 'green bins' for paper and cans was an utter waste of time and effort as well; after all, he often said sanctimoniously, paper was biodegradable, wasn't it? It wouldn't clog up the ecosystem if you simply buried it.

Carol knew that half the time he only ranted like this to push her buttons. She believed passionately in recycling and assiduously sorted their rubbish into three separate bins every week. She knew that Mark did occasionally ponder on the changing weather patterns and wonder aloud whether felling half the Amazon rainforests had anything to do with the fact that there hadn't been a dry summer in Dublin for the last five years, but he never outwardly admitted that there was a correlation between this and doing your bit for the environment. Mark was a financial controller. Unless it made business sense he wasn't interested.

So Carol couldn't quite believe his sudden desire to take the train and asked him outright if he had an ulterior motive while she worried as to what this ulterior motive might be.

'No,' he told her. 'And I really don't see why you're making such a fuss. I thought you'd like to get the train.'

'It's not a question of what I'd like,' Carol retorted. 'It's a question of you acting completely out of character.'

'Oh, for heaven's sake, for once I try to go along with one of your pet passions and all I get is abuse.'

'It's not that,' said Carol testily.

'What then?'

'I can't get dressed up if we go by train,' she told him eventually. 'It's a good ten minutes to the station from here and my shoes . . .'

'Wear a pair you can walk in for a change,' snapped Mark. 'Besides, it's a barbecue – you're hardly expected to get dolled up for a bloody barbecue.'

'I'm not going to Ben and Jill's looking like a wreck either,' retorted Carol. 'You wouldn't like me to turn up looking like a wreck, would you?'

'We're taking the train,' said Mark firmly. 'Tony and Finola think it's a great idea. Besides, Ben and Jill are only a five-minute walk from Seapoint station.'

Carol said nothing. She still didn't entirely trust Mark's motives.

But by Saturday evening when Tony and Finola arrived, she'd accepted the idea. She'd decided to wear a pair of slim-fitting jeans with an appliquéd design of red and green apples down one leg, which were short enough to go with her (almost) flat red shoes and which, she told herself, would be both dressy and practical. She teamed the jeans with a plain white T-shirt and spent an hour in the bathroom making herself look natural. She reckoned that her appearance was just about right for a cross-city journey on the train to the summer barbecue being held by her husband's boss. And friend. Mark considered Ben to be a friend. Carol knew that he wasn't.

Ben O'Malley and his wife Jill hosted a barbecue every

year for the staff of the communications company of which Ben was the managing director. Mark looked after the finances and Tony was director of sales. The three men had worked together for the last five years. They played golf together on the first Saturday of every month and represented the company in a yearly pro-am event. It was important, Mark often told Carol, to spend time socially with the people you worked with. And he sometimes asked her why the three wives didn't meet together more often since they all had so much in common.

Carol would shrug whenever he said this but didn't tell him that the first day she met Jill O'Malley she'd found her too pushy by far and an irritating stereotype of a corporate wife. She liked Finola Harris's company a little better but she really didn't feel that she had as much in common as Mark could possibly think with a woman whose main interest was in her two children and the spectacular success that she hoped they'd make of their lives. Carol much preferred to be with the people she'd once worked with herself – Chloe, Mags and Denise – all of whom she still considered close friends even though she didn't see them as much as she used to. Mark wanted her to be friends with people she didn't really like and she couldn't make him understand that she simply wasn't interested in cultivating friendships with his work colleagues and their wives.

The doorbell rang as she was spraying herself with her tried and trusted Chanel perfume. The same one she'd worn for the past fifteen years and which she'd never changed because she knew that it suited her. But one that Mark didn't notice any more.

'Come on, Carol,' he cried. 'They're here.'

She gave a last spritz in the general direction of her neck and grabbed her bag.

Finola and Tony were waiting in the living room sipping the gin and tonics that Mark had given them.

'Next train is in half an hour,' he said, noticing her quizzical glance. 'Just enough time for us to belt back a quick one before we go. One of the great advantages of public transport.'

'You'll get over it when the train is late,' said Carol darkly. 'Or if it doesn't turn up at all.'

'Rubbish.' Mark grinned and handed her a gin and tonic. 'I'm all for doing my bit.'

'It's because of the company, isn't it?' said Finola. 'Tony brought home that memo from Ben.'

Carol raised her eyebrows as she looked at her husband who shrugged.

'Ben's got on the waste-not-want-not tack,' he admitted. 'And he's trying to encourage people to use public transport to get to the office. Makes sense from his point of view – we have limited car-parking and at the moment we're paying a six-figure amount for additional spaces in another block. He wants to cut back.'

'Hoist by your own petard.' Tony grinned. 'You pointed out how much money we were spending on staff parking.'

'I didn't think that my space might be one that came for the chop,' said Mark ruefully.

'Will it?' asked Carol.

'The memo said that parking would be restricted to personnel who had essential use of their car,' Finola told her. 'Which means that Tony is OK because as a sales person he's out and about a lot. But Mark is desk-bound, aren't you, Mark, so it does look as though he might be getting the train a bit more often in the future.'

'You never said.' Carol looked at him over the rim of her glass.

'I was kind of hoping it wouldn't happen,' said Mark. 'I've been with them for long enough. I'm a senior person in the company. It's a prestige thing.'

Carol heard the defensiveness in his voice but remained silent.

'Maybe he'll retain spaces for senior management,' said Tony comfortingly. 'And then you won't have to worry.'

'Actually it makes sense,' said Carol eventually. 'You don't need the car, Mark, and you fume about the traffic every day.'

'It's still not the point,' he said irritably. 'It's a matter of perception for the rest of the company.'

'Well, perhaps Ben won't be in charge for ever,' said Carol, 'and things will change.'

Mark laughed. 'You don't know Ben,' he told his wife. 'The company is his life.'

*

According to the electronic board at the station, the next train to Seapoint wasn't for another twenty minutes.

'You must have read it wrong,' said Carol as she pulled her light jacket around her. Although the weather was warm, a cool breeze swept along the platform making her shiver.

'I didn't,' said Mark.

'Everyone knows that the timetable is just a fantasy,' Tony told him. 'Which is why it'll be a right pain in the arse for you, mate, when you have to leave your car at home in future!'

'Ha bloody ha,' said Mark while Carol grinned and Finola giggled.

The train, when it eventually came, was much fuller than they'd expected and all the seats were taken. Finola, whose shoes had higher heels than Carol's, complained that she'd have blisters by the time they got to Seapoint. Tony told her that she'd have been better off wearing sensible flatties like Carol and Finola had objected that Carol's shoes couldn't possibly be considered sensible even if they were flat – they were designer shoes, for heaven's sake.

'What does that mean, exactly?' Tony grabbed hold of the rail as the train pulled out of the station. 'Surely every-thing is designed by someone?'

'Ah but some are, you know, named designers,' said Finola.

'Everyone has a name,' objected Tony. 'It's all complete bullshit, you know it is.'

'It might be bullshit,' Carol agreed, 'but everyone kind of subscribes to it so you don't have any choice but to believe it.'

'Nonsense,' said Tony.

'Well, it's the same with cars,' Carol pointed out. 'You drive a Merc, don't you?'

'Not a big one,' Finola interjected.

'No, but it's a statement, isn't it? You could drive a different sort of car – cheaper but with exactly the same features, but you don't because the Merc says something about you.'

'At least everyone can see it's an expensive car,' said Tony. 'But nobody could tell whether your shoes were bought in Dunnes or a little boutique in Blackrock.'

Carol laughed. 'I can assure you that anyone who knows about shoes knows that they weren't bought in a chain store.'

Once the train had crossed the city they were able to get seats so that Finola had stopped complaining about blisters by the time they reached Seapoint. Ben and Jill's home was, as Mark had mentioned, a short walk from the station and her heels hadn't had time to chafe before they reached the white-bricked two-storey-over-basement house with its long, narrow garden to the front that opened out to a much wider one at the back.

'It's very seaside B&B, isn't it?' remarked Finola as they walked up the garden path. 'Reminds me of a place my parents took me to stay when I was a kid.'

'It's nothing like a B&B,' said Tony sternly. 'It's a work of art inside.'

But they didn't need to go inside to get to the barbecue. Instead they made their way to the open door in the honeysuckle-covered dividing wall between the front and back gardens. Ben had told them that there'd be about thirty people in all at the barbecue and, Mark realised, they were probably the last to arrive. Blast that bloody train, he thought angrily. He never liked being first or last. Somewhere safely in the middle was the most appropriate arrival time. Nevertheless he beamed expansively at Ben, held out his hand and introduced Carol.

'Nice to see you again,' said Ben. 'I hope you've been keeping well.'

'Very well, thanks,' said Carol. 'Your garden is wonderful.' She gazed at the masses of flowers and shrubs dotted around the perfectly manicured lawn.

'Thank you.' Ben smiled at her, his grey eyes twinkling. 'Jill does most of the work. Or at least Jill's gardener does most of the work. I haven't a clue what half the green stuff is but I do know that they seem to pick the right thing. Let me get you a drink. What will you have?'

'It's OK,' said Carol. 'I'll get myself a glass of wine from the table over there.'

'Fine,' said Ben. 'I'll talk to you later.'

Carol smiled at him again and drifted over to the table. She picked up a glass of white wine and began to sip it as she strolled through the garden. She knew quite a few people here because she'd met them at various company functions over the past few years. There was Lara Townsend, the wife of one of the accountants who worked with Mark; Gary Murphy who was something in sales but she wasn't sure what; Angela Harper, Ben's far-too-attractive PA . . . and, of course, Jill O'Malley, Ben's tall and elegant wife who looked as though she'd just stepped out of the pages of one of Ireland's top lifestyle magazines. Carol thought that Jill never looked like a real person, simply an artist's impression of what a modern company wife should be: stunningly attractive, coolly sophisticated and unbelievably youthful even though Carol knew that Jill was forty-four, seven years older than her. I wonder will I look that good at forty-four, she asked herself, and then clamped down on the smile that threatened to break out on her face. She didn't want to smile in case Jill thought that she was smiling at her. She didn't want to send the wrong signals to Ben's wife. Not right now anyway.

'Carol Greene, it's great to see you again!'

She turned at the sound of the voice and this time happily smiled in recognition at the young woman who was the deputy financial controller. A few years earlier Carol had worried about Sarah Jones and Mark and the close working relationship that they had with each other. Carol had been concerned that Mark might embark on an affair with the pretty copper-haired girl but it turned out that Sarah was very involved in a relationship with another woman, an actress who appeared on a national soap as a man-magnet. Carol had expressed complete shock to her at discovering both that Sarah was more interested in women than in men but even more that the vampish soap-star was a lesbian.

'I know.' Sarah's face had dimpled in front of her. 'Amazingly, nobody knows. They might suspect but they don't know. We don't go out together publicly. Not as lovers anyway. Most people just think we share a house. It's astonishing how gullible they can be.'

'I'd have thought that all the gossip papers would know,' said Carol.

'They know jack-shit really,' Sarah told her. 'Once you're discreet you can get away with a lot.'

'But you've told me,' objected Carol. 'I might blab.'

'I don't think so,' said Sarah. 'I feel that you're a discreet person. I think you keep a lot to yourself and you won't go talking about me. Why should you?'

'I wouldn't say a word,' agreed Carol. 'But what about everyone else in the company? Or everyone else who knows you?'

'Like I said,' Sarah told her, 'we're very discreet. Even your husband doesn't know.'

Sarah was probably right, Carol had thought after-wards. People whose names ended up in the papers over some big scandal or affair simply weren't careful enough. Sarah and the soap star were very, very careful. And stayed that way because there hadn't been a thing about them in the papers ever.

'How's things?' Carol asked now.

'Great,' said Sarah. 'Work's a pain, of course, but we're going on holiday soon because the soap's on a break so I'm looking forward to three weeks of doing absolutely nothing.'

'Mark'll miss you,' said Carol.

'I know.' Sarah dimpled again. 'I do most of the work.'

'Of course I have good staff,' Mark told Jill O'Malley as he stood beside her in the shade of an apple tree. 'Otherwise I wouldn't be able to do half as much as I do.'

'Ben knows how to hire good staff,' said Jill absently.

'Sure he does. He hired me!' Mark laughed and Jill smiled dutifully. But she wasn't really listening to him. She was watching Ben and his PA who were laughing together. She didn't like the way they laughed together.

'Anyway enough of the jokes,' Ben said to Angela. 'I'd better start grilling a few burgers and things otherwise the hordes will get rebellious.' He kissed his PA lightly on the forehead and took up his position behind the barbecue. He slapped some burgers onto the grill and watched a plume of blue-grey smoke rise into the air.

'What were you talking to her about?' asked Jill.

'Huh?'

'You and Angela.'

'Nothing.' Ben looked at his wife and frowned. 'I was telling her a joke.'

'I can't imagine what you could possibly have to say to her today,' said Jill curtly. 'Surely you have enough conversation with her during the week. Wouldn't you be better off talking to the O'Donnells or the Ryans? You haven't said a word to either of them and they are our neighbours after all.'

'Oh, don't be such a fool,' muttered Ben. 'Why don't you go and talk to them if you're that keen?'

'It doesn't do any harm to be polite,' snapped Jill. 'You're only ever nice to people you like.'

'It's worked till now.' Ben flipped over the burgers. 'Go and mingle and stop standing here as though you feel you have to bloody supervise me.'

'I do have to supervise you,' said Jill. 'You're not safe to be out on your own.'

'I'm the managing director of a respected company,' said Ben. 'Of course I'm safe to be out on my own.'

'Not socially,' said Jill. 'Unless it's with that gormless pair on the golf course.'

Ben grinned at her suddenly. 'They love it,' he said. 'It makes them feel important.'

'You're all the same,' she said eventually. 'Feeling important is what's important to you.'

She walked across the garden to speak to Moya O'Donnell. Her neighbour was a woman whose family had lived in their house for three generations. Jill knew that Moya considered her to be a blow-in. But that meant that everyone on Seaview Terrace was a blow-in as far as the O'Donnells were concerned.

Finola bumped into Carol as she refilled her glass with cool white wine.

'Good night, isn't it?' asked Finola.

'The usual,' said Carol dryly. 'Jill looking like Mrs Corporate Ireland, Mark and Tony getting pissed . . .'

'Ben doing his thing with the burgers,' interrupted Finola. 'But it's all a bit of fun. And it's easy-going because we know each other so well.'

'Do we?' asked Carol.

'What?'

'How well do we all know each other really?' she asked. 'I mean, I don't really know a thing about Jill O'Malley. I don't know anything at all about that fat woman over there standing beside the beanpole man.'

'That's one of the neighbours,' Finola told her. 'Very very old money and Jill is terrified of her. She's terrified of both of the neighbours.'

'That's totally ridiculous.'

'It's the old-money thing,' Finola said. 'Jill knows that she comes from somewhat more humble beginnings.'

'I've no idea about her beginnings.' Carol flushed as she said the words because she did, in fact, know that Jill was originally from Santry and that her father had been a window-cleaner. Not that it mattered to anyone except, perhaps, Jill herself; Santry was a perfectly acceptable suburb. But not in the same league as a south of the river, on-the-Dart-line, address.

'Anyway the woman is totally insecure,' Finola said. 'If I was rolling about in all the dosh that the O'Malleys have I wouldn't give a toss about my next-door neighbours but apparently she worries all the time that they think she's not good enough.'

'Stupid,' said Carol.

'Agreed.' Finola nodded.

'How do you know all this?' asked Carol.

'Tony is a terrible gossip,' said Finola, 'and he loves dishing the dirt on Ben and Jill whenever he can.'

Jill O'Malley watched her husband cooking burgers and chicken wings and wondered what it was about men and barbecues. He wouldn't lift a finger to help her cook anything in the normal course of events but bring a fire outside and he was prancing about like Ainsley Harriot or some other demented celebrity chef. She knew it wasn't just Ben. They were all like that. Aileen Moran had made the very same complaint about Dominic. And, Aileen had added, if he spent as much time helping to keep the place clean as he did messing about with his beloved car . . . she'd shaken her head and Jill had agreed with her.

He looked so ridiculous in that stupid chef's hat as well, she thought. It wasn't really appropriate of him to be wearing it, it took away from his gravitas. And Jill thought that it was very important for the managing director of a company to have gravitas. She'd worked at cultivating it herself, as the managing director's wife. She reckoned that she was good at gravitas, better than Ben, which wouldn't actually be too hard. She'd always had to push him, really, always had to make him realise how important his career actually was. How important he was. And then, of course, he had to go and act the complete moron in a chef's hat. She supposed she should be grateful he wasn't wearing one of those jokey PVC aprons with women's boobs on the top.

She turned away and smiled at Gerardine Ryan who was standing alone beneath the plum tree.

'You all right, Gerardine?' she asked solicitously. 'Anything you need? You're not too cold, are you?'

'Not at all.' Gerardine adjusted the fringed shawl around her shoulders. 'Plenty of warmth in this.'

Jill smiled tightly. Despite the accumulated wealth of the Ryan family, Gerardine would be definitely considered eccentric by most people. As well as the royal blue shawl, she was wearing a purple jumper and a red skirt and her salt-and-pepper hair was tied back in a plait which fell to her waist. Jill was afraid of underestimating Gerardine simply because of her appearance. She felt that the other woman was probably influential in lots of ways although she wasn't entirely sure what all of those ways might be.

'Your husband is having fun.' Gerardine nodded towards Ben.

'Oh, he loves the barbecue thing,' said Jill dismissively. 'It gives him the opportunity to behave like a caveman, I guess.'

'Men like to be in charge,' said Gerardine. 'Both of my husbands were like that. I allowed it of course, but only up to certain limits.'

'It's knowing where to draw the line that's difficult,' agreed Jill.

'Oh, I always knew where to draw the line,' said Gerardine. 'And they knew where it was drawn too.'

'Your first husband died quite young, didn't he?'

'He was thirty-nine,' said Gerardine. 'I was a couple of months younger. I was devastated at the time. But then I met Monty and everything worked out for us.'

Jill glanced over towards Monty Ryan who was deep in conversation with Sarah Jones.

'Sometimes you think your heart is broken,' said Gerardine. 'But it's never so broken that it can't be fixed.'

'You think?'

'Oh yes.'

'Desperately inappropriate they might be but I do love your shoes.' Mark smiled at Finola, his eyes slightly un-focused owing to the quantities of free wine and beer he'd consumed.

'Do you?' asked Finola as she extended her foot and rotated her ankle. 'I rather thought you despised them given what you said on the train.'

'I was just stirring it,' said Mark. 'I can't help myself.'

'I know,' said Finola. 'It drives Carol mad.'

'Does it?'

'You know it does.'

Mark frowned. 'No,' he said. 'I don't. She never says.'

'Probably tired of telling you.' Finola smiled. Mark noticed that her red lipstick seemed to shine on her lips. He noticed also, that her lips appeared fuller than they ever had before. He wondered whether it was anything to do with the lipstick. If so, he thought, he must buy some for Carol. His wife's lips were too thin. He'd always thought so. He especially thought so when she drew them into that harsh line so beloved of wives everywhere when they were displeased with some aspect of their husband's behaviour.

'You have gorgeous lips,' he said. 'Oops. Shouldn't have told you that. Sounds as though I'm trying to come on to you.'

'No it doesn't,' said Finola. 'You're a friend. I'll take it as a compliment.'

'Were they always like that?' Mark couldn't stop his mouth from running away with him.

'Like what?'

'Plump,' he said. 'Sexy.'

Finola giggled. 'I'm glad you think they're sexy.'

'I do,' said Mark. 'Really. But I've only just noticed. I can't help thinking I would've noticed before.'

'It's collagen,' admitted Finola. 'I got it done a few weeks ago.'

'Collagen?'

'Beauty treatment,' she said succinctly.

'Must get Carol to have it done,' said Mark. 'Looks wonderful.'

'I did ask her,' Finola told him. 'But she didn't want to.'

'Strange. I'd have thought she'd want to look sexy.'

'Carol always looks sexy,' said Finola loyally.

'No,' said Mark. 'She always looks well. But not always sexy.'

'I take your point.'

'More than that.' Suddenly Mark planted a firm kiss on Finola's collagen-enhanced lips. 'Take that too. Oh-oh.' He stepped back. 'My mistake again.'

'Actually,' said Finola, 'you're rather a good kisser.'

'That wasn't a kiss,' protested Mark. 'That was a peck on the lips.'

'Give us a real kiss then.' Finola put her glass of wine on the grass.

'People will see.'

'No, they won't,' said Finola. 'We're hidden by that ridiculous naked statue. And it's only a quick kiss. A friendly one. To check out how good you are. And to see if you really do like my lips.'

'Oh, OK,' said Mark and kissed her properly.

'Have you see Mark and Finola?' asked Tony.

Carol, who'd just loaded a paper plate with chicken wings and coleslaw, looked at him in irritation. 'Nope,' she said.

'Only I don't think Finola's had anything to eat and you know how silly she gets when she's drinking and doesn't have anything to eat.'

'She doesn't really,' said Carol.

'Oh, ever since she had the kids,' Tony assured her. 'Childbirth did something to her metabolism, you know. She can't hold alcohol at all.'

'I've never noticed,' said Carol untruthfully. Actually Finola got very silly when she drank too much. But she rarely over-indulged any more. She couldn't, she told Carol, when she had to face two children the next day.

'You, on the other hand, can knock them back with the best of us,' said Tony.

Carol grinned. 'What rubbish. If I drink more than a few I get the most horrendous hangover. Unlike Mark who really can drink without any ill-effects.'

'He doesn't, though, does he?' asked Tony. 'He's very proud of his abstinence.'

'He doesn't drink much during the week,' agreed Carol. 'But we usually have wine at the weekends.' She picked up a chicken wing and nibbled at it, the juices running down her chin.

'Bloody hell,' she mumbled through a mouthful of chicken. 'I'm destroying myself here.'

'Let me.' Tony picked up a green paper napkin and wiped her chin. 'Better?'

'Thanks,' she said. Her eyes locked with his.

'He doesn't know how lucky he is,' remarked Tony.

'Huh?'

'Your husband.'

'He knows,' said Carol although she bit her lip.

'I don't think so.'

Carol smiled although it didn't reach her eyes.

'Want some more?' Ben asked Carol who'd come up to the grill again.

'No,' she replied. 'Just wondering if you're having fun.'

'Are you?' he asked.

She grimaced. 'Not really.'

'It's a bit of a farce, isn't it?'

'Farce isn't the word I was thinking of.'

'Sham?'

'Perhaps.'

'Come on,' he cried as Lara Townsend walked over to join them. 'Get the last of your chicken wings here!'

They turned on the patio heaters as dusk fell and the air grew cooler. Instead of wandering round the garden, people began to gather in clumps beneath the heaters, pulling outdoor chairs or benches into the source of the warmth. The general mood had mellowed with the passing hours and the conversations became sillier and in the case of some of the employees, less guarded. The O'Donnells and the Ryans, Ben and Jill's neighbours, had stayed on, much to Jill's relief. Especially as they seemed to be having a good time even though she worried a little that they were talking about her and Ben, criticising them for not doing something as well as the previous inhabitants of the house might have done. Jill felt it was important for these people to think that she did the right thing. She wasn't sure why it mattered so much to her – she and Ben could buy and sell them, after all. Yet they managed to make her feel vaguely uneasy all the time, as though they pitied her, though why they should pity her was a mystery she'd never managed to unravel.

It was Tony who'd decided that enough was enough and that it was time to go home. He'd been waiting for Finola to come looking for him for ages but she'd been happily chatting to a variety of people and didn't see any necessity to leave. When he disengaged her from a group of women she told him that every time she'd had a glass of wine she'd also had a glass of water and it had made a huge difference. She wasn't in the slightest bit tired, she said, and was he sure he wanted to go? Tony hadn't mixed water with his drinks and was feeling very tired indeed.

He'd spent half an hour talking serious shop to Ben, wanting to sow the seeds of a possible further promotion in his boss's mind. He thought he might have succeeded. Then he'd spent another half hour being chatted to by Liam Shaw, one of the sales team, who clearly had a similar objective in mind. He was tired now and he wanted to go home.

'I'd better say goodbye to Carol first,' said Finola. 'I haven't seen her in ages.'

Her eyes narrowed as she tried to locate her friend in the darkness.

'I haven't seen her either,' said Tony, 'but there's Mark.'

They strolled across the lawn and Tony put his hand on his colleague's shoulder.

'We're off,' he said. 'Just wanted to say goodbye to you and Carol.'

'Off already?' Mark squinted at his watch. 'What time is it?'

'Late enough,' Tony told him. 'Where's the lovely Mrs Greene?'

'Dunno.' Mark shrugged. 'Last time I saw her she was talking to one of the neighbours. That was ages ago.' He looked around him vaguely. 'She can't be far.'

'Maybe she went inside,' said Mark. 'Needed to sit down.'

'Perhaps,' said Tony.

'I'll see if I can find her,' said Finola. 'Wouldn't want to go without saying goodbye.'

She walked into the house, slightly unsteady on her high heels. There was no one in the perfectly fitted kitchen, nor in the expensively carpeted hallway. She reflected, ruefully, that there was a big difference in the standard of living between a managing director and a mere sales director. There shouldn't be, she thought enviously. Tony worked just as hard as Ben. It wasn't fair.

She pushed open the door of the living room, noticing the expensive wall panelling and the carefully displayed bronze pieces dotted around the room. The carpet was soft and thick so that when she stepped inside she wobbled on her heels. There was no sign of Carol though.

She might, of course, be in the loo. There were two downstairs toilets in the house that had been used by the guests but both of them were unoccupied. Perhaps, she thought, they'd been in use when Carol had come into the house and she'd decided to use an upstairs loo instead. Finola felt a little daring as she walked up the wide stairway with its salmon-pink carpet. She stood on the landing and looked around for a moment then opened one of the doors. She realised at once that she'd opened the door to Ben and Jill's bedroom. The massive six foot bed was in the centre of the room with a circular canopy over it. Finola stifled a giggle. It was a bit over the top, she thought. She closed the door again and this time called Carol's name.

Her friend could be anywhere, of course. But Finola was suddenly sure that whatever Carol was doing it was something she'd prefer Mark not to know about. She'd seen Carol chatting for ages to a guy she didn't recognise – perhaps, with her inhibitions loosened by a few glasses of wine, Carol and this bloke had decided to look for a bit of privacy and . . . Finola grimaced. Maybe, she thought worriedly, maybe Carol had seen her and Mark together earlier and had got the wrong idea about their totally meaningless kiss. Though she didn't think it was the sort of thing that Carol would worry about. She'd been married to Mark for long enough to know that it was just a bit of harmless fun.

She walked downstairs and out into the garden again, realising that some of the guests had already left and that there weren't as many people around as earlier. Mark and Tony were standing together beside the still-warm barbecue.

'No sign?' she asked.

Mark shook his head. 'I saw her about an hour ago talking to some bloke but I haven't seen her since then.'

'Cormac Burton,' said Tony. 'He's a golfing mate of Ben's.'

'I don't know him.' Mark furrowed his brow.

'I met him last month when I went to the outing,' said Tony. 'Remember you couldn't come because you were testing the new system?'

Mark nodded.

'Nice bloke,' said Tony as he looked around. 'But he seems to be gone.'

'Where's Ben?' asked Mark. 'He'll probably know who's gone and who hasn't.'

'Yes, but Carol hasn't gone, has she?' Finola pointed out. 'She's just not around at the moment.'

'Maybe she went for a walk,' suggested Tony.

'On her own?' asked Mark.

There was an uncomfortable silence.

'Hey, Jill!' Finola waved at the other woman who'd just walked out of the house. 'Have you seen Carol at all?'

'Carol?' Jill looked at her in bewilderment.

'Carol Greene,' said Finola. 'Mark's wife.'

'No,' said Jill. 'I haven't seen her. I haven't seen Ben either. Not in ages.'

'Oh, for heaven's sake,' said Tony. 'Half the guests have gone home and the other half are missing.'

Finola laughed. 'Not quite,' she said. 'There's still a lot of people in the garden.'

'But not Carol,' said Mark.

'Not Cormac either,' said Finola.

'And not Ben,' said Jill.

'Well, they can't all have disappeared,' Finola said. 'Unless they're engaged in some kind of dastardly practice . . .' She stopped as she saw the expressions on the others' faces. 'I was joking!'

Sarah Jones told them that Cormac had left about twenty minutes earlier.

'He didn't say goodbye,' said Jill testily. 'That was very rude.'

'Maybe you weren't around at the time,' said Sarah comfortingly.

'But what about the other pair?' demanded Mark. 'What about Ben and Carol?'

'Well, Ben is obviously around somewhere,' said Finola. 'Mark, you and Carol didn't have a row or anything, did you? She wouldn't have gone off on her own?'

'Of course we didn't have a row,' snapped Mark.

They stood in silence and scanned the garden again. But neither Ben nor Carol were anywhere to be seen.

'Maybe Ben's gone to bed,' said Jill suddenly. 'I'll check.'

She went into the house. Finola didn't say that she'd been upstairs earlier and had peeked into the master bedroom. She wasn't sure that Jill would appreciate that.

'Oh, where the hell is she?' Mark was annoyed.

'Where the hell is he?' murmured Finola.

Jill walked out of the house again. Her face was pale. She had a letter in her hand. She gave it wordlessly to Mark.

'So.' Ben O'Malley pulled the car into the space in front of the tiny cottage and turned to look at Carol. 'How are you feeling?'

'OK,' she said tentatively. 'A bit nervous.'

'I'm not,' he said. 'I feel great about it.'

'They'll freak out,' she said. 'Maybe we should've done it differently.'

'I know we should have done it differently,' said Ben. 'We nearly had to, when your damn husband made you get the train. But this was more exciting somehow.'

'I could've done without the excitement of getting my stuff to you earlier in the week,' said Carol. 'I was terrified Mark would notice. It would've been so much easier to have shoved a case into the car tonight and let you transfer it across. Anyway, it's your fault. You and your environmentally friendly plans to stop people driving to work!'

'That's your fault.' Ben chuckled. 'You're the one who's made me see things differently.'

'Should I have, though? Will you be able to live a different sort of life with me?'

'Oh, yes.' Ben leaned across and kissed her. She put her arms around him and drew him closer. 'I can't wait to live a different sort of life with you.'

'I've always loved you,' she whispered. 'From the first moment I saw you.'

'I think I've always loved you too,' he said. 'And I love the way you don't want me for what I can give you.'

'I do want you for what you can give me.' She pushed him away. 'You can give me love and attention and all the sort of things that Mark won't.'

'I'm glad,' said Ben.

'And I can give you love and attention for yourself and not because you're the MD of some rotten company.'

'They'll be a bit miffed about my sudden departure,' said Ben.

'They won't. They'll scramble for your job. Tony and Mark and all the others.'

'Will it work out for us?' he asked.

'Yes,' she said.

'And them?'

'Jill will find someone else,' said Carol. 'Mark, maybe, if he gets the job.'

'You're being callous.'

'No,' she said. 'Practical.'

He grinned at her. 'Being with you is very liberating.'

'So is being with you.' She opened the car door. 'Come on, let's start the rest of our lives.'

Mark finished reading Ben's letter. The one in which he said that he and Carol had decided to make new, simpler lives for themselves. In which he said that they'd always been attracted to each other. That this was the only way.

'What a fucker!' Tony shook his head. 'I never would've believed it.'

'I would,' said Jill faintly. 'I always knew he'd mess it up for me one day.'

'He says he's leaving you everything,' said Mark. 'Which makes me wonder how they're going to survive in this simpler life.'

'Oh, he's probably been stashing a few bob away for years,' said Finola. 'Don't worry, Jill. You get a good lawyer and I promise you his life will be a lot simpler than he bargained for.' She turned to Mark. 'How're you feeling?'

'All right,' he said. 'I'll kill him, though. And her.'

'Give it time,' said Finola.

'I thought we were friends,' said Mark. 'Him and me. I didn't even guess . . .'

'You're among friends now, mate,' Tony told him. 'True friends. That bastard was never a friend. He's probably filled Carol's head with all sorts of nonsense.'

'Yes,' said Mark. 'Or she's filled his with worse.'

'Mid-life crisis,' said Finola. 'That's what it is.'

'What about the company?' asked Jill. 'What'll happen?'

'We'll have a management meeting tomorrow.' Tony looked at his watch. 'I'll call everyone first thing. We'll elect an interim chief and work from there.'

'I agree,' said Mark. 'It needs restructuring anyway.'

'Absolutely,' said Tony. 'I always felt the sales division could do with an injection of new blood.'

'Depends on the finances, of course,' said Mark.

'You'll work it out, I guess,' said Finola.

'Between you,' said Jill.

'No problem,' said Tony.

'We're friends,' said Mark.

'We all are,' Finola murmured as the two men smiled at each other.

HOT DATE

BLACKROCK

O K, I was quivering with excitement. I really was. Whenever I picked up a piece of paper I could see that my hands were actually shaking. It's kind of pathetic to get into a state like that about a bloke but, well, this was Richard Clavin. The smouldering, sexy, makes-Colin-Firth-look-like-Danny-DeVito Richard Clavin. And he was my date.

There wasn't a woman in Whizz-Bang Solutions who didn't think that Richard Clavin was sex on legs. He was tall (naturally) had dark-raven hair (expertly cut) deep blue eyes (which were whirlpools of emotion) and a jawline that any James Bond actor would've killed for. Oh, and he was excruciatingly intelligent, on the fast-track for promotion and had a wicked sense of humour. So, you see, anyone would want to go out with Richard Clavin. It wasn't as though this was an ordinary date. I was – to put it a little over the top – the chosen one!

And I'm never the chosen one. Never. My track record

with men makes Bridget Jones look like J-Lo. I'm hopeless. I pick the wrong one every time and I end up with my heart broken feeling as though 'dumped again' is emblazoned across my forehead in silver lettering as a warning to other stupid girls who think there's such a person as Mr Right. I usually pick the fuckwits, you see. The kind of blokes that shouldn't be let out without an emotional health warning tattooed on their anatomy. I never seem to get it right and I don't know why. Sometimes I think I must have been Cleopatra in a previous life and I'm still being punished for it. Sometimes I think that I was born hopeless. And then sometimes a bloke comes along and I forget everything that's gone before so I fall hard and fast for them and then remember the hopeless stuff a few weeks later when I'm on my own in the apartment playing 'Without You' at full volume while knocking back a few litres of Smirnoff Ice.

I didn't know what the Richard Clavin experience would be like but I hoped it wouldn't be too short-lived because I was getting fed up of 'Without You'.

He'd walked into the design department of our website company that morning and had looked around for a moment as though searching for the right person. And then those blue eyes had lighted on me as he smiled and said, 'Sadie, I've been given a free meal tonight. Would you like to join me?'

I looked at him, my mouth opening and closing wordlessly, and he smiled again.

'Dan McCormack's new restaurant in Blackrock,' he

told me. 'Remember we did their system? He said to drop in tonight if I could. I know you did a lot of work on the site. I wondered if you'd like to join me.'

Would I what! I clenched my fists together so that he couldn't see I'd already started to tremble and I nodded vigorously.

'Great,' he said as though he was totally unaware of my excitement. 'How about we meet in the pub near the train station? You know, the new trendy one?'

I cleared my throat. 'No, because I'm from the other side of town,' I said. 'But I'm sure I'll find it.'

'I can't remember the name.' He frowned. 'Topsie, Mopsie, Dropsie . . . something on those lines anyway.'

'No problem,' I assured him.

'About seven-thirty?'

'Perfect.'

'Great.' He beamed. (I forgot to mention that he had two rows of perfect white teeth.) 'See you then, Sadie.'

He strode out of the room and I almost dissolved at my desk.

'Oh, Sadie!' Anne-Marie Tarrant looked at me, her brown eyes full of envy. 'You lucky, lucky cow!'

'I know.' I could hardly keep the triumph out of my voice. 'He obviously realises my potential.'

'Yeah.' Noreen Smith looked at me with hostility. 'Your potential to be dragged into bed.'

'Tut, tut.' I gave her my best Cheshire Cat grin. 'Sounds like you're jealous.'

'No,' snapped Noreen. 'I just don't understand what all of you see in him. Self-opinionated shithead if you ask me.'

'Fortunately I didn't,' I cooed sweetly at her. 'Oh, and Noreen, don't bother telling me that he's all good looks and no brains 'cos we know that's not true.'

'All good looks and the emotional maturity of a complete fuckwit,' said Noreen nastily and stabbed at her keyboard.

I didn't like the fuckwit analogy. It reminded me too much of what could go wrong.

They were all jealous. I would've been jealous too if he'd come in and chosen Myra, for example. Or Helen. Or Susan. Or any of the others. But he hadn't. He'd chosen me.

I know what you're thinking. You're thinking that I'm getting into a state about someone who'll prove to be the emotional juvenile that Noreen thinks and who'll break my heart by making some crass comment about the size of my thighs or something. You're wrong. Richard Clavin isn't like that. He's kind. The day I dropped half-a-dozen crammed folders onto the floor beside the drinking fountain he stopped and helped me pick them up, commiserating with me and never once looking down the top of my (somewhat inappropriately) low-cut blouse. He'd said that it could happen to anyone and not to worry and wouldn't you think in a company like ours we'd have got rid of all that paperwork by now? He was nice to me. And he's emotionally mature.

*

Clearly, for such an important date, everything had to be perfect. It would've been better if I'd had a couple of days' notice because then I'd have had time to prepare myself properly. As it was I'd have to shave my legs when I got home that evening because I couldn't let him see them in their hairy glory – I was due to get them waxed in two days' time but that was no good now. Also, I knew that I couldn't do my favourite face-mask because that was a thing that needed a couple of days – otherwise I'd have spots on my face due to its 'remove all impurities' qualities. Finally (and a bit more worryingly) I didn't have time to get my hair cut but I rang the hairdresser and booked myself in for a wash and blow dry at half-five. After which I intended to go home, pop on my unflattering but useful shower cap to protect my newly styled mane from the steam, and sit in a scented bath surrounded by candles. The candles would calm my nerves and get my karma right for the night. (I'm not really into all that karma stuff but it can't do any harm, can it?)

I spent the rest of the morning pleasurably thinking about what I was going to wear – my new suede skirt with the cowboy fringe, perhaps. But I dismissed that because it was too jokey and light-hearted and I felt that dinner with Richard Clavin should be a more sophisticated affair. Even if it was preceded by drinks at Mopsies or Topsies or whatever it was called. My little black dress was, of course, totally sophisticated and a great standby for nights out when I wanted to look charming and elegant instead of sort of scatty like I usually did, but it was two seasons old and just a little tired. Buying something new would've been an option if our offices hadn't been located in the retail wasteland of Amiens Street and lunchtime restricted to a sandwich delivered to the desk because we were supposed to be working hard on Project X. (We always called the busy things Project X and sometimes they even had a hint of glamour, but this was a site for an electrical distributor and totally boring.)

I gazed into space. Perhaps my biscuit-coloured trousers and my moss-green Lycra top? Too businesslike. My Edina Ronay knitted dress? Maybe . . . but if it was warm in the bar (and it was sure to be warm in the bar) then my face would go red and would clash unbecomingly with the pink wool. I was still mentally mixing and matching when Jessica Ferris, our managing director, walked into the room.

'All hands to the pumps,' she barked. 'Anyone who's working on DomElectric get the finger out now. The head honcho and his sidekick are coming in to see us at five-thirty. I want to have something up and running for him.' She looked at me. 'You're working on it, Sadie, aren't you?'

'Well, yes,' I said. 'And Robert, of course.'

'OK you guys, get to it.'

I looked at my watch. I could get something up and running by Jessica's deadline but it would be hard. Also, I was due to be in the hairdresser at five-thirty.

'You won't need both of us at half five,' I remarked as casually as I could.

'Of course I bloody will,' snapped Jessica.

'But my hair appointment—'

'Sadie, cancel your appointment,' said Jessica.

'It's just that—'

'Sadie, these people are paying us good money and you will be there. So will Robert. Enough said.'

I groaned. Still, I thought, I only lived a ten-minute sprint away from the office. I could hang around for the presentation, get home and wash my hair myself. It wouldn't be the same as having it done for me but something usually goes wrong on a big date and missing my hair appointment wasn't the worst thing that could happen.

Of course it wasn't. Worse was to come, as Robert and I really struggled with the DomElectric, trying to get the links running as smoothly as we wanted. But we managed, just about, to get everything up and running by half five. Which was when Jessica walked in to say that they'd be a bit late but they'd be here by six. Six was cutting things a bit fine but it still wasn't a disaster. Even if I didn't get home till half-past I could have a really quick shower and do my speedy-getting-ready job. And it was a reasonably short hop from Connolly Station to Blackrock. But, I thought bleakly, as I moved the mouse over the image of a washer-dryer and wondered why on earth the description wasn't coming up like it was supposed to, this wasn't the preparation I'd wanted for my big night out.

They arrived at a quarter past six. I ran through the basics of the site with them while they asked the stupid sort of questions that people with no knowledge of technology whatsoever ask. And then they moved the mouse over the images themselves and the descriptions came up like they were supposed to, except when they clicked on the bright-green vacuum cleaner and the whole site crashed.

'No problem,' said Robert. 'That's just a glitch. I can sort that for you.'

His fingers flew over the keyboard while I looked surreptitiously at my watch. I would have to go really soon. It occurred to me that it would have been smart to have rung Richard Clavin's extension earlier and told him that I might be a bit late. But even if I'd thought of it I probably wouldn't have done it because he might have read it as (a) I'd changed my mind or (b) I was too busy to come out, and he might have asked Helen or Susan or – heaven forbid – even Noreen instead. So I hadn't rung him and maybe he was now at home thinking about me while I was still here struggling with images of vacuum cleaners.

'There,' said Robert in relief as the site finally came back. 'As I said, a minor glitch.'

'It looks good,' said one of the electric company honchos.

'I like it too,' said the other.

'Good work, guys,' said Jessica.

'I'm sorry to rush,' I said as apologetically as I could. 'But I have an appointment this evening and I really need to . . .' I allowed my voice to trail off as though there was nothing in my life more interesting than being with them but that this other appointment was interrupting us and, unfortunately, I had to deal with it.

All the same, Jessica looked irritated. 'If you must, Sadie,' she said.

'I must.' I grabbed my bag and legged it out of the building. The apartment I was sharing with my friend Ashling was on the quays. I ran down the street and was breathless by the time I'd punched the entry code into the keypad.

Ashling had already gone out. She had a steady boyfriend, the not-too-unattractive John, and she spent more time at his place than ours. In fact I sometimes wondered whether or not I would be needing a new flat-mate soon. A mental image of sharing my apartment with the gorgeous Richard Clavin drifted into my head.

'Come on, come on,' I told myself as I peeled myself out of my working clothes. 'No time for this.'

I jumped under the shower. It was freezing. Obviously Ashling had used up all the hot water. I swore as I hopped around under the icy spray and tried to rinse the suds from my hair. I hugged one side of the shower as I also tried to shave my goosebump-covered legs. I'd have words with the bitch later. Using all the hot water was simply selfish.

It was a quick shower. I got out and wrapped myself in a towel, still shivering. I grabbed my body cream, shook it and squeezed the bottle. A huge glob of white cream shot out and landed on my wet hair. I washed it in cold water again.

Do you want the whole litany of disasters? Do you want to hear about how my hair just wouldn't, absolutely wouldn't, dry properly? Do you want to hear about my mascara smudging and leaving a dirty black blob on my made-up face? Do you want to hear about how I decided that my denim skirt and white linen shirt would look good (even though not sophisticated) but how I managed to get make-up on the collar of the shirt anyway so that, at seven o'clock, I was still rummaging in my wardrobe looking for something to wear. I settled on my lilac dress, which actually is quite sophisticated but is a bit clingier than I'd like given the lack of success of my last diet in shifting poundage from my stomach area.

By ten past seven I was nearly ready. I picked up my hairspray to try and do a last-minute hold job on my errant locks. Or at least I thought I picked up my hairspray. What I had, in fact, picked up was my foot reviver spray. I realised this as the waft of mist drifted through the air and settled on my hair. It didn't make that much difference, I suppose. But it meant that my head now smelled of peppermint and athlete's foot lotion. I grabbed the correct spray, enveloped myself in a cloud of mist, and dragged my brush through my hair. I hoped that footspray and hair-spray weren't too incompatible. And then I picked up my bag and hurried out of the apartment.

It was twenty-five past seven when I got to the train station which was pretty good going. According to the board, the next train was in twenty minutes. It would be eight o'clock before I got to Blackrock; half an hour was a bit more than fashionably late. I'd been allowing for ten minutes of lateness. I could ring him, though. Everyone in Whizz-Bang had a card with staff mobile numbers on it. This was so that we could get called to some techno-logical disaster day or night.

Does the phrase 'total nightmare' mean anything to you? It was a total nightmare when I realised that I'd left the card in my other bag. I was comforting myself with the thought that it didn't matter, that he might in any event ring me, when I realised that I'd left my phone in my other bag too. The only things in the stupid bag I had with me were my purse (cash only, no credit cards – other bag of course!) and my make-up. (And the footspray. I had to wear high-heeled mules with the lilac dress and they were extremely uncomfortable. But they looked good. The footspray was a last-minute clever thought. Though not as clever as my phone would've been.)

Anyway, no more disasters. The train arrived, I got on,

there were no weirdos ready to spill Coke or paint or whatever on top of me. The Dart slid into Blackrock at eight on the button. I jumped off the train, landed awkwardly, and fell out of my shoes. The shoe that stayed on the platform was fine. The shoe that fell beneath the train was squashed to a pulp as the train pulled off. I sat on the platform, nursing my ankle that was swelling alarmingly, and started to cry. There was a stupid part of me that thought that people would care about what had happened. And, in fact, a couple of them had stopped when I fell and asked was I all right. I'd said yes, yes, fine, as dismissively as I could because of course I wasn't all right, I was mortified. They hadn't realised that my shoe was being pulverised beneath the train. They didn't know that the only difference between my ankle and a football – well, quite frankly, there wasn't much of a damn difference. And so they all disappeared out of the station and left me sniffing on the platform as my hair fell in lank foot-reviver tresses around my face.

I couldn't go to the bar now. I was late and I was a mess and I knew that some people might have been able to joke their way out of it but some people probably didn't care that I'd had secret fantasies about a date with gorgeous Richard Clavin for absolutely months and that those dreams were now as shattered as my poor squashed shoe. And I couldn't walk into a trendy bar with my face a mess, my hair still smelling of peppermint and athlete's foot lotion, wearing one shoe and sporting a swollen ankle. Call me vain, but there you are. It clearly wasn't Richard Clavin who was the fuckwit in this scenario.

I got to my feet and hopped toward one of the bright-green benches. I didn't know what to do. The shrill noise from my bag made me jump with fright. It was at that point that I realised that 'fuckwit' wasn't even half appropriate enough a word for me. I did have my phone after all. I'd shoved it into the little side compartment in the bag. But I still didn't have the card with everyone's phone number on it. That was in my credit-card folder and I knew that the folder was very definitely in my other bag.

I took out the phone and hit answer.

'Where are you, Sadie?' Richard Clavin asked loudly above the beat of a music mix. 'This bar is crowded and you might be here but I can't see you anywhere. And if you're not here then you're really, really late. And I don't mind you being late but I do mind if you've decided to stand me up.'

I hadn't managed to get a word in edgeways even if I'd known what word to use.

'Um, well, actually—'

'Is there a problem?'

'Sort of,' I said.

'What?' He wasn't yelling now and I realised it was because he must have stepped out of the bar.

'I had a bit of a disaster,' I told him.

'What sort of disaster?'

What sort of disaster did I want to confess? That I'd

been late and had a cold shower and put cream and then footspray in my hair? That I'd fallen off the train like a gawky teenager and lost my shoe? Or that there had been a crisis at the office and I'd had to stay to sort things out and I was sorry for not having phoned him before now because I'd been so very busy but I'd meant to call him immediately I'd got a moment. Which of those things would make Richard Clavin like me and ask me out again?

'Just a disaster,' I said. 'Sorry.'

'Where are you, Sadie?' he asked.

'Look, it doesn't matter, I can't see you tonight.'

A train screeched into the station and drowned out my words. I thought about getting on it until I clicked that I hadn't crossed the platform.

'Are you on the train?' demanded Richard.

'Look, Richard, sorry. I'll talk to you again.'

I closed my phone and shoved it back into the bag. I wondered would he ring again but he didn't. I buried my head in my hands. I was a hopeless, useless fool of a woman who wasn't safe to be let out on her own. And who clearly wasn't mature enough to go for sophisticated evenings with men like Richard Clavin.

'Sadie?'

This time I nearly jumped five metres into the air. Only the fact that I couldn't actually move stopped me. I looked up.

'What's the problem?' Richard Clavin was standing beside me, doubtless intrigued by my mascara-tracked cheeks, my bird's-nest hair and my single-shoed state.

'What's the problem?' I almost laughed. 'What's the problem!?'

'There is, obviously, a problem,' he said. 'Otherwise you'd have left the station and come to the pub.' He waved at Topsie's which was only a few yards away and clearly visible through the rails. 'I heard the train on the phone at the same time as I saw it go by and realised you must be here.'

'I'm sorry,' I said. 'I've had a shit day.'

'I have those all the time.' He grinned.

'And I really can't have dinner with you because I have athlete's foot in my hair and no shoes.'

He looked at me in puzzlement. 'Would you like to run that by me again?'

So I explained about working late and the mix up with the sprays and falling off the train, and I could see him trying very hard not to laugh and I wanted to curl up in a ball and die.

'I guess Dan McCormack wouldn't be too impressed if I brought a woman with a headful of athlete's foot into the restaurant,' he agreed.

'Anyway, I'm not really your sort of girl,' I told Richard. 'This kind of thing happens to me a lot. I'm a walking disaster area. I split up with my last boyfriend because I reversed his car into a bus stop.'

This time he did laugh. It was gorgeous and sexy. Naturally.

'Besides,' I told him. 'Everyone thinks you're too good-looking to be decent boyfriend material.'

'That's a bummer,' he said. 'Besides, who said anything about boyfriends?'

I winced. He was a fuckwit. And so was I.

'Can you walk at all?' he asked.

'I can hobble,' I told him. 'My ankle is sore. And I only have one shoe.'

He looked at me appraisingly. 'We can make it as far as the car park,' he said. 'Which is where I'm parked. And then I'll drive you back to my place and I'll strap up your ankle and we can order a takeaway. If that's all right?'

Gosh, I thought. How decisive. That's probably why he was one of the top guys in the company. He didn't mess about.

'I don't sleep with people on the first date,' I said.

His deep blue eyes opened wider. 'Neither do I.'

I winced again. I'd wanted to sound as decisive as him but maybe I'd just been a bit silly.

'Can you hop?' he asked. 'Or do you want me to carry you?'

'I can hop.' Although the thought of being carried was pretty appealing.

He helped me into the car and then turned to me.

'I thought you'd stood me up,' he said.

'I wouldn't do that,' I told him.

'That's what I reckoned.' He smiled at me. 'That's why

98

I like you, Sadie. That's why I asked you out. You seem a really nice person.'

'A bit of a walking nightmare though,' I said.

'Not so much of the walking.' He laughed as he started the car.

He wasn't an emotional wreck. He was gorgeous and funny and just plain nice. I wasn't too emotionally wrecked either. I didn't sleep with him on the first date. Because there were lots of other dates to follow. I didn't try as hard for those and I didn't have any disasters either (well, not major ones – there was the night when I thought we were supposed to be meeting in the Morrison whereas he'd said Morrissey's but we sorted that out). There were other ups and downs, of course. He wasn't perfect and neither was I. But we managed to work things out. Which just goes to show that sometimes the really gorgeous blokes are meant for people like me after all. And I mustn't have been Cleopatra in a previous life. Maybe I was her assistant.

WALK ON BY ● ━━━━━━━━━━━●━━━━━━━━━━━

SYDNEY PARADE

When my mother phoned to say that she was coming home for a visit I almost dropped the receiver in shock. The last time she'd set foot in Ireland was ten years before and she wouldn't have been here then except that I'd married Bernard in Dublin and she'd felt obliged to turn up. But she'd hurried back to the States almost immediately afterwards, claiming that Dublin was a cultural backwater and that I had succumbed to suburbia. I didn't respond to the accusations. They were true, to a point. But I was quite happy to settle down in her perceived creative desert of the Dublin suburbs with the man I loved.

I guess if I'd been born now, if the whole thing had happened today, the newspapers would simply run a feature story telling their readers that Michelle Morrissey was pregnant, and there'd be pictures of her in *Hello!* and *VIP* and *Heat* with her bump hanging out over her Stella McCartney jeans as she strolled along Grafton Street looking chic and happy. Maybe some of them would call me a 'love-child', although that term isn't as common as it once was. But I suppose it's better than bastard or illegitimate which were the terms of the 1960s. It was to avoid those names and a far less sympathetic press that my mother moved to France with her then lover, my father, Luc Tricot. I don't know if they avoided the newspapers completely but the French journals didn't give a damn about unmarried pregnant women.

My mother, Michelle Morrissey, was famous in the 1960s. Actually she's famous again now because there was a resurgence of interest in her a few years ago when her record company released a 'Greatest Hits' album following her Oscar nomination for the theme tune to a Hollywood blockbuster. You know how it is with those things, all sorts of people buy the damn record whether they like the music or not. So it got to number one in all the album charts and re-introduced her to the listening public. What with the resurgence in sixties nostalgia and the Oscar thing I suppose it would've been surprising if it didn't do well.

She was a great singer back then. Still is, even now, though obviously she finds it harder to hit the top notes than before. Her voice takes over a room, her music takes over your mind. It's similar to Joan Baez but with a kind of scratchy, earthy quality that you don't get in Joan's voice. Their songs are similar, though, all very sixties, all concerned with love and change and messing up the world. Maybe that's why they're popular again.

Naturally my mother was known as the Irish Baez, which irritated her immensely. She used to say that she wasn't an Irish version of anyone but herself. I understood her feelings. It's probably the only thing I really ever understood about her.

She was at the height of her fame when she met Luc, fell deeply in lust and got pregnant. She told me once that it had happened in the back of a purple Volkswagen van just outside Orranmore. I would've preferred the Santa Monica Boulevard or something more exotic, but a van in Orranmore was the best she could do for me.

She never really thought about staying in Ireland once she realised that I was on the way. She'd heard whispers before, about how so-and-so was 'in trouble' and how she'd been packed off somewhere until the whole thing was over. She'd heard the stories too, about how unmarried mothers were treated like criminals in hospitals, how they were persuaded to give up their babies for adoption, how they were made to feel like sinners, transgressors, evil women. She wasn't sure whether or not she'd be treated like that, or whether she'd be treated even worse. It was all very well to be a famous singer who'd appeared on *Top of the Pops* wearing an emerald-green chiffon mini-dress covered with gold-sequinned harps but that wouldn't cut any ice in an Irish maternity hospital.

I don't really know whether things were any better in France. She says that she was treated well and that she was happy, firstly in Paris where I was born, and then in a town near Avignon, which I remember as dry and dusty and always hot.

She went through a lean period then. Music was moving on, away from save-the-world ballads and into glam rock. It wasn't her thing. Fortunately it didn't matter too much at the time – the royalty money was still pouring in; she bought a small farmhouse and brought me up on her own. Luc hadn't come to Avignon with us. The affair had fizzled out after I was born and he left for Nashville where he thought the action would be better. I've never met Luc, never even seen a photograph of him. It doesn't bother me though.

You'd think that I'd be close to my mother, living together on the French farm (although it wasn't really a farm, just a farmhouse – we got all our supplies from the village), but it didn't work out like that. Apparently for the first two years she was besotted with the idea of being a mother and would sit for hours with me in the poppy-filled field behind our house, chattering to me in a mixture of French and English, making me feel loved and wanted. And then Roger Madison came into our lives. He was a record producer who'd tracked my mother down. He wanted to update some of her songs; he wanted – he said – to make her famous again.

It was complete horseshit really. Nobody who was famous in the sixties could hack it in the seventies. I think my mother knew that really. But she was flattered by

Roger's attention and she agreed that we needed to go to London to be where the action was.

I remember London more than Paris. We lived in a flat near the King's Road. It was always full of people coming and going, friends of Roger, friends of my mother, friends of friends. She and Roger had become lovers by then. They also took recreational drugs. She'd missed out on the drug scene in the sixties so I suppose she thought it was the thing to do. It reinforced her potential rock-chick credentials. She didn't neglect me, exactly, but I wasn't the highest priority on her list. Booze and marijuana were – and who's to say she was wrong?

It didn't work out with Roger. He didn't make her famous again. Dorian Carmody, a different producer, was the next person to lie to her about fame. He also became her lover. He didn't make her famous either. He introduced her to different recreational drugs. There was a piece in the paper about them. And I was mentioned too – the little girl who knew the difference between talcum powder and cocaine.

My grandparents arrived from Dublin to see whether or not the stories were true. My mother did her best to appear coherent, and then Dorian turned up and she kissed him hungrily in front of them. I remember that very well. I didn't like seeing her kiss him like that. And I knew that my grandparents didn't like it very much either. They brought me home with them. My mother protested weakly but she didn't care very much. Dorian had become her life now. Dorian and what he could give her.

I settled down quite well back in Dublin. I liked being in my grandparents' home in Terenure. It was a very ordinary three-bed semi with a big garden, two apple trees and an ornamental pond, and it made me feel ordinary too. I wanted to be ordinary. I didn't want to be the focus of attention of adults with white faces and unnaturally glazed eyes. I wanted to be told to eat my vegetables. I wanted to go to school every day. I wanted to have a dog.

My dog was called Punk and he was a mixed breed.

Sometimes I spoke to my mother on the telephone and she always said that she'd come and get me as soon as she'd made her money again. I knew, though I didn't want to know, that most of it had gone on the recreational drugs. I knew that she'd left Dorian or he'd left her and she was now living in a flat in Notting Hill. They hadn't made the film, of course, and sometimes she called it Grotting Hill. Then she'd cackle with uncontrollable laughter and I'd feel very uncomfortable and hang up.

And then she simply stopped calling. My grandparents said that she'd gone to the States. I wondered if it was to be with my father again but apparently not. She'd gone to make some low-budget movie. It wasn't porn, or even soft-porn, but she appeared naked in it all the same. Among other things it raised her profile again. Years afterwards she told me that the nudity was absolutely essential to the plot. In reality, though, I think it was absolutely essential to getting paid.

I didn't hear from her for ages. My grandparents didn't talk about her either. I went to school, studied hard, developed a reputation for being a bit boring and got spectacularly good results in my exams. Then I got a pretty good job in a bank where I met a number of men but eventually fell in love with Bernard. He was intrigued to learn about my mother. Most people were. They'd heard of her, of course, and they couldn't believe that I was her daughter. Although, they'd sometimes say, look-ing at me critically, you do look a bit like her, Amelie. You have the same hair. Red curly hair. Irish hair. But not her brilliant-green eyes. Or her wide mouth with its pouting lips. I must have resembled my missing father.

I wasn't sure whether or not my mother would come to my wedding. It really wasn't her sort of thing. She'd graduated from her seventies 'Goth' look to embrace the wide shoulders, big hair and dolly-mixture colours of the eighties. She'd also given up the recreational drugs. More or less. I still knew the difference between talcum powder and cocaine.

The newspapers heard that she'd come back for the wedding. Photographers turned up at the church and afterwards her picture was plastered all over the papers.

At the reception, she walked around the tables telling people about her 'film career' and how someone was looking for her to sing the theme song to a new movie and how she was thinking of cutting a new album – it all sounded horrible and fake and I felt sorry and embarrassed for her and wished she hadn't come. She'd worn the kind of dress that Cher was known for wearing – see-through with rhinestones – which was obviously the reason why the only photos in the paper were of her!

Bernard said that she was certainly an interesting woman. She said he was the most boring person she'd ever met. She wanted to know what our sex life was like. I told her it was none of her business. She supposed it was as boring as him. I wanted to shout at her that it wasn't, that Bernard was a thoughtful and surprisingly inventive lover, but I didn't. Instead I said that at least both Bernard and myself knew the name of the person we were making love with, which was more than could be said of her most of the time. And I said that her music career had been short-lived and forgettable. And that her film career had been an embarrassment. And that she was nothing more than a slut. I didn't feel the slightest bit guilty when I saw the flash of hurt in her brilliant-green eyes before she laughed throatily and told me that I was a product of my sadly suburban upbringing. And I said that at least my grandparents had been sober and clean enough to bring me up. She walked away from me and the next time I saw her she was sitting on the best man's lap.

But she sang at my wedding reception and I realised, with a shock, that she really did have a wonderful voice. And that everyone stopped and listened. They couldn't help themselves. Even I couldn't help myself. I was surprised, at that point, that she hadn't made a comeback because she was so bloody magnetic and brilliant when she sang.

A couple of months later the Hollywood blockbuster-type movie was released and my mother sang the theme tune. It was the song that was nominated for the Oscar. She was at the ceremony, squeezed into a dress by an up-and-coming designer, looking twenty years younger, her brilliant eyes glittering at the crowds. To me she looked triumphant and accusing even though someone else won. And despite not getting the trophy, my mother's song spent longer in the charts.

So finally she was famous again. And, I thought, laughing at me. I didn't bother to call and congratulate her. Besides, she was now living in LA with her latest lover, somewhat amazingly not a record producer but a doctor. I suppose she'd gone to see him about her drug dependency. Or maybe he was a shrink. I didn't know, I didn't care, and neither of us made contact. Occasionally I'd read about her in the magazines, but not very often, even though she was now earning pots more money than ever before.

As all this came flooding back, I stood holding the phone in shock. A voice across the transatlantic silence brought me back to myself. 'Are you there, Amelie?' my mother asked.

'Yes.'

'So I will be arriving next Tuesday,' she said. 'You will be able to meet me?'

'Hasn't your record company organised a limo?' I asked sarcastically.

'This is a private visit, *ma fille*,' she said. (I hated when she threw in the French words. It was pretentious and unnecessary.) 'Why would they organise anything for me?'

'Because I thought that's the way it worked,' I said. 'I thought you stars were always treated like minor royalty.'

She chuckled, deep and throaty. 'Major royalty,' she corrected, 'if that's what we want. But I thought you would prefer if I arrived quietly, *non*?'

'Whatever.'

'You will meet me?' She sounded vaguely anxious.

'Sure,' I said ungraciously. 'I'll pick you up. Where are you staying?'

'With you,' she said as though she'd been an honoured guest a hundred times before.

I put down the phone and stared into space. I was still staring into space when I realised that it was time for me to pick up Catherine from school. My daughter is six years old. She doesn't know the difference between coke and talcum powder.

Bernard was equally surprised when I told him of my mother's impending visit. His black eyebrows almost disappeared into his head as he opened his eyes wide and wondered aloud why she was coming.

'Broke up with the doctor?' he asked.

'She's never visited me after a break-up before,' I reminded him. 'Hardly this time either.'

'Perhaps she's ill.' He looked anxiously at me. 'You've got to accept that she might be ill, Amelie.'

'For heaven's sake!' I snapped. 'The woman was a cokehead and an alcoholic. I've been expecting her to die for years.'

'You're upset,' he said.

'Of course I'm upset,' I retorted. 'She upsets me. She always has.'

She'd flown under an assumed name so that there weren't any photographers at the airport. I didn't like to say that there probably wouldn't be anyway, it was Dublin she was coming to, not celebrity-mad LA, but I kept my mouth shut. Actually, I wondered whether or not I'd recognise her. The last photo I'd seen of her had been at some awards ceremony where she was handing out a prize. Her glorious red hair had been piled into an exotic creation on top of her head, she was dressed entirely in her now trademark emerald green, dripped with borrowed diamonds and looking like an Irish colleen on acid.

I didn't quite miss her as she walked out of the arrivals hall but I could easily have done. She was wearing a fawn jacket, black skirt, black shoes, fawn cashmere top. Her hair was pulled back from her face. Her earrings were tiny drop pearls. And she wasn't even wearing sunglasses.

'Hi.' I stepped out to greet her.

'Hello.'

I'd been half-expecting an effusive LA-style greeting, or at least a double-cheek-French-style peck, but she simply smiled at me.

'This it?' I nodded at the case – Louis Vuitton so at least she still had the trappings. Though on closer examination I could see that the clothes were expensive and I assumed that the pearls were real.

She followed me to the car park, looking around her as though trying to accustom herself to the smallness that was Dublin. But she was still uncharacteristically quiet.

I drove along the motorway and towards the bay.

'I used to come here as a kid,' she remarked as we crossed the toll bridge, and the striped towers of the Poolbeg chimney stacks reached up into the china-blue sky.

'Wouldn't have thought it was your thing,' I said.

'Of course it was,' she said. 'I wrote songs about the sea and the birds and the bloody great blot on the landscape that these are.' She pointed to the chimney stacks.

'Oh.'

We drove in silence again. Eventually I turned into our road and pulled up in front of our house. She got out of the car and looked at it appraisingly.

'Too cluttered,' she said.

'I beg your pardon?'

'Too close,' she amended. 'To everyone else.'

It was a four-bedroomed house, built in the 1940s, the

same decade as she'd been born. I liked it. It was similar in appearance to the one where my grandparents had brought me up, solid and stable. And it had two apple trees in a long garden that backed onto the railway line behind us.

'Would you prefer a suite in the Conrad?' I asked coolly.

'No,' she said. 'This is fine.'

'Good,' I told her. 'And remember that this is my home. It's where I live. So leave off the snide comments about suburbia, will you? Besides, this is an expensive part of town and we don't think of it as the suburbs.'

'Whatever.' She followed me inside and stood in the hallway. I knew that the décor – pastel colours and the kind of Edwardian country-house feel – wouldn't be her thing. But it was my thing. I liked it. I loved my home.

There were two reception rooms downstairs divided by a double door which we normally left open. It made them bright and airy. Less cluttered, which might appeal to her. Anyway she had a nerve to complain about space and clutter. The flat on the King's Road had been tiny and overflowing with junk.

'Would you like tea?' I asked.

She nodded.

'I've put you in the room on the left upstairs,' I told her. 'Do you want me to carry your case up for you?'

She looked at me scathingly. 'I do think it's something I can manage.'

'You've had a long journey,' I said. 'I thought you might be tired.'

'Not that tired. Besides,' she looked at me trium- phantly, 'I'm accustomed to travelling these days. I do a lot in the States.'

'I suppose you do.'

I left her to carry her own bags upstairs and filled the kettle while she pottered around. Though 'pottered' isn't a good word to use about my mother. Pottering describes someone older, laid back. My mother – even when she was singing ballads – was never laid back. And I didn't consider her old.

But, of course, she was getting older. In her sixties now, though she certainly didn't look it. Yet it must slow her down. God knows, I was only thirty-five and already I felt slower than I used to be.

Was she here because of illness? She didn't look ill either but how would I know? I hadn't seen her in so long. Maybe the radiant glow about her was more to do with prescrip- tion drugs from Doctor Lurve than actual good health. And if she was ill – cancer, I supposed – what did she want from me? To forgive her for being a shit mother? To tell her that the mornings I'd woken to find her slumped in the armchair stoned out of her head didn't matter? To say that it had been a difficult time but, hey, I'd got through it and it was all part of life's rich experience? And did she want me to hug her and hold her and tell her that despite everything I'd always loved her? Always thought of her?

The truth was that from the moment that Grandma and Grandpa Morrissey had taken me back to Dublin I'd barely thought of her at all. And when she became famous again I really didn't think of her as anyone related to me. She was a distant figure, someone I'd heard of but had no real connection to any more. She didn't matter. She'd never really mattered.

'D'you want it black?' I asked as she came back into the kitchen.

'I don't suppose you have lemon?'

Wordlessly I took a lemon from the fruit basket and cut a slice. I poured the tea into a porcelain mug, dropped the slice into it, and handed it to her.

'Where's Catherine?' she asked.

Bernard had picked her up from school that afternoon and taken her to the cinema. I hadn't been sure whether or not I wanted them to be there when I arrived home. Right now I rather wished that they were.

I told her where they were.

'What time will they be back?' she asked.

I looked at my watch. 'In about half an hour.'

The sudden whoosh of a Dart going by caught her attention.

'How can you live here?' she asked. 'There's a train running through your back garden.'

'Don't be silly,' I said. 'It's not in my back garden. And I like it. I like seeing people's faces as they go by.'

'But they can see you too,' she said.

'It doesn't bother me.'

'It'd bother me.'

'Strange,' I said. 'Given that you've spent so much of your life being watched by people.'

'That's different.'

'No it's not.'

She sipped her tea. I walked out into the back garden. The sun was lukewarm.

'Bit of a change, weather-wise,' I said.

She nodded.

'Why are you here?' It came out more abruptly than I intended and she winced slightly. I knew then it was an illness. I wished I hadn't asked.

'I wanted to talk to you,' she said. 'About everything.'

'I don't want to talk to you about anything,' I said. 'I accept that you're probably sorry about my childhood but it's irrelevant. Our lives are irrelevant. We're joined by a biological incident, that's all.'

'I rather hoped it was more than that,' she murmured.

'I don't think so.' I looked at her. 'But so what. I've lived my life, you've lived yours.'

'Are you happy?' she asked.

'Yes,' I said.

'The little things?'

'Yes,' I said.

'I wasn't,' she told me. 'For a long time.'

'I don't need to know,' I said. 'It's over.'

'I'm not sorry,' she told me.

I raised an eyebrow.

'I'm not sorry because I did what I had to do.'

'Fine,' I said.

'But I am sorry that I ridiculed what you did.'

'Oh?'

'The suburban thing,' she said.

'I said it doesn't matter.'

'You see, I was rebelling against it,' she told me.

'No, you weren't,' I said. 'You were a Catholic girl who got pregnant and who left home. Lots of you did it and I don't blame you one little bit for that.'

'No?'

'It's afterwards that bothers me,' I said. 'Luc going. Roger, Dorian – the others, I know there were others. And the drugs.' I shrugged. 'It's not that I'm criticising you but you had a kid and you should've known better.'

'Do you think I was hopeless?' asked my mother.

'Pretty hopeless,' I said.

'But lots of kids want to be different,' she said.

'No, they don't,' I said. 'Most of us want to be the same. We want ordinary mothers who get up every day and bring us to school and make us our dinner and give out to us for not washing our hands. We don't want spaced out, washed up has-beens.'

'But I wasn't washed up,' she said. 'I was nominated for an Oscar.'

'True.' I nodded.

'And I would've liked you to be at the awards.'

'Cut the crap,' I said. 'What's the prognosis?'

'Prognosis?' She looked at me in surprise.

'Look, I presume you're here because you've been told you have some incurable disease and you only have a few months to live,' I said. 'And I suppose you want to make your peace with me and tell me that you never meant to hurt me.'

She looked at me in amazement.

'And it's fine,' I continued. 'But I don't want to do the whole forgive and forget thing. I just want to forget.'

'Really?' The look of hurt was in those fabulous eyes again. 'You'd rather forget I existed?'

'You forgot about me,' I reminded her. 'Which wasn't a problem, it didn't bother me. But I don't see why we have to go through a charade of pretending.'

'I suppose you're right.' She looked at me thoughtfully. 'Though of course I never forgot about you.'

'So you're welcome to stay but I really don't want any drama,' I said as though she hadn't spoken.

We watched each other in silence.

'What is it?' I asked.

'What's what?'

'The disease.'

She looked embarrassed and for a moment I thought that maybe it was AIDS.

'There is no disease.'

'Huh?'

'I came here for a different reason.'

'Oh?'

'But now I'm not sure . . .' she looked at me nervously, her brow creased.

'What?' I asked. I realised that her expression was exactly like Catherine's when she was puzzled about something.

'I'm embarrassed because I'm afraid you'll laugh at me,' she said. 'Or think the wrong thing.'

I looked at her quizzically.

'It's just that – don't laugh,' she said suddenly and fiercely. 'Just don't.'

'I won't.' I was intrigued now.

'I wanted you to be – to be a bridesmaid for me.'

'What?'

'Me and Guy,' she told me. 'My doctor? You know, the man I've been living with for the past few years. He's been great to me. Made me see things differently. I love him, Amelie. We're getting married.'

I remembered the scathing words she'd used when she heard about me and Bernard. Words about bits of paper and legal commitments and the complete sham it all was. I was going to remind her about them but suddenly I didn't. I saw the pleading look in her eyes, willing me not to remind her, not to make an issue over it.

'When?' I asked instead.

'In a month's time. In LA.'

'I can't come to LA,' I said.

'Not on your own,' said my mother. 'Bernard and Catherine too.'

'Why?' I asked.

'Why what?'

'Why the marriage? Why us? Why now?'

'I've turned sensible.' She looked at me with an expression of horrified amusement. 'And I realise that I love him.'

'And that you loved me too?' I asked dryly.

'Hard to quantify that one,' she admitted. 'I didn't want you.'

'I know.'

'I didn't want to give you up either.'

'That wasn't very obvious.'

'Yes, well, I was spaced at the time. But it's true.'

I looked at her fine-featured face, still beautiful. It was hard to imagine that she was the same woman I'd seen puking down the toilet. It was hard to imagine that she was a grandmother, for heaven's sake! And it was very hard to imagine that she was getting married.

'OK, here's the deal.' She grinned at me and I struggled to keep my own face expressionless. 'I was a crap mother and I should say sorry but what's the point? I was pretty horrible about you getting married and about your suburban dream and that might have been worse because it was sheer nastiness. And I know I've said that it's all a bit crowded here but I was just saying what was expected. Actually it's OK.'

'OK?'

'I should use a better expression,' she said. 'But I can't think of one.'

'What do you want from me?' I asked.

'I don't really know,' she said. 'More than I gave you, I suppose. I want you to understand me.'

'I never wanted to understand you,' I said. 'I never wanted to care one way or the other.'

'Maybe if we hugged?' she suggested tentatively.

'Is that what they taught you in LA?'

She looked shamefaced. 'Um, yes.'

I laughed. I don't remember ever laughing with her before.

'So . . .' she broke off doubtfully. 'D'you want to hug?'

'I'm not a very huggy person,' I told her.

'Neither am I.'

'But we could try,' I suggested.

As a hug it wasn't much. But it was the first time and so we could be forgiven our awkwardness.

'Tell me about the doctor,' I said after we'd broken apart a little uneasily.

'Guy's wonderful,' she said. 'I love him. I really do.'

'And you're going to marry him and we're all going to be at the wedding.'

'If that's what you want.'

'Maybe,' I said. 'But not if you're going to wear something see-through.'

'I'm sixty-two,' she said. 'I'm a bit old for see-through.'

'Surely you've had a few nips and tucks?'

'I'm afraid of surgery,' she said.

'Me too.'

We smiled cautiously.

'I'm not going to wear anything see-through either,' I added.

'Pity.' There was a sudden, wicked gleam in her eye. It was a look I remembered from a long time ago. 'There was a dress in a shop on Rodeo . . .'

And this time we both laughed.

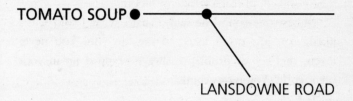

TOMATO SOUP

LANSDOWNE ROAD

The bowl slid in slow motion across the counter and then fell to the floor, an arc of bright red soup cascading onto the tiled surface and forming a sticky puddle on the porcelain beneath. Jennifer gasped in horror as she watched the puddle begin to spread across the kitchen floor and she flinched as his words bounced around the room.

'You stupid, stupid bitch.'

She wrapped her arms around her chest and held herself tight.

'I've been out all day and the best you can do is soup?' His tone was harsh. 'Not only that but you're trying to give me tomato soup. You know I fucking hate tomato soup!'

'No,' she whispered. 'You like it. You said you liked it before.'

His hand cracked against the side of her face again, this time sending her spinning against the wall. She blinked a

123

couple of times and then touched the side of her mouth where she could feel a trickle of blood.

'Minestrone soup,' he said. 'That's what I told you I liked. You just don't listen to me, do you? You never listen, that's your problem. Always wrapped up in your own world. You never think.'

'I—'

'Oh, shut up.' His face was red with anger. 'Don't give me one of your pathetic excuses. Just don't.'

'But—'

'I'm warning you.' His hand was raised again and she fell silent. She was afraid of him, afraid that this time he would really hurt her. Afraid that it would be more than a heavy slap to the side of the face and that maybe she might pass out. And she couldn't afford to pass out. She had to stay conscious. Focused. Aware of what was happening around her.

'I'm going out,' he said shortly.

The front door slammed and the parrot-head umbrella that had been propped against the wall of the porch slid downwards with a damp thud. Jennifer slid downwards too, her back against the wall, easing herself into a hunkered position, her legs tucked up beneath her chin, her arms hugged around her knees pulling them close to her. She could feel the blood from her cut lip trickle down her mouth but she didn't care. Now that he was gone all she wanted to do was to hold her body together because she was afraid – silly though some part of her already knew – that if she didn't she would, quite literally, fall apart. Every one of her joints seemed to be disconnected from each other. She could see her fingers but not move them. She could feel the throbbing in her head but couldn't be certain that it was her own head, her own pain. She closed her eyes and emptied her mind while letting the steady tick of the old-fashioned clock on the kitchen wall soothe her.

It was the sound of a Dart hurtling northwards behind the house that finally jolted her back to reality. Brian hadn't wanted to buy a house so close to the railway line but she'd liked it, she enjoyed watching the trains going by every day and felt a connection with the people who took them. She rarely took the train herself. She had a car, a little A-class Mercedes, which Brian had bought for her birthday two years earlier. It had been the most extravagant present he'd ever given her, eclipsing the diamond necklace of the previous year and the antique gold ring she'd received the year before that. He was the most generous person she knew. He adored her. He told everyone how much he adored her. But he'd hit her. Again.

She remembered the first time, just over a year ago. He'd come home late and she'd been angry because she was supposed to be going out herself only he'd phoned earlier in the day to say that he'd forgotten his house keys. She was surprised at that because they were normally on the key ring with the ones for his car but he reminded her that the car had been in for a service and he'd separated the two sets and he was really sorry but she couldn't go out until he got home. Which wouldn't have been a problem if he'd been on time but he didn't get in until nearly seven. She was supposed to meet the girls in town at seven and she was hopping up and down in a frenzy of anxiety by the time he opened the hall door.

'Where the hell were you?' she demanded as she gathered up her belongings.

'Don't talk to me like that.'

She looked at him in amazement, surprised by the harshness of his voice and the aggression in his tone. He smelled of beer and smoke but he wasn't drunk.

'I'm late,' she said mildly. 'I was waiting for you.'

'And is that so difficult?'

'No,' she said. 'But I'm supposed to be somewhere else. You should've remembered. I phoned you but you'd switched your mobile off.'

'That's because I don't have to be at your beck and call every minute of every day,' he snapped.

'Oh, for heaven's sake.'

She moved to push past him and he grabbed her by the arm, whirling her around so that she was facing him again.

'You're hurting me!'

'I'll show you what hurting really means.'

He slapped her, a stinging blow across the side of her face that left her cheek hot and sore and brought tears to her eyes. She wasn't able to speak. She stared at him, her dark eyes two pools of black in her now chalk-white face.

126

'Oh, Jesus, Jenny – I'm sorry.'

And he folded her into his arms, hugging her, stroking the back of her hair, telling her that he hadn't meant it, that he'd reacted badly, that it was all his fault. She hadn't been able to say anything, shocked beyond belief that he could have done this to her. She'd allowed herself to be held in his arms while he apologised repeatedly and told her that it would never, ever happen again. And then he'd placed his finger under her chin and tipped her face up to look at him and asked her to look straight into his eyes and believe that it had been a terrible, terrible mistake.

And she'd agreed with him that he had a hot temper which he did well to keep under control and that perhaps the drink he'd had with a couple of colleagues after work had contributed to his loss of control. Then she told him that if he ever laid a finger on her again she'd leave him. If there was one thing she'd learned from reading magazines and watching talk-show programmes it was that you didn't give men who hit you a second chance. This wasn't a second chance though. This was her putting a line in the sand. Because he hadn't really meant to hit her this time, it had been a reflex action that she knew he already bitterly regretted. He was still apologising to her as she said again that she'd leave him if he ever repeated it.

But she wouldn't, he replied, because it wasn't going to happen. He loved her. He'd always loved her. He always would.

Jennifer didn't go to meet the girls after all. She was

too shaken. She'd phoned Denise and explained that something had come up at home and that she was really sorry but that she'd catch them at the next get-together. And then she went into the living room and watched TV while Brian hovered around solicitously, making her cups of unwanted tea and fussing over her in a quite unaccustomed way.

In bed that night he'd held her close to him and made love to her with a gentleness that she hadn't experienced with him before. He swore that she was the only woman in the world for him and said that she had absolutely no idea how much he loved her. And she'd fallen asleep in the circle of his arms, the duvet tucked tightly around them, binding them together.

Two months later she discovered she was pregnant. Brian was ecstatic at the news. He'd always wanted a family. He loved kids – Jennifer knew that he was good with them. Every year his company organised a Christmas dinner for the struggling families in the surrounding area. Every year Brian dressed up as Santa Claus and distributed presents to hordes of screaming children. He enjoyed it as much as they did.

Throughout her pregnancy he was wonderful. He sympathised with her bouts of morning sickness, he brought her dried toast and tea in bed (even though she actually disliked breakfast in bed, but she didn't want to discourage him); he went to all of the antenatal classes he could with her. He was the perfect father-to-be. They were a perfect couple. Jennifer had never been happier. And their baby, Rosa, was absolutely beautiful.

The second time he hit her, Rosa was present. She'd been about to bathe the baby when he suddenly snatched her out of Jennifer's arms and then, holding Rosa in one arm, slapped Jennifer with the other. He missed her cheek this time and had caught her on the nose, causing it to spurt blood down the front of her white T-shirt.

'You didn't test the water,' he told her. 'You could have scalded her.'

Jennifer *had* tested the water. He hadn't seen her dip her elbow into it before getting the baby. She tried to tell him this but he wouldn't listen. He told her that she wasn't fit to be a mother, that his daughter was the most precious person in the world to him, more precious than anyone else, even her. And she stared at him in complete shock, unable to believe what had happened.

He insisted on bathing Rosa while she held a tissue to her nose and wondered whether he'd ever believe that she truly had tested the water first. She was afraid to leave him alone with the baby, but then she realised that his anger had been directly solely at her and that Rosa wasn't in any danger. She went into the bedroom where she changed her T-shirt and combed her hair.

He entered the room a few minutes later with Rosa wrapped in a fluffy pink towel and he sat behind her on the bed and apologised.

'I was so anxious,' he explained. 'I was afraid for her.'

'You didn't have to hit me.'

'I didn't mean to hit you. I was trying to stop you.'

'You could've simply asked me to stop. You only had to say.'

'I know. I'm sorry.' He sighed deeply. 'It's work. I'm under pressure. We're so busy and I guess I'm on a bit of a knife-edge.'

'Maybe you need to see someone.'

He looked at her then, his eyes scornful. 'I need a good night's sleep,' he said.

She understood that. Rosa woke up a lot during the night and, even though Jennifer was the one to get up and comfort her or feed her, she knew that Brian woke up too.

'I'm sorry,' she said. 'I know it's difficult.'

'I don't mind it being difficult,' he said. 'I love her. I love you. I'm just so tired.'

He put his arm around her and drew her closer to him and to baby Rosa, and he whispered that they were the best family in the world.

Another train flashed by, disrupting her memories, bringing her back to the present. She shivered. She realised that despite the heat of the house, she was freezing. She flexed her fingers but she couldn't feel them properly. Slowly, she tried to stand up but her legs wouldn't support the weight of her body and she slid back down again. Her head was pounding. This time he'd really hurt her. The other two times – the times that she didn't really count because there'd been reasons for them – those times the blows had been glancing, not heavy. They'd hurt, of course, but in a quick, stinging way. And her nosebleed had been awful but then nosebleeds were. She'd been in pain and shock but she hadn't felt as though she'd been really hurt. But this time, this time her head felt as though it might explode. She felt as though her brain was pulsating within her skull and every movement made it throb even more. But she had to get up. She couldn't stay here like this. She had to move.

Her nose started to bleed. She felt the sudden gush of warm blood and she pushed her hand against it. Then she forced herself to stand up and grab some kitchen towel from the roll on the pine holder attached to the wall. She was shivering again, her teeth chattering. She felt sick. She stood over the kitchen sink but nothing happened. She turned on the tap and cupped some cold water in her free hand while keeping the kitchen towel pressed against her nose. She didn't really know what she was doing, didn't feel as though she was inside her body at all.

Then Rosa's sudden wail made her draw on resources she didn't know she had. She hurried up the stairs, ignoring the pain that seared through every muscle and pushed open the door of the baby's room. Rosa's face was red and angry and Jennifer realised that it was time for her feed. She picked up her daughter and walked carefully down the stairs. She was glad that there were bottles already made up just waiting to be heated. She knew that she wouldn't have been able to measure out the formula properly. And the delay would cause Rosa to scream even louder, which would mean that perhaps she was a bad mother after all.

She sat in the big armchair and nestled the baby into her arms. Rosa sucked impatiently at the teat of the bottle, her cheeks working furiously to get at the milk. Jennifer's breathing was ragged as she fed her baby, not helped by the crust of blood around her nose. Rosa's frantic sucking slowed down as her hunger was abated and her eyes began to close. She was a beautiful baby, thought Jennifer. She knew that every person believed their own child to be the most beautiful in the world but Rosa was undeniably lovely. Her baby skin was soft and clear, her eyes were buttons of topaz in her round face and her black tufts of hair stuck up endearingly from her head. She was a perfect image of babyhood when she was asleep, when awake she was cheerful and inquisitive. Of all the things she'd ever done, Jennifer thought, creating Rosa was the best.

Creating Rosa with Brian. She could also see Brian's genetic legacy in her daughter. The way Rosa would suddenly look at something and stop quite still, staring at it in complete wonderment. The way she crinkled her nose just before she laughed. The way sometimes she heaved an enormous sigh. Jennifer knew that these were all parts of Brian.

He's not a violent man, she told herself as she rocked the baby in her arms. Really he's not. That first time was a complete mistake and the second time was because he was so worried for Rosa. It wasn't as though he'd set out to hit her. It wasn't like he came home every night and beat her up for the fun of it like other men did to their wives. He'd hit her as a reaction to something that had happened and, even though he shouldn't have done it, she could understand why.

They'd talked about violence in the office where she'd once worked. It was before anything had happened. And the girls had agreed, as she had, that you didn't give a man a second chance. That if he touched you, you threw him out. But it was easy to say something like that when you weren't in the actual situation, Jennifer thought. It was easy to talk about domestic violence when what you really meant was living with some psychopath. Brian wasn't a psychopath. He had a quick temper. But he wasn't someone who liked using force. He didn't even kill spiders, for heaven's sake!

Jennifer brought Rosa back upstairs to her cot and carefully placed her on her back, then covered her with the pretty pink quilt. She walked into her own bedroom and sat in front of the mirror.

The reflection was of a woman she hardly knew. A woman with a pale face surrounded by dark hair with ink-blot eyes staring out from beneath a straggled fringe and red weals across her white cheeks. She examined her swollen lower lip and the dried blood on her chin and around her nose. I'm a mess, she thought. A disaster area. Who would've thought that such a minor incident would leave me looking like this.

She picked up her brush and began to draw it gently through her hair. Every stroke hurt as though each individual hair was protesting at being touched. She stopped after a few seconds. It was too painful. She took a facial wipe from the box beside her and dabbed at the dried blood, wincing as the astringent lotion stung her cut lip. She looked better without the blood.

She eased her stained sweatshirt over her head and dropped it into the laundry basket. Then she opened the dresser drawer and took out a soft yellow cashmere cardigan which she fastened around herself, her still-trembling fingers struggling with its tiny pearl buttons. The cardigan was a big improvement. She was starting to feel much better already. She changed from her jeans into a pair of soft trousers. Then she went slowly downstairs, back to the kitchen, and took two Panadol tablets from the first-aid box in the cupboard. She filled the kettle and switched it on. She'd feel better after a cup of tea. Her mother always put on the kettle when she needed to be soothed. Jennifer did too.

She sat at the kitchen table and clasped the mug in both hands. The trembling had stopped now and her headache had eased. Her mouth was still sore and her nose was tender. But she no longer felt as though she was going to disintegrate. She felt more solid somehow. More real again.

Why had he hit her this time? That was the worrying part. Surely not over a bowl of soup? Besides, he *did* like tomato soup, he'd had it before, the exact same brand. He'd devoured the soup with the same variety of brown bread which earlier she'd piled on the plate beside it, and he'd enjoyed it then. There must have been something else, something she'd said or done to upset him. He wasn't an irrational man, wouldn't have flown off the handle like that for no reason at all. He was a decent man. He really was. But there was something wrong right now. Maybe he should see a doctor. Maybe it was a physical thing. He might be feeling unwell and anxious about it and this was how he was expressing it. Because he wasn't a violent man. He just wasn't. She repeated it over and over to herself, reminding herself that truly violent men spent their time in pubs, then came home and beat up their wives for no apparent reason. Brian hardly ever went to the pub. He belonged to a golf club – he was the captain there. And he was in a gym. He looked after himself. He wasn't a wife beater.

She finished the tea and put the cup in the dishwasher. Then she noticed the congealed soup on the kitchen floor. It was hard to bend down to clean it up but she had to do it. He wouldn't be too happy to come home and find the floor still smothered in tomato soup. She wiped ineffectually at it, and then took a bucket from the utility room and filled it with water. She squirted lots of pine-fresh cleanser into it and then mopped the floor until it was perfectly clean again. She emptied the dirty water down the drain in the back garden.

Her head was beginning to hurt again. She had to sit down. She was utterly exhausted.

Jennifer was in bed by the time Brian came home. She woke up, instantly alert, when she heard his key in the lock. It was eleven o'clock. He'd been gone for nine hours. Where had he been, she wondered, for nine hours?

She heard his footsteps on the staircase. He was walking quietly so as not to disturb her or Rosa. A shaft of light entered the bedroom as he pushed the door open. She stirred in the bed.

'Are you awake?' he asked quietly.

'Yes.'

He sat down beside her. 'I'm sorry,' he said. 'I really, really am. I don't know what happened, Jennifer. I don't know why I did what I did. I said before that I was stressed and that's all I can think of. You know I would-n't hurt you for the world.'

She said nothing.

'I knew the moment I did it that it was wrong. I didn't mean to but it was like my hand had a will of its own. But I promise you, on my mother's grave, Jennifer, that I won't let it happen again. I know how terrible it was. I didn't mean it.'

'Where were you?' she asked.

'I went to the golf club. Had to swing the club a bit, sort my head out. And I did.'

'Were you drinking?' She couldn't smell alcohol from him.

'I had a glass of wine with some food,' he told her. 'That's all.'

She hadn't had anything to eat. She hadn't felt the slightest bit hungry.

'Jennifer, you're my wife. You're the most important person in my life.'

'I thought Rosa was.'

'Rosa depends on me,' said Brian. 'But I depend on you.'

Jennifer said nothing. She closed her eyes again. She listened to the sounds of him getting ready for bed. Using the bathroom, brushing his teeth, hanging up his clothes. She lay still as he pulled back the covers and slid in beside her.

'I love you,' he whispered as he put his arm around her. 'I know I didn't behave like it today but I do love you.'

'You hurt me,' she said.

'I know.'

'You did it before.'

'I know. But it's behind us. I swear.'

'I loved you,' she told him.

'You still love me.'

'But how can I be sure . . .'

'Ssh.' He touched her face gently. She jumped.

'Oh, Jen.' His voice was cracked with emotion. 'I never meant to do this. Look, I can't do it again. I just can't. It was something . . . I don't know . . . I didn't mean it.'

'I know you didn't mean it.'

'Because you know I love you.'

'I guess so.'

'I love you and I cherish you and I'll care for you,' he promised. 'There's nothing that you can't have. Nothing.'

'Don't be silly.'

He held her even closer.

'So, we're all right now?' he asked.

'We're all right.' She bit her bruised lip as she lay beside him and stared through the darkness.

THE MARTINI GIRL

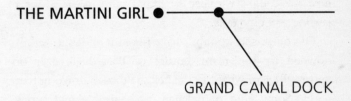

GRAND CANAL DOCK

Kimberley Blake never told Greg Donnelly she was pregnant. She had no intention of ever telling him. She'd told the truth when she'd said to him, nine months before, that she took total care of these things, that he shouldn't worry about it and that life was too short. She'd said those words because, at that exact moment, she'd wanted him more than anything and she'd ignored the voice in the recesses of her head that told her she was taking a chance. Right now – lying in the labour ward of Holles Street maternity hospital – it seemed an insane risk for such fleeting pleasure. But she'd been totally turned on by him, noticing him as though for the first time because that evening he was wearing jeans and a T-shirt instead of his usual boring suit. And the casual look seemed to set off his George Clooney jawline and his brilliant blue eyes so that he was suddenly transformed from an attractive, though irrelevant, manager in the office to someone she didn't want to resist.

Now, as she stared at the white ceiling, she wondered how she could have been so stupid as to risk it all for a jawline and blue eyes.

Of course she wouldn't have risked it all if she hadn't downed far too many bottles of Bacardi Breezer or Smirnoff Ice or whatever the hell she'd been drinking that night. Some kind of defence mechanism would surely have kicked in if she'd even been half-sober instead of smashed out of her head, wouldn't it? It had been a point of honour with all of the more junior staff to get smashed out of their heads on the company booze at the party – after all Cooper & Simpson weren't exactly over-generous when it came to salaries; the least they could do, everyone agreed, was fund their Christmas drinking.

And then she'd been egged on by the other girls. Cathy had been the one to insist that Greg Donnelly fancied her and Kimberley had laughed it off, saying that most of them fancied her because of her long, long legs and her big, big boobs and her tiny, model-sized waist. She told Cathy that she really wanted them to fancy her for her mind and Cathy had shrieked with laughter and asked when that had ever happened. Since Kimberley had a better body than Giselle, she said, the least she could do was use it. Sorcha suggested that a bit of judicious flirting could help Kimberley move from Accounts and get the job that she was angling for in Client Services – after all, wasn't Gorgeous Greg Donnelly the Senior Manager in Client Services? And a little flattery might go a long way with him. Kimberley had dismissed the girls' comments but she'd kept her eye on Greg because she really did quite fancy him even though he was a good bit older than her and, as far as she knew, was happily married.

'They're never happily married at the Christmas party,' Sorcha had told her. 'They're always up for it then. And why not?' Sorcha had been in the company three years longer than Kimberley.

'Isn't it a bit difficult?' Kimberley had to squint at Sorcha to keep her in focus. 'After all, we have to work with them afterwards.'

'Oh, nobody bothers about afterwards,' Sorcha assured her. 'It's like everything that happens at the Christmas party happens in a bubble. It doesn't count towards real life.'

She wouldn't have believed Sorcha if she hadn't been so pissed. She would've listened to the part of her brain that told her people never forgot even if they didn't say anything. Sex with someone in the office was very different to sex with someone else, and having it off with the Client Services Manager might not seem such a good idea the next day. But then Greg Donnelly had walked right past them and had smiled at her and something inside her had simply flipped over and she'd been consumed with desire for him.

Consumed with desire. It sounded impossible now.

She hadn't been consumed with any desire other than to see her feet again in ages. Some of the magazines she'd bought told her that during her pregnancy she might find a sudden surge in her libido but she'd found quite the opposite. Feeling fat and frumpy, Kimberley couldn't imagine how anyone could get enjoyment out of any physical activity apart, perhaps, from eating an entire tub of Ben & Jerry's Phish Food ice cream in one go.

She wished she hadn't thought of Phish Food. It was making her hungry and queasy all at the same time.

She'd smiled back at him. She knew she had a good smile. Some of her friends told her she looked like Julia Roberts when she smiled because, like Julia, she had a wide, generous mouth, even if she didn't have the whole girl-next-door look. She was, Kimberley knew, more sophisticated than that. At least usually. Maybe not after all that alcohol – she'd no idea how she looked when she was out of her tree with drink.

But she must have looked all right because Greg Donnelly stopped in his tracks and turned to her.

'Enjoying yourself?' he asked.

She gave him the benefit of her widest smile again.

'Great,' she told him. 'A bit pissed though.'

'It's Christmas,' said Greg. 'And I'll let you into a secret. I'm a bit pissed too.'

'Surely not,' she said (it came out as 'shuurley'). 'And you the Manager of Client Services.'

Greg had laughed at that. He had white, even teeth

although one had a tiny chip out of it that made him look even better. Not so perfect.

'Client Services managers are known for their love of getting pissed,' he told her. 'That's part of our charm.'

'What else makes you charming?' They were standing side by side now, their heads close together to hear each other through the din of a hundred people gathered in the boardroom.

'My nose,' Greg said. 'Everyone likes my nose.'

She giggled. It was a perfectly ordinary nose.

'And my smile.'

'No.' She shook her head. 'It's my smile. That's my charming thing.'

'Sure is,' Greg agreed. 'You have me charmed, for sure.'

'Really?'

'Really.'

It had been such a silly conversation. Not that you could expect much else at midnight on the Friday before Christmas but even so . . . Kimberley sighed. She should have known better.

They danced together. She'd laughed when he knew the words to the songs because they were old eighties numbers and, though they were vaguely familiar, she didn't really know them. Greg said that they were classics and she giggled and told him that she preferred garage. He'd shaken his head at that and said that he'd never wanted to be like his parents and say that modern music was complete crap but that garage was unlistenable to. And then the DJ for the night, Ricky (from her department) had played 'Three Times a Lady' which, of course, she couldn't help knowing and Greg had held her close so that she could feel the heat of his body against her own.

She didn't know whose idea it had been to go to his office. She didn't think that they'd gone there simply to have sex on Greg's modern white ash desk. They'd gone for some peace and quiet, she thought, simply to be together for a while, to talk about things.

Hell, she thought now, what kind of things would we have found to talk about? What on earth did we have in common?

He'd closed the door behind them and she'd seen him lock it but she knew it was safe. And then he was standing beside her, suddenly looking a little uncertain, as she was pulling his face to hers and kissing him.

He'd been surprised, she knew, at the kiss. Maybe he'd come from a generation of people where it was the men who did the kissing and the women who waited around, pathetically grateful for whatever they were offered. But she didn't. She knew how to get what she wanted. And right then, in Greg Donnelly's office, she knew what she wanted.

Well, why not? she asked herself, as she slid her hands beneath his T-shirt. What harm will it do? The girls are right. Christmas is different. Office parties don't count.

He paused as he pushed up her short suede skirt and asked her about protection. She was surprised that he had asked, and pleased too. It meant that he wasn't a complete moron. And she'd told him not to worry, she looked after all that.

Usually she did. But she hadn't brought her bag down to his office with her, and she wasn't going to stop this moment to go and get it. Because she was afraid that if she stopped it now, then Greg Donnelly would have second thoughts, and she didn't want him to have second thoughts – she wanted him to make love to her.

And she thought that, just for once, it wouldn't really matter. How many girls thought that, she wondered. How many other women were lying in labour wards around the country because they thought it would never happen to them? And how many of those women were there on this September afternoon because of a moment of passion at a Christmas party – a moment they thought they could simply forget about?

She grimaced. If only the moment of passion had been the worst of it. If she'd known, back then, that they'd been followed downstairs by that sadistic shit Liam O'Reilly, she would have stopped things immediately and that would have saved her. She knew that Liam was the sort of bastard that thought it was funny to take pictures of workmates doing things that they shouldn't have been doing. And the photo which eventually found its way into everyone's e-mail inbox was one in which

Greg's hand was clearly underneath her skirt (if you looked closely you could see, in fact, that his fingers were twined around her thong) while she leaned back on the desk.

So, as far as she was concerned, the Christmas party was not something that she could simply forget about. Everyone knew that she and Greg had been in his office and everyone knew exactly what they'd been up to.

'Oh, so what?' said Sorcha the following week when Kimberley had received the e-mail attachment and disappeared into the loo refusing to come out. 'All the blokes are jealous that it wasn't them and, God knows, all the women are jealous that it was you and not them! Apparently he used to be a bit of a rover before he got married but not since. They're all disgusted that it was you he strayed with.'

'I don't care what they're jealous about. Everyone's laughing at me.'

'If they are, they're laughing at him too,' said Sorcha.

'No they're not.' A fat tear slid down Kimberley's cheek. 'They're slapping him on the back and telling him he's a great man but they're looking at me and thinking I'm a slut.'

'Don't be silly,' said Sorcha. 'That's such an outdated way of thinking.'

'It would be if it wasn't true,' said Kimberley bitterly. 'I'm telling you, my career here is fucking finished and it's all my own fault.'

'It's just as much his fault as yours,' said Sorcha. 'Come on, Kim. Head up. Go out there and don't let them get to you.'

Kimberley didn't want to leave the sanctuary of the ladies. But she couldn't stay there all day.

'Hey! It's the Martini Girl!' David Dolan grinned at her as she walked across the office back to her desk. She looked at him in puzzlement while some of the other staff giggled.

'What is he talking about?' she hissed at Sorcha who looked uncomfortable.

By that afternoon she was getting e-mails with Martini Girl as the subject and copies of the photo as an attachment. She trashed them all without looking at them. She was doing a really good job of not looking at anyone or anything all day.

'It's from the ad,' Sorcha told her later. 'You know – any time, any place, anywhere.'

Kimberley hadn't ever seen the famous series of ads for a drink she hardly knew existed. But she knew what they meant all right. Her face flushed.

'I'm not coming back,' she told Sorcha. 'I can't. That's what they all think of me. An easy lay. Any time, any place, anywhere.'

'They'll forget about it in a week,' said her friend. 'You can't just walk out on your job, Kim.'

But she did. She sent a letter of resignation in the post that was accepted by return. She put her name on the register with an employment agency and thought that she was lucky to get something almost straight away because suddenly jobs in Dublin weren't as plentiful as they'd been when she joined Coopers & Simpson.

She was glad to get back to work even though the new job was paying slightly less than before. But it was conveniently located close to her flat in Grand Canal Dock which meant that she no longer had to bother about getting the train across the city, thereby allowing her an extra half-hour in bed every morning.

She didn't actually realise she was pregnant until her period was nearly two months overdue. She didn't have any other symptoms – she hadn't once felt sick or had sudden cravings for lumps of coal – so it simply hadn't occurred to her. In any event the potential outcome of having unprotected sex with Greg had been overtaken by the e-mailed photo and her metamorphosis into the Martini Girl. When the test showed up positive, she stood in the bathroom of her studio apartment and cried for an hour.

She'd heard from Sorcha that Greg Donnelly had also left the company and that he was now working somewhere in Baggot Street. She was slightly bothered by this since Baggot Street wasn't far away enough, in her view, from Grand Canal Dock. But she knew that the likelihood of bumping into Gorgeous Greg was pretty remote. She thought, bitterly, that he probably wouldn't even recognize her if they did meet. Then, later, she heard that his wife had left him.

Thrown him out, Sorcha told Kimberley in hushed tones, when they met for lunch one day. Literally. Dumped all his clothes into the garden and set fire to them, apparently. Or maybe she'd thrown them all into their ornamental fish pond. Flung them at him anyhow as she ordered him to leave. Sorcha was a bit hazy on the details. But bottom line was that Helena had freaked out and told Greg to leave. Anyway now that neither Greg nor Kimberley was around any more, the office gossip had moved on; apparently Ruth McCarthy was having an affair with Dermot Gaviston but it was being kept very, very quiet.

Kimberley said nothing to this.

'She was right to throw him out,' Sorcha told her, 'given the way he behaved.'

'With me,' said Kimberley. 'He behaved that way with me. So I'm as bad, don't you think?'

'Oh, no, Kimberley. Of course not. He took advantage of you.'

'You think?'

'Sure he did. He was senior management. You were legless with drink. He should've known better.'

'So should I.' Kimberley's hand slid unconsciously towards her stomach. She jerked it away. She didn't want Sorcha to know about the baby. She didn't want anyone to know. And she knew what Sorcha would say. That she should get support from him. That it was his baby too. That he had a right to know. As far as Kimberley was concerned he had no rights about anything any more. And she didn't want him offering support. The bottom line was that they'd had a shag at the Christmas party, no strings, no declarations of undying love, and now through her own fucking stupidity she was pregnant. Besides, if his wife had thrown him out because she'd found out about the sex, Kimberley didn't really think that he'd be in a position to offer much anyway.

The pain hit her in an agonising burst and she yelled out. She'd expected it to hurt. No matter how much she'd heard about how manageable the pain should be, Kimberley still got the impression that it would hurt like hell. And she was right.

She wished there was someone with her. Anyone really. She didn't care who. Well, not Gorgeous Greg Donnelly of course, but someone who'd hold her hand and tell her that she was a great girl and that it would all be over soon. She'd phoned her mother as soon as she'd arrived at Holles Street but she'd got the answering machine on both the home phone and the mobile – Kimberley guessed that Anna Blake was out on the golf course and couldn't be disturbed. Which wasn't to be critical of her mother, because the baby hadn't been due for another two weeks and Anna had promised to be available night or day by then.

She flinched as another wave of pain overwhelmed her.

Her mother had been good about it. More or less. But Kimberley had seen the disappointed expression shadow Anna's face before she'd smoothed it over with a mask of stoic acceptance and told her that these things happened and that she'd do her best to help. She'd been less stoic about Kimberley's insistence that the father of the child was absolutely not in the picture and never would be and she had tried, to no avail, to discover who he was. Kimberley knew that if her mother discovered the father's identity she would confront Greg and tell him about his child. The last thing that Kimberley wanted was a semi-repentant Greg telling her that he'd do the right thing. A Greg who thought, perhaps, that he should be involved with their child. A Greg who might think she was a suitable substitute for the wife who had thrown him out, or that Kimberley's baby could take the place of the daughter that he'd left behind.

She hadn't known until she left the company about Greg's other child, Dana. And when she heard about her, Kimberley felt as though she wanted to die. Greg had been thrown out of his home and it was partly her fault. It was so bloody unfair because it was only supposed to have been a bit of fun and why, oh why, did the consequences have to be so damn far-reaching?

The biggest wave of pain hit her and quite suddenly a nurse was beside her muttering about dilations and all sorts of stuff that Kimberley didn't want to take in. She'd gone to her antenatal classes but she'd avoided listening to as much of it as possible on the basis that she didn't want to know anything. The baby would be born one way or another and she didn't care what stage of labour she was at because it wasn't going to make any difference, was it? She wanted drugs, she told the nurse, whatever they could give her and as quickly as possible. This was ridiculous pain. She couldn't cope with it. There was a design flaw in the human body if you were supposed to endure all this simply to have a baby. Why not lay an egg, she demanded, like an ostrich or something? Wouldn't it make more sense? We were supposed to be an evolved species, she cried. How fucking evolved was this?

And when, at last, her baby boy was placed in her arms she simply closed her eyes and said that she was too tired to care. She slept.

Her mother was sitting beside her bed when she woke up. Anna Blake smiled at her daughter and told her that the baby was utterly gorgeous with his black hair and his navy-blue eyes and that he didn't look red and wrinkly like most newborns but was sleek and handsome. Kimberley made a face and said that her mother was talking complete nonsense but Anna got up and put the baby into her arms. Suddenly Kimberley was overwhelmed by it all and started to cry.

Five minutes on the desk and this was the result, she thought. But better, maybe, than the result of other work that had happened in Greg Donnelly's office. Better than the memo that had gone around about the new client care programme that had been developed. Better than memos about time-keeping and tidying the desk every night. But God, she thought, much longer term than any of them.

'You still haven't told the father?' Anna looked at her enquiringly.

Kimberley shook her head. 'I can't,' she said. 'And I won't.'

'I don't like to think of him getting away with it,' said Anna. 'I don't like to think of you having all the responsibility.'

'It's the way I want it,' said Kimberley. 'It's my choice.'

'Fine,' said Anna. She stretched out her finger and laughed as the baby's fist closed around it. 'What are you going to name him?' she asked.

'I don't know,' said Kimberley. 'I haven't decided yet.'

'After your dad, perhaps?' Anna asked tentatively.

Kimberley laughed shortly. 'I don't think so,' she said. 'Not after what he did to us.'

'Men have affairs,' said Anna. 'They leave their wives. I can't honestly say I've forgiven your dad but I've got over it.'

'I know you have,' said Kimberley. 'You're a great inspiration to me in the getting-over of things. I was thinking, maybe, of calling him Adam.'

'After anyone at all?' Anna asked.

Kimberley shook her head. 'No. No baggage. Me and him doing it for ourselves. Nothing else.'

'You always could do it for yourself,' said Anna. 'Any time. Any place. Anywhere.'

Kimberley stared at her.

'What did you say?'

'That you always could do it for yourself.'

'No, you said "any time, any place, anywhere"?'

Anna laughed. 'I know. I was trying to reinforce the message.' She looked quizzically at her daughter. 'Is something the matter?'

Kimberley shook her head slowly. 'Someone else said that to me once.'

'See.' Anna smiled brightly. 'I was right.'

'They weren't being complimentary,' said Kimberley.

Anna stared at her. 'How did they mean it?'

'It doesn't matter,' said Kimberley.

'Was it him?' demanded Anna.

'No.' Kimberley sighed. 'It didn't work out too well for him either.'

Anna opened her mouth then closed it again. 'You're a good girl,' she told Kimberley after a few minutes. 'You are. No matter what anyone says.'

'Thanks.' Kimberley smiled faintly.

'And you're strong.'

'Strong but stupid,' she said.

'No,' said Anna. 'We all do stupid things at least once in our lives. It's part of living. You're just strong.'

'I hope so,' said Kimberley as she kissed Adam on the top of his head. 'I really hope so.'

'You'll always be strong,' Anna told her. 'Every time, every place, everywhere.'

'Maybe more of a vodka martini than just a martini?' suggested Kimberley.

'Exactly.' Anna put her arms around her daughter and held her close.

CONNECTIONS

PEARSE

Helena hesitated for a moment before she stepped out of Pearse station and emerged into the dismal grey of Westland Row. The last day she'd done this – the day before she'd finally given up her job at Coopers & Simpson to stay at home with Dana – had also been grey and miserable. And the lowering clouds had seemed to skim across the tops of the dreary old buildings in exactly the same way. Suddenly it didn't seem that long ago and yet, she told herself as she walked along the cheerless street, more than five years had gone by. Five years in which her life had changed and changed again in ways that she couldn't have expected.

It felt odd to be back in an area of the city that she always associated with work. She never bothered with this part of town any more. Westland Row, Merrion Square, Mount Street – all with the old Georgian buildings that tourists loved to photograph, idealistically believing them to be people's homes but which were mainly warrens of offices where people like her put in their seven-hour day. She'd been part of it all for so long, the bitching at the photocopier, the sneaking out to buy some fresh scones from the deli round the corner, the office gossip, office politics, office romances . . .

She gritted her teeth at the memories of the office romances and glanced towards Fitzwilliam Square where her old company had been before they'd relocated to a purpose-built block in the East Point Business Park.

She was out of that world now and part of a different one, although it hadn't been until she'd struck up friendships with some of the other parents in the Killiney suburban estate that she'd really got to grips with everything. After they'd moved in there, it had taken time to get to know the other women, because she wasn't a naturally outgoing person and she found it hard to strike up conversations. Besides, she had a terror of becoming a Stepford Wife type of suburban woman – a house-proud, husband-pleasing robot who spent her time having coffee mornings with the girls and talking about the best way to remove dark stains from pale carpets. But it wasn't like that. There were one or two mothers who fitted into the very house-proud model but most of them muddled along happily, making time for the kids but also making time for themselves. Between them they did the carpooling and the emergency child-collecting and all of the other things that they shared in order to make life a bit easier. She joined a book club where they read the kind of novels that she'd never had time for before and she enrolled in morning classes on 'Confidence Building for Successful Living'. Greg had laughed at that, told her that she was the most confident person he knew and asked what did she need to learn, for heaven's sake? And she'd replied that being at home all day, nice though it was in principle, often meant that you lost touch with the skills you'd built up in earlier life. Sometimes you needed to remind yourself of them, she said. At which point he'd reminded her of some of the skills that had attracted him to her in the first place, which made her laugh, and suddenly they'd made love in the hallway, not stopping even when there was a ring on the doorbell.

All of it had seemed so right, she thought as she crossed into Clare Street, head bent against the buffeting wind. He hadn't been unhappy, she hadn't been the sort of wife who nagged him about being home more often (at least, not much). He'd occasionally look at a picture of an actress or model in the glossy pages of the gossip magazines she brought home and say that Liz or Giselle or Sophie was a bit of all right, but she'd expect that from just about any bloke who saw a picture of an attractive model dressed in a wisp of chiffon.

'No,' said Helena out loud, 'we had a good marriage. We were partners. We loved each other.'

She looked up and saw Annette standing outside the gallery waiting for her. She waved, though her friend was staring blankly in front of her, not noticing the people who were thronging past. But she finally spotted Helena and her face broke into a smile. Helena smiled too. It was a long time since she'd seen Annette; it was difficult to talk to even close friends because she felt so humiliated by everything.

They walked into the gallery and joined the queue at the restaurant. Years earlier Helena and Greg had often met at the gallery for lunch, but since then the new annexe had been added and the restaurant updated and moved, so meeting Annette here didn't cause the pang it might have done. Helena chose a green leaf salad from the healthy-looking selection and Annette raised her eyebrows and asked if her friend wouldn't prefer something a bit more substantial.

'Not right now,' said Helena. 'I might have dessert.'

Annette knew that Helena was fobbing her off. The other woman, as slender as she'd ever been, never ate desserts. They sat down at a marble-topped table.

'So,' said Annette, breaking the silence that had descended awkwardly between them. 'How're you keeping?'

Helena bent her head as she drizzled oil over her salad.

'Pretty OK,' she said eventually.

'And Dana?'

'She wants him back,' said Helena. 'But she's pretty OK too.'

'And how are the lawyers?'

Helena laughed bitterly. 'Being lawyerly, I suppose.'

'You were right to throw him out,' said Annette. 'You've got to remember that.'

'Of course,' said Helena. 'I remember it every day.'

She wondered when the day would come that she didn't remember it. The day she'd wake up in the queen-sized bed that Greg had insisted they have (even though it was ridiculously expensive and took up far too much of the bedroom) and think of something else other than the fact that her husband had made her into the laughing stock of the city and that she hadn't had any option but to tell him to get out.

She swallowed as she remembered the day she'd seen the picture. There'd been a bundle of envelopes in the post, a mixture of bills and New Year junk mail. She'd flicked through them without opening them although she was the one who looked after the household finances. But she hadn't been in the mood to discover how much they'd spent on turning Christmas into a lifestyle experience when actually all that either of them wanted was a few days together and the joy of watching Dana unwrap all her presents.

Nevertheless, she'd opened the white envelope, hand-addressed to herself, simply because she hadn't a clue what it was and she was curious. She took out an A4 page folded in half. On the back was written 'And who do you want to get into your stockings this Christmas?' When she opened it out she saw the picture of her husband and a woman in his office. The woman's face was half-hidden but what wasn't hidden was the length of her legs and the fact that Greg's hand was at the top of one of them. And that the girl was pulling him close to her. And that Greg wasn't saying no. Even remembering it now, so many months later, made her feel sick. In her head she always continued the story of the picture, Greg's hand moving still higher, the girl undoing the belt of his trousers, the indignity of them falling around his ankles (didn't men ever know how stupid they looked like that) and the final betrayal of him having sex with this woman when he was married to someone else. Married to her. His wife. His stupid, stupid wife who believed him when he told her things like she was the only woman in the world for him.

'Helena?' Annette's voice shattered her mental images. 'Are you OK?'

She closed her eyes and opened them again. 'Of course I am,' she said. 'Sometimes I remember it and it makes me feel . . .' She shook her head. 'I hate remembering.'

It had been the first week in January. He'd gone back to work after the long break. They'd spent Christmas together as usual, made love as usual, shared private jokes with each other as usual, enjoyed Dana's excitement about the whole festive season – all exactly as they'd done before – only this time he was saying and doing all these things while knowing that he'd betrayed her with some tart from the office.

Christ, she'd thought, we met at an office party ourselves but we never had it off on anyone's desk. We barely got around to snogging each other in the lift! But with her, with this tramp, he just hadn't cared. He hadn't cared that he was doing it in the office and he hadn't cared who saw him. Somehow that was even worse. She wanted to think that he'd at least have been discreet about it. But he hadn't been. He'd screwed that girl without thought. He was a complete and utter bastard. And there was no way that he could say anything to appease her.

He tried though. He'd arrived home that night, in fine form, laughing and joking about some incident in the office which went right over her head. She'd originally intended to confront him straight away because Dana should have been at her friend's house to watch her new DVD, but Shannon Smith had caught a bug and Dana was at home. Helena had to wait until Dana was in bed before she wordlessly handed him the printed picture.

'I can explain.' His face was ashen.

She stared at him.

'It wasn't exactly what you think. I'd had a lot to drink. We both had.'

She listened to his miserable, pathetic excuses. It was a party. They were drunk. He hadn't meant to. It didn't mean a thing. He hardly even knew her. He hadn't spoken to her since. Just sex.

She'd practised all the things she was going to say to him before he came home. She'd said them to herself in front of the bedroom mirror until she could do it without bursting into tears. But in the end she just yelled at him that he was a miserable cheating bastard and if he thought for one second that she would put it out of her mind and carry on as before then he had another think coming.

Then he'd tried to put his arms around her and she'd pushed him away, running up the stairs and shutting herself in the bedroom. Not my finest hour, she thought. I'd had all that time to do something far more useful like changing the locks on the doors so as he couldn't even get into the house but all I did was practise saying things that I never said and then ran away and hid.

Greg slept in the spare room that night. She thought again about changing the locks the next day, but didn't, because she wasn't sure whether or not she was legally entitled to do something like that and she didn't want to do something he could blame her about afterwards. So she spent the day sitting mindlessly in the kitchen, not answering the phone when it rang and completely unable to do anything useful at all. She brought Dana to school and home again. She watched some kid's programme with her on TV. She went through the motions but it was all meaningless. And when he came home that evening with an enormous and extravagant bouquet of roses she threw them into the bin straight away. There was another argument that night too, but a quiet one, so that Dana wouldn't wake up. She asked him to leave.

He protested at that, said that he wasn't leaving the house (she often wondered afterwards whether he'd had advice on this particular confrontation) because, he said, it was his house too, that he was the one paying the mort-gage and that it had been a bloody mistake. 'A mistake, Helena,' he hissed. 'You know what that is. Something that won't happen again.' She'd responded that he was bloody right, it wouldn't happen again, and it had all got messy and ended in him spending the night in the spare room once more.

He left eventually. He said he was doing it for the sake of Dana who was aware that something was wrong. He'd called Helena a selfish cow who cared more about herself than her daughter and told her that he wouldn't be keep-ing her in the lap of luxury for her whole life. And then he'd broken down and cried and told her that he was really, really sorry and that he loved her and Dana and hoped he'd be able to come home soon.

As he'd taken his suitcases to the car she'd spotted his woolly golf-hat on a peg and thrown it after him. At that moment, Myra Walters, the road's favourite purveyor of gossip, walked by. Helena had felt like a cast member on *Fair City* or *EastEnders*. She certainly hadn't felt like herself. She certainly hadn't imagined that her life would've turned out like this.

'Helena, you can't brood on it.' Annette interrupted her thoughts. 'You've got to move on.'

'I have moved on,' Helena said. 'Mostly I have. We're working on the separation details and then I'll file for divorce and everything will be over and done with.'

'Does he still call out every week?' asked Annette. 'It

really upsets you, doesn't it, when he comes to the house?'

Helena exhaled slowly. 'Partly because I'm always afraid I won't be able to get rid of him again,' she said. 'Partly because Dana gets so upset when he leaves. And partly because it's so hard not to do as he asks and give him another chance.'

Annette stared at her. 'I didn't think you wanted to give him another chance,' she said.

'I don't.' Helena poked at a lettuce leaf. 'I don't want to forgive and forget, Annette. He did an awful thing.'

'Maybe he doesn't think it's so awful.'

'He doesn't.' Helena laid her fork on the plate. 'For weeks he kept saying that it was a mistake that happened because of drink and that no real harm was done.' She bit her lip. 'Maybe no real harm was done to him or to her, but to us, me and him as a couple, he changed everything. So, when he calls out, I'm like this ice maiden who's really not me at all and I know he thinks I'm a hard bitch who simply wants to take him to the cleaners and get my revenge but it really isn't like that.'

'I know,' said Annette.

'And he doesn't come as often now. I suppose it got a bit broken up when I took Dana away on holidays during the summer. He got out of the habit of coming then. I think he plays golf again some Saturdays.'

'So how often?'

'Once a month now,' said Helena. 'I prefer that.'

'Does Dana?'

'Thing is, she misses him but there are other things on Saturdays that she wants to do,' Helena explained. 'There's a creative expression thing on in the school at the moment and that's from twelve till two. She loves it and even though she wants to see Greg she doesn't want to miss the creative expression.'

'What the hell is creative expression?'

'Oh you know, dance, music, drama – all that sort of stuff,' explained Helena. 'She's a born show-off, which is why she likes it so much.'

'And how does Greg feel about it?'

'He wants to do what's right for her,' said Helena. 'But it doesn't always work out that way.'

'What about Sundays?' asked Annette.

'We usually go to my mum on Sunday,' said Helena.

'And what about his parents?'

Helena pursed her lips. 'They call round from time to time. But his mother bangs on and on about letting bygones be bygones and that everyone makes mistakes. I wish I'd kept the picture. That'd soften her cough.'

'Will you have to sell the house,' asked Annette, 'once the lawyers are finished dividing the spoils?'

'I hope not,' said Helena. 'We're settled in Killiney. We love it there.'

'Hard on him though,' said Annette.

'Oh for God's sake!' cried Helena. 'Whose side are you on? He's the one who had it off with that girl. He's the one who can bloody well pay for it.'

'I know, I know,' said Annette hastily. 'And I wouldn't even consider saying that you shouldn't get everything you can out of him. I just feel a tiny bit sorry for him, that's all.'

'Well I don't,' said Helena. 'He betrayed me and Dana. OK, he had to leave his job because everyone had seen that picture – it was sent round as an e-mail, you know, so he couldn't really stay after that . . . so it was traumatic too, but it was a trauma for us as well because we didn't know whether or not he'd get something with the same salary . . . I might have had to go back to work.'

'Maybe you'd be better off,' said Annette.

'I gave up work because I couldn't do everything,' snapped Helena. 'Do you really think I'd be better off as a single parent?'

'No.' Annette sighed. 'I'm sorry, Helena. I'm trying to be open-minded and fair to both of you.'

'Why should you be fair to him?' demanded Helena. 'He wasn't fair to us.'

'I guess he wasn't.'

'And he totally humiliated me.' Helena swallowed the hot tears that had suddenly welled up in her eyes. 'Everyone in that damned office knew about it. People I knew and worked with before I left! Girls who were envious of me before because I was the one who snared Gorgeous Greg. Laughing at me now. Sorry for me now. I don't want them to be sorry for me!'

She couldn't stop the tears that slid down her cheeks and plopped onto the salad leaves.

Annette looked at her helplessly. 'I'm sorry,' she said again. 'I swore I wouldn't even talk about it!'

'It doesn't matter.' Helena sniffed. 'And I don't mean to get so upset. God knows, Annette, I've had time to get over it. It's just that whenever I think about it, whenever I think about him and that girl . . .'

'Forget him,' said Annette. 'He was never worth it really.'

'The problem is that I thought he was,' said Helena miserably. 'I thought we had a good life together and I thought he was happy.'

And that was the whole point of it. If Greg had been happy with her then he surely wouldn't have felt the need to be with that other woman no matter how attractive or seductive she was and no matter how drunk he might have been. She knew that people did stupid things at Christmas parties – it was part of the whole scene. But she didn't think that her husband would be one of them. She really didn't.

She pushed her plate to one side. Why was it so hard to get over him, she wondered. Why hadn't she managed to rebuild her life by now? Other women did it – Caroline Devlin's husband had left her six months ago and Caroline had found another bloke and was having a great time with him. Luckily for her he also got on famously with her two children. But Helena hadn't even gone back to the book club yet, she simply wasn't able for it. Even though her friends on the estate were totally supportive and talked about her getting out and about. Aoife had suggested that she was still a good catch for the right man. Helena had laughed sourly at that. She didn't think so somehow.

Not that she actually wanted another bloke at this point anyway. She wasn't sure what she wanted any more, only that she still wanted for it not to have happened. She knew that he thought she was brutal towards him, chillingly cool whenever he called out to the house, totally intransigent in her determination not to forgive him. But she was cool because to be any other way would have her in floods of tears and potentially forgiving him. And she couldn't ever forgive him.

He didn't blame himself enough, for all the apologising he did. He blamed the sender of the printed photo, saying that someone wanted to destroy their lives. Someone was jealous of their happiness and saw this as a way of getting even. She'd ranted at him then about trying to portray himself as a victim when he was the one who'd caused all the trouble. That had been one of the earlier Saturdays when he'd called to pick up Dana. She'd shoved the picture under his nose and asked him how, exactly, he was being the victim there? There wasn't anything he could say in reply.

She sighed. She hated him now anyway. There was no way back from that. At the start, perhaps, she might have forgiven him but her friends stood firm behind her and agreed when she said that it was impossible to forget. And they agreed when she said that he'd broken her trust and that she'd never be able to get that back again. Only sometimes now she wondered whether or not she was wrong about it. Whether she would've been able to forgive him if the opportunity had been there.

Well, it was too late now. Especially since the summer when he'd stopped calling out every Saturday at twelve to take Dana to places she didn't really want to go. Those had been the days that had broken her heart, the days when she knew that she was most likely to give in and tell him she wanted to give it another try. After she'd come back from her summer holiday in Benalmadena with Dana he'd told her that he'd run out of interesting places to bring the little girl. And that he couldn't compete with holidays anyway. He'd sounded beaten and depressed and quite unlike the Greg she'd once known. And she'd allowed Dana to enrol in the creative expression classes so that there'd be something else for her to do.

Damn it, she thought furiously, why do we muck up our lives so much? He did a stupid, stupid thing and I was right to throw him out but I'm still miserable and I don't know when I'll get over it.

Annette glanced at her watch. 'It's getting late,' she said. 'I have to get back.'

Helena nodded. 'Do you still enjoy it?'

'Well, it's not as much fun as Cooper & Simpson used to be but they're a nice crowd and I like being with people,' said Annette. 'So, yes, I do.'

'I don't think I could do it any more,' said Helena. 'It's so much damn organising.'

'It might be good for you. Or if not a job in town, how about something in Killiney?'

Helena shook her head. 'I don't think so.'

'You can't stay depressed for ever,' remarked Annette.

'I know,' said Helena. She smiled suddenly and her face was transformed, looking years younger. 'I keep on meeting old friends and getting it off my chest. Maybe one day it'll work.'

'I hope so.'

'You know what I tell myself?' said Helena, as she slid her arms into the sleeves of her coat. 'I tell myself that the last few months have been a miserable time but that it's only a small part of my overall life. So I will get over it. Honestly. It's just taking more time than I thought.'

Annette smiled too. 'Maybe you're on the way there.'

'Maybe.' Helena grimaced. 'And, honestly Annette, I don't obsess about it every day. I just haven't started thinking of myself as a single woman again yet.'

'You're a fine single woman,' said Annette.

'You're a liar,' Helena told her. 'But a good friend.'

They walked out to Clare Street. The clouds were even lower now, scudding across the sky in banks of grey. Helena hugged Annette and promised to be in touch again. She shivered as she turned towards Grafton Street. Since she was already in town she might as well take advantage of it and do some shopping. A new winter coat, she thought. She could do with a winter coat. Or maybe something frivolous and silly. A winter coat might be a more useful buy but she hadn't splashed out on something frivolous in a long time.

It was her own fault that she collided with the young woman pushing the buggy – a girl really, she thought, very beautiful and very young. She apologised as she helped her gather up the contents of the bag that had fallen from the buggy's tray.

'I'm really sorry,' she said. 'I wasn't looking where I was going.'

'It's OK,' said the girl. 'I was rushing to get him home before the skies open. I wasn't really looking either.'

'No, it was definitely my fault,' said Helena. 'I was in a kind of dream world, thinking of spending money.' She smiled. 'He's lovely.'

'How did you know he was a he?' The girl pulled the drawstring on her bag and put it back on the buggy's tray.

'I don't know,' said Helena. 'I just did.'

'Well he's a demon who's due his feed,' said the girl. 'So I'd better get going before he roars at me.'

'Absolutely,' said Helena. She turned back towards Grafton Street trying to clamp down on the sudden pang of jealousy towards the woman who was clearly besotted with her lovely baby and who probably had a loving husband who didn't go round shagging office tarts on his desk. Although with a wife like that he wouldn't even think about it. She wondered whether, if she herself had

had that wide mouth, those luminous eyes and tumbling dark-red hair, Greg would ever have strayed with the slut.

As she stood at the traffic lights waiting to cross the road, the young woman's eyes followed the tall and slender stranger who'd been unexpectedly nice about the fact that she'd nearly had her ankles taken off by the wheels of the buggy. She wished that she, too, could spend time shopping in town without having to worry about feeding times and someone to watch over her baby. Some women didn't know how lucky they were. And then she leaned down and kissed baby Adam on the top of the head because she didn't, for one minute, want him to think that he wasn't the most important thing in her life and that she wasn't happy to have him.

A GOOD SENSE OF HUMOUR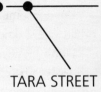

TARA STREET

I arrived early. Nearly half an hour early, in fact. It was unlike me to be quite so ahead of time but I wanted to observe everyone who came into the foyer of the trendy riverside hotel during my wait whilst remaining unnoticed myself. Being early meant I could pick a decent vantage point where I could see without being seen. That way I could choose to stay or I could get out before I had to introduce myself. I knew there was a flaw to this plan. The man I was meeting could've had the same idea. Even now, he could have been lurking behind a pillar or sitting in one of the stylish armchairs holding a newspaper up to his face, with exactly the same intentions as me. Only I didn't think so. Because when I'd arrived at seven o'clock the foyer was deserted and I had the choice of lookout points.

I sat behind a tall plant and wondered why I was in this clichéd set-up in clichéd surroundings and I wished, fervently, that I hadn't been so intensely stupid as to reply to the ad in the Personal Column. I'd never have done it if it hadn't been for Sara, who practically forced me into it.

'I'm not some sad individual who can't meet a man any other way,' I objected.

'Don't be silly, Cathy,' she said. 'It's a perfectly practical twenty-first-century way to meet people. Louise met a lovely guy, didn't she?'

'Louise is different.'

'This one sounds sweet.' Sara ignored me and jabbed her finger at the ad from someone who was 'late thirties, tall, dark, attractive, solvent, emotionally secure, sincere, likes animals, eating out, good movies and travel to warm places. GSOH.'

Everything else is optional but a Good Sense of Humour is obligatory.

My sense of humour is average. I laugh at *Frasier* and *Friends*, enjoy *Absolutely Fabulous*, smile at *Sex and the City* and find *South Park* utterly unfunny. I don't like practical jokes. I had a horrible feeling that meeting a perfect stranger in the trendy riverside hotel was, somehow, a practical joke of monumental proportions. No matter what his SOH was like.

My heart raced as a man walked into the foyer. He was tall and very attractive, and walked with a confident stride up to the desk. Unfortunately, he was wearing a navy suit and dark tie and was carrying a briefcase. My guy would be wearing pale chinos and a blue jumper.

It was seven-fifteen.

Maybe he had arrived before me and found an even better place to hide than behind the cheese plant. He could've checked me out already and decided that someone who was size fourteen, had mid-brown hair and grey-green eyes, and was wearing (unusually for her) a lilac cotton dress didn't look like the sort of woman who was ready for a possible LTR with an NS. It was Sara who told me that LTR was a long-term relationship. I figured out the Non-Smoking bit all by myself.

At half-past seven I went to the loo and re-did my lipstick. Then I repositioned myself behind my friendly plant. There were more and more people coming into the hotel now and I observed them all covertly, wondering what their senses of humour were like and trying to decide whether or not any of them were suitable long-term-relationship material. By a quarter to eight, I decided that my own 'likes cinemas and restaurants, cuddly, attractive' description wasn't good enough for a NS bloke with a GSOH who'd probably had better offers. It hadn't worked with most of the men I knew already, why the hell should a complete stranger be taken in by me?

I made a hasty exit out the side door of the hotel. I wondered if, by a cruel twist of fate, my NS with the GSOH was entering by the front door at the same time. That was the way my life worked, wasn't it? Nothing ever went according to plan. My non-smoker could've been the perfect man for me and we might have had a happy, sincere, fun-filled life together (with his animals). But he was late and I'm passionate about time-keeping. I didn't know the accepted abbreviation for Can't Stand Unpunctuality.

I walked to Tara Street to catch the train home, feeling stupid and miserable. It's bad enough being dumped by someone you know, but being dumped by someone you haven't even met is worse!

The train pulled into the station and a couple of teenagers, who'd been larking about a bit, knocked my bag from my hand. Then they bumped into the man who was standing a few metres away from me. They looked embarrassed as they piled onto the train, while I rescued my bits and pieces from the platform.

'This yours?' The man who'd been bumped into handed me a lipstick.

'Oh, yes. Thanks.'

'Bloody kids,' he said. 'Should look where they're going.'

He sounded like Victor Meldrew even though he was only about thirty-five. My sense of humour stretched to *One Foot in the Grave*.

'It was an accident,' I said.

'Oh, I know,' said the man. 'But I don't see why everyone has to spend their time pushing and shoving each other these days. Even if it is supposed to be fun.'

I wanted to laugh. Exactly like Victor Meldrew, I thought.

'I mean, having a laugh is one thing, but they should think about what they're doing.'

I bit my bottom lip.

'After all—' He stopped suddenly and looked at me. 'Are you laughing at me?'

I shook my head but I didn't trust myself to speak.

'You are!' He stared at me. 'You're laughing at me.'

I shook my head again. 'It's just—'

He grinned suddenly and then I realised that, thankfully, he didn't look like Victor Meldrew.

'I'm sorry,' he said. 'I've had a bad day. I've been working late, my career is in terminal decline and I'm supposed to find something funny to say about heartburn.'

'Heartburn?'

'Copy writing,' he said. 'They want something different. A new approach.'

'Oh.'

'Heartburn isn't funny,' he said. 'Not remotely.'

'Don't you have a Good Sense of Humour?' I asked.

'Pardon?' He looked at me in amazement.

This wasn't the man I was supposed to meet. He was only average height, his hair was sandy and, if he had a good sense of humour, it was clearly in abeyance. I liked him a lot.

'Would you like to go for a drink?' I asked, shocked at my own directness. 'You can bounce the ideas off me and I can tell you all about the funny side of indigestion.'

'There is a funny side?'

'Absolutely,' I said.

'You're on.'

So me and the man with no sense of humour left the station and went for a drink. And we talked about lots of things. Funnily enough, though, heartburn wasn't one of them.

REBEL

CONNOLLY

The newly built glass-walled office was so close to the railway line that sometimes, when the train slowed down or stopped, I could almost read the words on the computer screens through the carriage window. It was as though the train became part of the office. It wasn't just the computer screens that came into view. I could see the copies of the *Irish Times* folded on the desks, the half-full waxed coffee cups, the occasional tabloid newspaper or glossy magazine. The glossy magazines weren't the usual ones you'd find in an office though. I knew this because I only ever saw men working there and men don't buy *Glamour* or *New Woman*. So I guessed the mags were *GQ* or *Motoring Life*. Or maybe some computer games magazines. Dommo loves computer games magazines.

The office was part of a bigger company. There were three desks near the window and another slightly further back. At first, when people moved into the place and it changed from a new building into a working environment, the three desks were used by men who wore almost-identical suits – dark suits, usually black or navy – and the men hung the jackets over the backs of their chairs every day. The brown-haired guy who I christened Brownie (oh, OK, not original but accurate) usually wore a plain tie in blue or red; the sandy-haired bloke (Sandy) preferred spotted ones on garish backgrounds and the dark-haired man (Blackie), wore vibrant ties in deep purples and maroons (he was probably the snappiest dresser). I bet to myself that if I got a close-up look at their ties his would be pure silk while the others were some kind of mix.

They started work early. They were always at their desks when the train went by at seven-thirty so they must have had to be in by seven. And they were usually there when I was going home too, although it was harder to see them in the evenings because the train was usually on the far side of the track.

I wondered if it was a security risk, the fact that I could see so much of what went on, or more probably the possibility of someone being able to read what the men in suits were typing onto the screens. Maybe a competitor could see their latest plans for a brilliant new product; or – and this was my favourite scenario, given that they always looked so official – perhaps they were working on some kind of top-secret project of national importance that would all go horribly wrong because a passenger on a train read about it and blabbed to the press. I was interested in them, in whatever their job might be, whatever kind of secret-agent work they might be doing, and I worried about their security arrangements.

OK, I know it's complete rubbish. I know that nobody in an office near Connolly station is a secret agent and that Ireland probably doesn't have offices full of secret agents anyway. Only, I like to imagine these things. It makes the daily commute that bit more interesting. Let's face it, there isn't much to interest you on the train when you're heading in for another day's grind, is there? Although I suppose that depends on what that grind might be.

In my case the grind is for a good cause. My name is Tamzin Burton and I'm a secret agent myself . . . no, sorry, my name isn't Tamzin at all, I just like it better than Anne, which is the boring name that my mother dumped on me when I was too young to object. Anne Kelly to be exact. It's not as exciting as Tamzin Burton, is it? Anyway, when I'm on the train and listening to my Walkman I'm Tamzin Burton, model with a secret life. You know, like all those girls with attitude on TV – Sydney Bristow in *Alias* and Max in *Dark Angel* or even *Buffy the Vampire Slayer*. (I've gone off Buffy a bit, she can get really irritating with that whispery, whiney voice. Whereas Max is a much more interesting character, I think, what with her genetic messing about and everything.) And, of course, Halle Berry as Jinx in *Die Another Day* was truly brilliant: gorgeous, sexy, clever and handy with a gun! I desperately want to be one of those kick-ass girls and when I'm Tamzin I am. But Anne Kelly is a receptionist at McReady

Motors, a main dealer for the luxury car market. Which means that I meet lots of people who can afford brand new Merc coupés and convertibles and little sporty numbers and that sort of thing while I drive a six-year-old Polo myself whenever I can get it away from Dommo, who owns half. Naturally, in my Tamzin persona, I drive an Audi TT, which I think is the kind of car that a model/secret agent would drive. Clearly I'd love the Aston Martin as driven by James Bond but the original doesn't have power steering and since I'm five foot two and weigh about seven stone I don't think it's the kind of car that I'd be able to use in a frantic chase down Amiens Street.

You see, there I go again. Sizing up cars for driving in chases as though there's the faintest chance of that ever happening. The only chasing I ever get to do is clattering up the steps to the train and trying to throw myself through the closing doors. But it's nice to day dream about it.

My favourite dream is of being sent on a kind of Lara Croft mission where I have to go somewhere tropical to retrieve some ancient artefact which has the potential to change the world. Only problem with that is the fact that I'm massively allergic to mosquito bites and I don't have any of Lara's more physical attributes. (I'm a 32A cup size, for heaven's sake. I don't even look like I have boobs unless I stuff a Wonderbra full of cotton wool.)

So there you have it. You can believe in Anne Kelly,

twenty-three, day-dreaming receptionist with a flat chest. Or you can decide that I'm giving you a cover story and I really am Tamzin Burton, 36C, attitude-girl. Anyway, it was in my Tamzin Burton mode that I noticed the new bloke in the secret agents' office, the man who didn't wear a suit at all, the man who took over the desk a little bit away from the window.

I had to wonder about him, you see, because he didn't fit the pattern. If it was a suit company then why was he wearing a denim shirt over cargo pants? Why did I know that he didn't even possess a tie let alone a spotted one, or a royal blue one or something vibrant in pure silk? How come he had one of those short and spiky Keanu Reeves kind of haircuts instead of something a bit more businesslike? And why didn't he read the *Irish Times* like everyone else? (OK, he might have got the *Irish Times* but I couldn't be certain because his desk was a bit too far back to see everything.)

I noticed him for three mornings in a row as he sat at the desk, staring at his computer screen, sipping his coffee from the standard waxed cup. (It may or may not have been coffee but you have to make assumptions sometimes and I didn't see him as a tea drinker. I thought it might be espresso, though. He had the look of a bloke who liked a caffeine hit.)

The fourth morning he was standing at the window as the train slid to a halt. I was listening to my James Bond movie theme CD when I looked at the building and straight into his eyes. They were a startling blue and his face was lightly tanned. His eyes were set off by the lighter blue of the denim shirt. (I was kind of hoping he had more than one denim shirt at that point.) But still. He was gorgeous; really sexy and hunky and definitely some kind of intelligence operative. And he was looking straight at me. I made my own gaze flinty and cool. One spook to another, I thought. Give him the vibe that I'm a finely honed professional, just like him. And then he grinned at me.

I was so startled I almost dropped my own cup of coffee. I get one every morning before I get on the train in the hope that it will wake me up sufficiently to make me appear bright and cheerful when I arrive at McReady's garage. I knew that I blushed, which was very embarrassing, but I hoped he wasn't able to see that. And, of course, I didn't smile back. We secret-agent types can't afford to get involved.

I thought about him during the day, though it was in my Anne Kelly role, as I took the flak from customers whose cars hadn't been delivered or who were freaking out because the labour costs on their service bill were so high. Those people don't seem to understand that servicing a car is a skill and needs to be paid for. Nor do they understand that it isn't my fault all their brake pads need to be replaced. You should see my TT, I tell them silently. New brake pads every second week what with the high speed chases and everything.

It was a busy day and I was late leaving the garage. The

Men in Black, as I'd christened them, would have finished for the day. And so, presumably, would my new man. I couldn't really call him a Man in Black. He was more of an anti-hero. I named him Rebel. I craned my neck to see into the office as we travelled northwards. The lights were still on and I was sure that I caught a glimpse of him as we went by, but I couldn't be certain. I looked at my watch. After seven. Hard worker or industrial spy?

Do you think I'm crazy? Do you think there's something wrong with a five-foot-two receptionist who wants to save the world?

When I got home my brother, Dommo, had already helped Mum to have her dinner. I rang him when I realised that I'd be late because I knew she'd start to fret. Despite the fact that she's in a wheelchair a lot of the time and that, since the car accident shortly after I was born, she has limited use of her legs and her left arm, she's a cheerful kind of person who does most things for herself. But she gets tired easily and anxious about us when we're not around and that's why I don't tell her that my secret life is that of a secret agent. She'd worry for me, you see. She worries for both of us.

Dad died in the car crash. It wasn't his fault, another car came hurtling out of a side road and ploughed right into them, killing him instantly and causing those serious injuries to Mum. After the accident we all went to live with my grandparents and it worked out just fine even though, as you can imagine, it wasn't always easy. But you have to get on with things, don't you? Like James Bond being socked on the jaw by the latest villain you have to shake yourself down and keep going.

Anyway, Dommo went out for a while after I got in and I sat and watched TV with Mum. She likes action-packed things too so we had a really good time overdosing on a re-run of *Die Hard* followed by a *Buffy* classic episode. Even though Buffy annoys me I do like the fact that some of the vampires are women too. We're not all sugar and spice.

I dreamed about Rebel that night. I dreamed that he was locked into the glass-walled office and that it was packed with C4 explosives and that I only had five minutes to get him out. I was running out of time when my alarm clock went off.

He was standing at the window that morning too, wearing a stone-grey T-shirt and jeans. And our eyes met again. This time I couldn't help smiling. For the next two weeks I saw him every morning. And each morning he'd smile at me and nod in recognition. Once or twice he raised his waxed cup towards me and I'd lift mine towards him too. By the end of the fortnight he was mouthing 'Hello' and 'How are you this morning?' at me and it gave me a peculiar little thrill to know that he was waiting for me.

On the third Monday he wasn't there and I was shocked at the depths of my disappointment. The Men in

Black were at their desks as usual but there was no sign of Rebel. As far as I could see, his computer wasn't even switched on. But he was back the following morning and gestured manically towards his mouth which made me think that he might have been at the dentist the day before. I was relieved that he was back. It hadn't been the same without him.

And so our early morning greetings continued for the rest of the month. But then he disappeared again. At first I thought it must be another dental appointment; after all, they rarely get anything done the first visit, do they? It's always, 'Come back for another few fillings.' But when he didn't reappear the following day or any day that week I felt devastated. Of course, I realised, he could be on holiday. It was the start of May after all and the weather was just moving from cool spring to the promise of something warmer. Maybe he'd gone to lie on the beach for a couple of weeks and tan his toned body. Or maybe he'd just got bored waving to me every morning. Maybe it had meant more to me than it had to him.

I allowed him two weeks holiday time and then I began to worry. After all, I reminded myself, that company was a hotbed of secret agents. I'd forgotten that in the past few weeks of grinning idiotically at a bloke I didn't know. Perhaps he'd been sent on a mission and perhaps he wasn't coming back. Nobody else seemed to care. The Men in Black continued to tap away at their keyboards every day. They weren't missing him at all.

I took the next morning off work. The garage manager was quite surprised because I rarely take days off. I'm committed to my job – it's an excellent cover, after all. But I told him I had personal matters to attend to and he just nodded at me and said, 'Fine, no problem, have a nice lie-in tomorrow.' Of course I'd no intention of staying in bed late, I was going to get my usual train into town – but on this day I would get off at Connolly station and find out what had happened to Rebel.

The next morning, I dressed in a suit. Obviously neither Rebel nor I were suit people but I thought that it would be easier to find out the information I wanted if I looked like a competent business person. I slapped on some make-up, although it's not something I particularly like to wear. Still, secret agents have to be prepared to do anything for their cover. As the train pulled in to the platform I looked at the office window but there was still no sign of him, just the Men in Black beavering away.

I got off the train and walked out on to Amiens Street. I had to do a bit of searching to find the office – although it was clearly visible from the platform, you couldn't really see it from the street. I looked at the brass plate outside the door which read 'Final Solutions' and pursed my lips. Final Solutions. Sounded like they might be in the assassination business. I didn't like to think that Rebel might be an assassin, but if he was doing it for the sake of his country . . . thing is, assassins are notoriously screwed-up people. Remember Bridget Fonda in *Nikita*? Deeply disturbed. (The French version was much better, though, more realistic.)

I adjusted my skirt and pushed the revolving door. The security man didn't even look up from his newspaper. I wondered if I could make it past him without his noticing. Surely that would be impossible. But the whole thing depended on looking confident, as though I knew what I was doing.

I pressed the button on the lift and that sparked his attention.

'Where are you going?' he asked.

'Fourth floor.' I'd worked it out from the train.

'You've got to sign in,' he said.

I walked over to his granite desk and signed Tamzin Burton from Terminal Answers. He hardly even looked at it. I strode purposefully back to the lift, which arrived at the same time as me. I stepped inside and immediately pressed the 'close door' button followed by the one for the fourth floor. I leaned back against the smoked mirror.

My plan was simple. I would ask to see Rebel and, when they denied all knowledge of him, I would tell them not to waste my time, that this was an important personal matter and that I needed to contact him urgently. After that, I'd play it by ear.

The doors opened and I stepped out onto the fourth floor. I was faced with a wood-panelled wall and a corridor leading to open-plan areas at either end. I mentally adjusted my position within the building and decided that I needed to turn left. I followed the corridor and walked to the open-plan area. I'd got it right. A train went by just as I arrived.

The Men in Black were at their desks. I looked around for Rebel. I have to admit that my heart was hammering in my chest and, quite suddenly, I wondered what the hell I was doing. I was in the office of some company I'd never heard of, standing among people who hadn't a clue what I wanted, looking for someone whose name I didn't know and who had nothing to do with me whatsoever. I wanted to turn and run but then the sandy-haired Man in Black looked at me and frowned.

'What d'you want?'

I cleared my throat. 'I'm looking for . . . for . . .'

'For what?' he asked. 'If you're Julian's new assistant and he's sent you for the copy on the Harrison campaign, you can just go back and tell him that I'll have it to him when it's done and not before and I don't appreciate being harassed like this.'

'No,' I said and then mentally kicked myself because Sandy had just given me a way out and I'd blown it. 'I'm looking for—' I took a deep breath, '—for Rebel.'

'Rebel?' He stared at me as though I'd lost my marbles completely.

'Dark-haired bloke,' I said. 'Wears denims.'

'Oh, you mean Frank.' The brown-haired Man in Black looked up from his computer and regarded me speculatively. I glanced at the screen. The document said something about product placement and brand imaging.

192

'He never told us his nickname was Rebel.'

I shrugged.

'He's not here,' said Sandy. 'He's gone back.'

'Back?'

'Are you his girlfriend?' Blackie suddenly looked interested. 'Has he given you the elbow, darling?'

'Of course not,' I snapped. 'I – I've worked with Frank. I need to talk to him.'

'Would've been a lot easier to phone,' said Brownie.

'Maybe,' I said. 'But I need to see him in person.'

'Like I said,' Sandy told me, 'he's not here any more. Breezed in, did a bit of messing about with the systems, breezed out again. But that's Frank for you.'

'And where is he now?' I kept my voice steady.

'Galway, I think,' said Brownie. 'Where else?'

Where else indeed? I hadn't a clue why Rebel – why Frank – should be in Galway. I'd no idea why he would've been in Dublin either. I was a complete idiot who'd let some ridiculous fantasy run away with me. Suddenly I felt my legs begin to tremble.

'I'd better get going,' I said.

'OK.' Blackie was looking at me intently. 'You're sure you're not Frank's girlfriend? Only I'm certain I've seen you before.'

'I doubt it,' I gasped as I turned as quickly as possible and walked back to the lift.

By the time I'd emerged from the Final Solutions building and back onto the street I was shaking from head to toe.

And I was feeling incredibly stupid. What the hell did I think I was doing, walking into a place like that and looking for a complete stranger? And signing my name Tamzin Burton, for heaven's sake. If the security guard had asked for my ID he'd have discovered that my driver's licence and credit cards all belonged to someone called Anne Kelly. He'd probably have called the cops. Was I completely insane?

I staggered into the mainline station and grabbed a cup of coffee in Oslo. (That's the name of the bar/restaurant. I wasn't in some Norwegian fantasy.) I felt better after the coffee and my legs stopped shaking. Nobody had come after me. Nobody really gave a damn. I'd gone into the building pretending to be someone else and I'd actually found out that Rebel's name was Frank and that he was now in Galway.

I sighed. I couldn't really go to Galway and start looking for him. Besides, I told myself, using the first bit of common sense I'd discovered in a long time, Frank wasn't a secret agent. Frank was some kind of systems analyst. And he'd obviously been sent to Final Solutions to do some work for them. Although . . . I frowned . . . maybe they had a branch office in Galway. Maybe I could find him that way. I got up from my chair. I wasn't going to find anyone. I was going to get back to work and remember that I was just a receptionist in a garage who had an over-active imagination.

I wasn't able to go back to being Tamzin Burton. Somehow, once I'd gone home that evening and taken off my Tamzin suit, I felt more comfortable being Anne Kelly than I ever had before. I don't know why. I sat in the living room with Mum and we watched *My Best Friend's Wedding*, which made us both giggle and tear-up a bit at the end. And afterwards I didn't bother switching over to the repeat of *Dark Angel*.

I stopped looking into the Final Solutions offices. I concentrated on being a better garage receptionist. I think I might have grown up a bit. A little piece of me still wondered whether or not I could find Frank, the systems analyst, but I knew there was no point.

It was about three weeks after my covert operation in Final Solutions that I saw him again. I was sitting in the window seat, my head resting on the glass, listening to a 'Now That's What I Call Music' compilation. And he was on the platform. I jerked upwards in surprise. That's when he saw me. His face broke into a wide grin and, as the doors to the carriage opened, he pushed his way inside.

Because of the crush he wasn't able to get near me for a couple of stops. I watched him, my heart in my mouth, as he made his way towards me. A couple of stops later more people got off the train and Rebel – Frank – sat down beside me.

'Hello,' he said.

'Hi.'

'Long time no see.'

'Yes.'

'I missed you,' he said.

'Oh?'

'Absolutely.' When he smiled, those blue eyes just sparkled. I could feel my legs turn to jelly. 'I was in Dublin for a few weeks working on our company systems. I liked seeing you every morning. It brightened up an otherwise dreary day.'

'Really?'

He nodded. 'I thought you enjoyed seeing me too.'

'I did.' As a conversationalist I was failing miserably.

'Anyway, I had to go back to Galway to do some other work. And I missed you.'

I smiled tentatively.

'So, I decided to come back to Dublin this weekend. I took today off specially to be at the train station.'

'Really?'

He nodded. 'You've kind of got under my skin,' he said softly. 'I kept making up all sorts of fantasies about you.'

'What sort of fantasies?' I asked, suddenly afraid that he was a serial killer or something.

'Oh, you know.' He laughed shame-facedly. 'Rescuing you from a burning building, that sort of thing.'

'Really?' I looked at him in surprise.

'Oh yes. I kind of fancy myself as the kind of bloke who could rescue women from burning buildings. Though the truth is that I'd probably just run screaming.'

I laughed. 'I don't think so.'

'Anyway,' he said, 'I was wondering if you'd like to come out with me tonight?'

'Where?'

He shrugged. 'Dinner, drinks, movie? Whatever.'

I hesitated.

'Don't feel obliged to say yes just because I've travelled over two hundred miles to be here.'

I grinned at him. 'Well, in that case, yes,' I said.

'Excellent.' He beamed at me. 'My name is Frank.'

I almost said that I knew. But I didn't.

'Anne,' I told him. 'Anne Kelly.'

'Pleased to meet you, Anne,' he said.

'Glad you found me,' I replied.

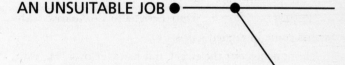

AN UNSUITABLE JOB

CLONTARF ROAD

I sprint along the coast road towards Clontarf Road Dart station, aware that I've already missed the nine thirty-nine train but hoping that I won't miss the next one as well. I look up at the railway bridge, willing it to stay empty because if the snaking green train slides along the tracks I know that I'll never make it on time. The bridge leads into the station itself but it's a longer walk (or run) than you think through the car park before you can buy a ticket and push through the turnstiles. I've just reached the entrance to the car park when I hear the ominous rumble and feel the vibration through the tarmac.

'Shit, shit, shit!'

My high heels, not my usual footwear, are not exactly designed for running and I've already slithered a couple of times on my hurried dash from the apartment. Normally a fifteen-minute stroll away, I've made it to the station in seven. But my feet hurt and I can feel a blister forming on my little toe. I make one last effort and clatter to the ticket office. The bloke behind the window is leafing his way through the *Sun*. He looks up languidly.

'Return . . . to . . . Dún Laoghaire . . . please.' My words come in ragged gasps.

He punches out the ticket and hands it over. He isn't being deliberately slow but he isn't exactly hurrying himself either.

'Your change!' he calls as I grab the ticket and shove it into the turnstile. I don't care about the change, I just want to make the train on time. I run up the steps and pop onto the platform like a cork from a bottle of champagne. The train sighs its way gently out of the station, without me.

'Shit, shit, shit!'

I grit my teeth and squeeze my eyes shut in frustration. I wasn't meant to be late. I'd planned everything perfectly. Now I'm hot, sweaty and furious. As well as being late. And I don't want to be any of those things.

The reason I'd decided to get the train to my interview in the first place was because of the taxi-drivers' protest in the city. It's not actually that far from Clontarf to Dún Laoghaire, especially when you use the toll bridge, but the taxis had formed a cavalcade along the approach roads to the bridge earlier that morning, effectively blocking any chance of using it and forcing other drivers to divert through the city centre. With the interview scheduled for ten-thirty, I'd made the decision to leave my car at home and get the Dart. And, because I reckoned that there'd be extra pressure on the train service that day, I'd chosen to get one that was due to arrive in Dún Laoghaire by ten, building in a possible delay as well as giving me plenty of time to rehearse what I was going to say to the interview board of Enchem who, I hoped, would be dazzled by my experience and my confidence. I'd selected my wardrobe with care – a soft chocolate-brown suit with a pale cream top and the high-heeled shoes to emphasise my legs. Donald always said that my legs were my best feature (though personally I prefer my bum, because it's small) but since the interview board consisted entirely of men I bowed to Donald's superior knowledge in these things and wore the shoes. The self-help books advise wearing something comfortable for an interview and I'm most comfortable in my loose-fit jeans and ancient Timberlands. But I'm confident in the brown suit even though it's a few years old by now. It makes me look intelligent and efficient.

I am, of course, both of these things anyway. It's not generally considered good form for anyone to admit that they're intelligent – especially a woman. We're meant to pretend that our brains are some lucky accident, and we're aware that nobody likes us boasting about our ability to use them. But I know I'm intelligent – I've done the tests and got the results to prove it. Mind you, that doesn't actually mean I've any more common sense than the next person. Probably less, to tell you the truth. But in the case of my job interview I'm hoping that the IQ factor would wow them. Thing is, the IQ is meant to go hand-in-hand with that efficiency part of me, and now I'm worried that the efficiency part has fallen down badly. Because I'll never make it to Enchem by half-ten.

It isn't my fault. I was actually on the way out the door when the phone rang and I picked it up, thinking that it might be the company to change some detail of the interview. But it wasn't. It was Donald.

'Don't panic,' were his first words, which immediately sent my heart leaping into my mouth with fear. 'Everything's fine. Tasha had a bit of a fall and she wanted to talk to you.'

I bit my lip and held the receiver more tightly.

'Mum,' Tasha's voice quivered, 'I bumped my head.'

'Did you?' I asked. 'How?'

'I fell.'

'Off what?'

'Off the breakfast counter.'

'Off the breakfast counter!' My eyes widened. 'What were you doing on the breakfast counter in the first place?'

'Watching Dad make my lunch.'

'He let you sit on the counter while he was making your lunch?'

'I always sit on the counter when he's making my lunch,' said Tasha. 'It's what we do.'

'OK,' I said lightly. 'So how did you fall?'

'I was leaning over,' said Tasha, 'and I slipped off. And I banged my head.'

'On what?'

'The handle of the washing-machine door,' she said.

I closed my eyes and visualised it. Black-marble counter. Shaker-style integrated units. Brushed-steel handles. I winced.

'Did you cut yourself?'

'Yes.' Tasha paused melodramatically. 'It poured blood.'

The taste in my mouth was metallic. I hate thinking about blood. I even hate the word. It makes me feel ill.

'But it's OK now,' continued my daughter. 'Only Dad says that I can stay out of school because I have a bump the size of an emu's egg on my head.'

'Can I talk to your dad?' I asked, as I looked at my watch and realised that I was going to miss the train. I relaxed my shoulders. No problem, I told myself. I had a built-in time delay. I could afford to miss it. And it was more important to find out about Tasha.

'She's fine, Joely,' said Donald. 'She's right about the bump, it's shocking. But she's OK.'

'How do you know?' I asked.

'I know.'

'Is there a chance that she's concussed?'

'No,' said Donald.

'Should you bring her to hospital?'

'Joely, stop nagging me. I know what I'm doing. I'm keeping her home this morning and I'll see how things go.'

'But—'

'Joely!' His voice was firmer this time. 'Give it a rest.'

'I'm not . . . I want to be sure—'

'And you think I don't?' Donald asked.

'No, of course not, but—'

'I only rang because she wanted to tell you,' he said. 'Otherwise I wouldn't have bothered you. I know how you feel about being bothered.'

'I need to know if something happens to her,' I told him tightly. 'I have a right to know.'

'Sure you have,' he said. 'I know all about your rights.'

'What's that supposed to mean?' I demanded. 'I never gave you grief about rights. Never! So don't start at me now. I'm concerned about Tasha, that's all. I've a right . . . I'm entitled to be concerned.'

'I know.' His voice was softer this time. 'I'm sorry. I didn't mean to get at you.'

'It doesn't matter,' I said wearily. 'Neither of us ever means it, do we?'

'Nope.'

'So everything's all right?'

'Yes,' said Donald.

'And I'll see you as usual on Sunday?'

'Yes,' said Donald again.

'OK then.'

'She wants to talk to you again.'

There was a scuffling noise and then Tasha's voice, not quivering any more.

'Dad says I'm going to have a massive bruise.' Her tone was self-satisfied now. 'He says it's going to be an absolute corker. Like as if someone punched me in the head.'

'Lovely,' I said. I glanced at my watch again. I was beginning to cut things a bit fine for the next train too. I was starting to panic, then I heard the word 'stitches'.

'What?' I was alarmed.

'I want to have stitches.'

'No you don't,' I told her. 'You'd have a scar.'

'I'd love a scar,' she said wistfully.

'You'd hate a scar,' I said firmly.

'But it would be cool!'

'Maybe now,' I agreed. 'Maybe when you're six it's cool. But when you're sixteen you wouldn't like it.'

'Why?'

'Because it would spoil your beauty,' I told her.

She giggled. 'Dad says I'm not beautiful,' she informed me. 'He says I'm like you. I have character.'

'Does he indeed?'

'Yip.' I could almost see her turn towards Donald. 'Don't I, Dad?'

'What?' His voice was faint.

'Have character?'

He told her that she did, indeed, have character. Just like her mother. I felt a lump in my throat. Then I looked at my watch again.

'I have to go,' I told Tasha.

'Work?' she asked.

'Yes.'

'OK.'

'I'll see you soon.'

'OK.'

'I love you.'

'Me too.' She hung up and I ran out of the apartment.

But it was too late and now I'm standing on the platform with images of my husband and my daughter in my mind, messing up my head, getting in the way of the interview plan of campaign that I'd worked through earlier.

Enchem is an engineering company and the job is a much bigger one than I have now with a good deal more responsibility (and a better salary). I'm an engineer. People look slightly surprised when I tell them what I do for a living and I know they're thinking that it's not politically correct to say that you don't see that many female engineers, especially ones at my level. But you don't. I'm good at it. It's all I ever wanted to do. And getting this job is important to me because it'll make up for everything else. It's not that I feel the need to make up for everything else but . . . well, maybe I do. Maybe I need something solid to replace what I thought I had. Me and Donald and Tasha. A family. But not any more.

That wasn't anyone's fault either. Donald and I are as different as two people can be. He's an illustrator for children's books. He does really fantastic drawings of bug-eyed animals and round-headed children, which seem to jump off the page at you. He's won awards for his illustrations and he deserves every one of them. He's creative and messy but he gets things done and he works from home.

That's why he has Tasha. It makes more sense. He's always been at home for her and just because he and I have split up it doesn't mean that I should put up some kind of fight to have her with me. I never want Tasha to be some kind of pawn in our game, someone to fight over. I want what's best for her. I really do. It's not that I don't miss her like crazy. It's not that I don't want to cry sometimes when I'm in the apartment on my own. But I don't work from home and I wouldn't be able to give her the support that Donald gives her, so it's better for her to be with him.

Besides – and this is really hard to admit – I'm not half as good with children as he is. He comes from a big family and he loves them. I am an only child. And I don't take to kids easily. I love Tasha, of course, but I'm not a natural with her. When they first put her in my arms I sat like a statue, afraid to move in case she stopped breathing or something. I pulled a muscle in my neck because of the tense way I held her. But it was no big deal to Donald. He slid his hands under her tiny body and held her close to him in the kind of nurturing way that I knew I'd never master.

And that's how things carried on. I tried feeding her myself for a while but it didn't really work and when I eventually gave in to bottles Donald sighed with relief and slotted himself in to feeding duty. She was more relaxed with him, too, fed better, slept better, smiled more. I suppose she knew that I was afraid of her, afraid of what I might accidentally do to her. And even though I told myself that I was managing fine, I was glad to get back to work and leave Donald with the responsibility of our daughter.

Is that so awful? Is it? I hate telling people about it because it truly makes me feel totally inadequate. And, like I said, I'm not. I'm eligible for Mensa, apparently. Maybe that's why I feel inadequate about so many other things.

Like being a wife. Not that I think I was the worst wife in the world and not that half of everything that went wrong wasn't Donald's fault. But every time we had an argument, every time something didn't work out, I would clam up and stare at him and wonder why he was getting so harassed about things. I couldn't figure out why it bothered him that on my way home I'd forgotten to pick up the takeaway he'd ordered, or that I didn't remember our wedding anniversary or lots of other silly things that didn't really matter. After all, I could simply go out again for the takeaway, couldn't I? And what was our anniversary after all, except a date? We'd been living together for ages before we got married so the actual day didn't really mean that much in the end. It was fun, of course, but hardly earth-shattering.

Whenever I say that (which is pretty rare) people look at me with a wide-open gaze and say, 'But Joely, your wedding anniversary!' as though it was the most important thing that ever happened to me. I can't seem to explain that it wasn't. I love Donald – loved Donald – but getting married wasn't such a big deal. The best day of my life was getting my degree and I'm sorry if that's not romantic enough for most people, but it's true.

My relationship with Donald was a different thing altogether. We met by accident at an apartment block near the seafront. It was at a time when finding somewhere to rent was an almost-impossible task and the letting agent had scheduled a number of us to look at this place at the same time. But the agency had made a mistake in the advert which had said that it was a one-bedroomed apartment suitable for a single person. As it turned out it had two bedrooms and the rent couldn't possibly have been paid by one person, unless they were into organised crime or something. But it was lovely, set slightly back from the main road with landscaped gardens to the front and a view over Dublin Bay. Not that the Dublin Bay view from Clontarf is particularly pretty – much of it is of the port so you're looking at storage tanks and cranes – but I like storage tanks and cranes and when the tide is high there are often windsurfers flitting across the water which softens the skyline a bit. And the apartment was very convenient for me because I work from an office close by. I desperately wanted it. But I couldn't afford it.

Donald felt the same way. Because it was on the top floor of the block it had skylights as well as wall-to-ceiling front windows and it was incredibly bright. He needs light to work and he likes it to be natural. The two of us stood on the tiny balcony and moaned at each other about how the letting agents had wasted our time and what a pity it was that the apartment was for two and how convenient it would have been for either of us. Which is when he told me about the illustrating and I told him about being an engineer and he asked me if it wouldn't be a good idea to share.

Sharing an apartment had never even crossed my mind. I'm not really a very sociable person and I wasn't sure that I could possibly get on with a complete stranger. But he laughed and said he was pretty unsociable too so it would be ideal. And next thing I know (completely out of character for me) we're agreeing to give it a go and we sign the lease and I really have no idea why I've just done what I've done.

At first we hardly ever saw each other. Then we started spending Friday nights together in front of the TV watching *Will & Grace* and *Frasier*, both of which we both enjoyed despite the fact that I didn't think blokes liked either of those US sitcoms (well, *Frasier*, perhaps). On Saturdays we'd occasionally walk to Clontarf and share a pizza in the little Italian bistro. On Sundays Donald would cook breakfast while I went out and got the papers. It was all very easy and totally platonic. Women phoned up looking for him.

He went on dates. I pretended to go on dates. (I'd split up with a boyfriend a few months earlier and just wasn't interested in the whole dating thing.) We congratulated ourselves on being good friends. And then, almost inevitably, we slept together, thanks to a romantic comedy from the video store one evening (actually it was *When Harry Met Sally* so kind of appropriate for us I guess), a bottle of Pinot Noir and a sudden inexplicable desire on both our parts to try it out together.

The sex was good. Better than I could've imagined. And afterwards we weren't awkward and edgy with each other. We just laughed. Donald told me that we'd probably been building up to it. I disagreed. We argued. We made love again. And then we were an item.

And then I got pregnant.

But it was OK. We'd already decided that we loved each other. We got married, me carrying an extra-large bouquet to cover my bump. My friends all confessed to being jealous of me and Donald. Jealous that it had happened so easily for me in the end – especially as I was the benchmark against which they used to be able to compare their relationships. I might be bad with men, one or the other would say, but at least I'm not as bad as you, Joely! And we'd all laugh, me the most.

It was a bit of a shock to be married and pregnant. And though the company couldn't say a word about it, I know that they were thinking that this was the problem with women engineers. They got married. They had kids. They were hopeless afterwards. Clearly none of the other engineers had ever gone on maternity leave before. My boss talked uneasily about it to me, worrying that he'd have to find a replacement, wondering if I was coming back at all. (I don't think that he's legally allowed to wonder about that but you can't blame the bloke, can you?) I was emphatic about my return to work. I knew I'd want to work after the baby was born.

And I did. Although it was harder than I'd expected to leave Donald and Tasha together that first morning. And I thought more about her and her feeding times than I did about the pipework I was inspecting that day. But we got into a routine which worked for us and so I never really noticed that I was taking Donald totally for granted, or that sometimes I was impatient and rude and downright patronising to Donald because he'd spent the day at home and I'd been out there working my butt off. The reason I was sometimes impatient and rude was because my workload had increased and I certainly wasn't having anyone saying that I couldn't keep up just because I was a woman with a child. I wanted to prove that I could do it regardless of my personal circumstances. Besides, there were lots of men with kids on the project. Only they didn't have the guilt.

Oh, of course I was guilty! There's a gene built-in to women that makes them guilty, there really is. I felt guilty about leaving my baby even though she couldn't have cared less because Donald was such a brilliant father. And

I felt guilty about the fact that I had got over leaving her so quickly because, to be perfectly honest, I'm better with inanimate objects than squirming, real-life babies. I pretty much felt guilty about everything. And I took it out on Donald.

But we soldiered on. We bought a house about ten minutes away from the apartment and that kept him extremely busy because, naturally, it had to be practically rebuilt before it was habitable. Plus he was doing his own work and looking after Tasha. When people work from home everyone else tends to think that it's terribly cushy on the basis that they can get up whenever they like and slob around the house in their pyjamas if they want, but of course it isn't really like that at all. Donald had loads of deadlines to meet so he couldn't spend the day lazing round drinking cappuccinos. It was just that, because the project I was working on meant that I was leaving the house at six every morning, I couldn't help feeling he had the better part of the bargain. So I nagged at him and then he got stroppy with me and before we knew where we were it was impossible for us to have a conversation without implying that one or the other of us was a lazy sod who took all and gave nothing. Even making love was an angry thing. We didn't make love actually. We just had sex. But sometimes, when we'd least expect it, we'd find ourselves laughing at the same joke, or thinking the same thing at the same time, or connecting on a different level. Then we'd look at each other and smile and everything would seem OK again.

But it wasn't OK. It was even less OK the morning I called back to the house unexpectedly and found Donald and a strange woman having coffee in our newly decorated kitchen. Clearly it would have been worse to have found them in bed but I didn't need to find them in bed to know that they'd slept with each other. I might be an unromantic engineer but I'm not totally blind to these things. Donald introduced her as Linda, the mother of one of the children in Tasha's crèche. (Before she went to school Donald arranged for Tasha to spend mornings in the crèche so that he could get some uninterrupted work done. He'd pick her up around lunchtime. I believed the guff about getting uninterrupted work done until the day I met Linda.)

Anyway, she finished her coffee and left and I looked at Donald and knew that he wasn't even going to deny it. In fact all he said was, 'Well, we haven't done it much lately, have we?' I said nothing. He asked if I wanted to talk about it. I shook my head. I'd already decided to leave.

I don't know if Tasha even noticed that I wasn't living there any more. After I'd moved out and into a tiny one-bedroomed apartment, in a block close by to the one where Donald and I had originally shared, I worked out that she'd only ever seen me in the evenings and at weekends anyway. And seeing Tasha in the evenings was unusual since I was often working late and she was asleep by the time I got home. On those occasions, I'd sit with her for a while, as I thought she'd sense my presence and it would comfort her to know I was there. But she probably didn't have a clue. So I comforted myself, when I left, by telling myself that she didn't care very much, that she was happy with Donald, that Donald was happy with Linda (or whoever might eventually take her place) and that I was happiest being on my own, that I'd never really been any good at the wife and mother thing anyway.

I wasn't lying to myself. Being on my own meant not feeling so guilty any more. I didn't have to worry about being out late. I didn't have to adapt my way of life for Donald or for Tasha or for anyone. I could do my own thing and concentrate on my job and become a top professional in my field. And that's exactly what I did.

Which is why I was asked to go for an interview with Enchem who were the top company professionals in engineering. This was everything I'd ever hoped for and worked for. I was going to knock them for six. I would get the job. I'd justify my faith in myself and everything would be worthwhile.

I stare down the tracks. The next train is due in another ten minutes. I might not actually be very late after all. I just won't be early, as I'd wanted. But there is no point in getting upset. I exhale slowly and allow my heartbeat to slow down. I try to think restful thoughts. That was something Donald was always trying to get me to do. 'Relax,' he'd tell me when I came in frazzled about the fact that we'd suddenly hit rock where rock wasn't supposed to be or something equally traumatic. 'Don't take everything on your shoulders. Don't blame yourself if other people make mistakes.' I don't blame myself for other people's mistakes but I do rather like to anticipate them.

By the time the train arrives I'm much much calmer, although the blister on my little toe is really sore. It's lucky that the Enchem building is only five minutes away from the train station in Dún Laoghaire. I'll be able to grit my teeth and pretend I'm not in agony as I hurry towards it.

All the seats in the carriage are taken when I get onto the train, but a woman (in her mid-thirties I reckon) with two young children sitting on the seat opposite her tells the boy to get up and let me sit down. Maybe she can tell I have a blister despite the fact that I'm trying to look serene. The boy, aged about eight, stares at me mulishly and eventually offers me his seat as ordered. I accept, mainly because I don't want to undermine the authority of his mother but also because, despite thinking that women can do most things a million times better than men and hating all those old-fashioned movies that have men treating us like cut-glass or china, I do think it's kind of nice if a bloke, even an eight year old, goes to the trouble of offering you his seat, and believe that the least you can do is take it as graciously as possible. And not think that they're offering it to you because you look like some middle-aged crone who won't make it to the next station without falling over.

I breathe a sigh of relief as we leave the station. Then the train stops again, about 100 metres or so down the track. I frown and catch the eye of the woman opposite who shrugs her shoulders. I'm sitting with a grim expression on my face when the voice of the driver comes over the speakers and announces that there's an obstruction on the line at Connolly and it'll be a few minutes before we get going again.

I'm not bothered by this now. If I'm going to be late I might as well be very late. I ring Enchem and speak to someone there and explain that I'm stuck on the train. She clucks sympathetically and says not to worry – they'll slot me in when I arrive. Slot me in? I suddenly wonder how many people are being interviewed for this job!

As I end the call I exchange looks with the woman opposite again and she smiles at me and says, 'Hope it doesn't affect your chances.'

'Pardon?'

'I couldn't help hearing your call. I hope the interview goes well.'

'Thanks.' I'm dismissive.

The boy who gave me his seat starts to climb one of the poles in the centre of the carriage. His mother tells him to get down at once and I can see him wondering whether or not he'll obey her or whether he'll make an issue of it. The little girl, who's now sitting beside her mother, looks at both of them with interest. She's weighing up the possibility of her brother disobeying a direct order and wondering whether or not that'll lead to trouble. I can see her thought processes as clearly as if I had some way of accessing her brain directly. She sees me looking at her and she grins. It's a wicked, cheeky grin and I can't help laughing. She sticks out her tongue at me.

'Amanda!' Her mother looks annoyed. 'Don't be so rude.' She sighs and apologises to me and I assure her that it's OK.

'They're such devils at this age,' says the mother. 'They really are.'

Amanda is about the same age as Tasha I think, though nothing like her in looks – Tasha is dark whereas Amanda is peaches and cream. But they seem to have similar personalities. Tasha has a bit of a devil in her too, always pushing to see how far she can go. Which is probably why she fell off the breakfast counter this morning. I wonder why the two children on the train aren't in school.

'Burst water pipe this morning,' says their mother, as though she's reading my thoughts. 'We get to the school and we're told that the place is flooded. I thought I'd bring them on an educational trip on the Dart. They never get to go on the train.'

'When will it start again?' Amanda asks petulantly.

'Will I get out and fix it?' Her brother looks hopeful.

'It's not the same as a toy train,' says their mother. 'You can't fix it, Gus.'

'I don't see why not.' He looks determined. 'I fixed the video, didn't I?'

I'm impressed. Despite my engineering degree and high IQ, mastery of the video is one skill that constantly eludes me.

'I know,' says his mother.

'And I can fix computers and electrics and everything,' says Gus.

'I know,' says his mother.

'And I can—'

'Enough,' she says, although she's starting to giggle.

He laughs as well. 'I'm better at fixing stuff than Dad.'

'True.'

'So I could probably fix this.'

'It's an obstruction on the line,' I tell him. 'Which means that the tracks are blocked. It's not broken.'

He looks at me in disgust and I realise, again, that I am not connected with the world that children spin around them. Just like I never really connected with Tasha and all of the fantasies that she created. I am so bloody hopeless!

'That's the thing about boys,' says Amanda confidently. 'They don't listen.'

I stare at her in amazement and can't help laughing. So does his mother, though Gus looks annoyed.

'They're like this all the time,' says their mother. 'They have me and their father driven demented. Our lives aren't our own any more. But you wouldn't be without them.'

I smile half-heartedly. I know what she means. Only I am without my daughter.

I stare out of the window. I'm without her because I couldn't live with my life not being my own any more. And because I was too selfish to change. And because I didn't give Donald the respect that he deserved. And because I thought there were more important things to care about.

And yet I'm watching this mother and her children and they're having fun together even though they're testing boundaries all the time. I was always hopeless at that – if Tasha did something she shouldn't I'd snap at her and if she tried again I'd lose my temper. Not harshly, because I knew she was a child, but I'd rage inside because she couldn't see what my problem was. Though how the hell was she meant to understand?

Could I blame Donald for sleeping with Linda? Well, yes, because he didn't have to run into the arms of the first comforting woman that came along. He could've talked to me first. Only, he'd told me afterwards, he never found the time to talk to me. Or maybe it was I never found the time to talk to him.

I can't understand why today of all days I'm obsessing so much about Donald and Tasha. It's not just the woman and her kids because I was thinking about my husband and my daughter when I woke up this morning, before the phone call. I think about them every morning, I realise suddenly. I'm forever thinking about them. But when I was with them, when we all lived together, I was forever thinking about my job. 'It's not the most important thing in the world, Joely,' Donald would sometimes say. 'The world won't stop spinning just because you can't bore a hole where you want.'

The train eventually begins to move. Gus and Amanda whoop with glee and their mother sighs with relief. I look at my watch. Not that it matters since Enchem are going to slot me in. And I'm going to do the interview of my life with them because I want this job so badly. And yet I'm wondering, as we travel through Fairview Park, how much more demanding than my current job it'll be. And how little time I'll have left for myself if I get it. But then again, I don't need time for myself.

Suddenly all the things I was so sure about are shifting in my head. I can't seem to grasp what is and is not important any more. I don't know what I am and am not good at. And I sure as hell don't know why because today is a day the same as any other.

But it's the day that my daughter phoned me to tell me that she'd hurt herself. She'd wanted to talk to me. No doubt Donald had picked her up and comforted her and hugged her and done all the things that he'd normally do with her but she still wanted to tell me that she'd hurt herself. And even though I was late I'd listened. And there was a little part of me, a tiny part of me, thinking that maybe I wasn't such an unsuitable mother after all. And that maybe I would get better at it some day.

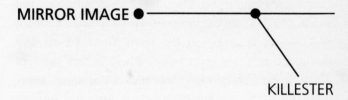

MIRROR IMAGE

KILLESTER

It was an ordinary mirror: full length, from the Argos catalogue, with a mahogany trim. Well, fake mahogany. Mahogany veneer. I couldn't have afforded the real stuff. And even if I could I wouldn't have bought it unless it was from a sustainable forest. I was trying to be 'green' these days. The kids at school were inundated with environmentally friendly catch-phrases which Mikey parroted to me every day and I suppose they were right. But I was finding it hard to know what was acceptable to buy any more – wood, coffee, paper – everything seemed to have an agenda of its own. And I couldn't remember what was what. Although that had nothing to do with the information overload. It was just that I didn't seem to be able to remember anything much these days.

But I remembered buying the mirror. It had been a treat. A sort of treat anyway. I suppose it was a sad state of affairs when I considered that buying a mirror was a treat. Buying clothes or jewellery or perfume should be a treat. Buying a figure-hugging dress or cripplingly high boots was something exciting. Not bloody furniture. But I didn't have a full-length mirror at home and I'd seen it as I walked by Argos in the Jervis Street Centre and thought that it was great value with its twenty per cent discount. So I bought it. It was kind of liberating, something I used to do but hadn't done for ages. Impulse shopping. Even if it was a mirror.

I felt pretty macho as I drilled holes in the wall, stuck grey plastic Rawlplugs in the gaps and then screwed the mirror into place so that it was dead straight. (Well, OK, maybe not dead straight but it was straight enough!) I was pleased with myself, pleased with the knowledge that I knew how to do these things. That I was able to be everything I needed to be. I was both pleased and sorry for myself in equal measure. I stood in front of my full-length Argos mirror and looked at the reflection of the thirty-two-year-old woman who stared back at me.

And I frowned because I knew the woman in the mirror should have had mouse-brown hair falling into her eyes, dusty denim jeans and a juice-stained sweatshirt (courtesy of Mikey who hadn't yet managed to get through a day without spilling something). That was the reflection I'd seen for the past few months because all I wore lately were dusty jeans and grubby sweatshirts; I hadn't had time to get my hair done so it always fell into my eyes and it was definitely mouse-brown because I hadn't even had time to use the colouring kit I'd bought three months ago. Because I'm not worth it, I muttered. And I'm tired. So tired that I've even forgotten what I look like. I closed my eyes.

I heard the train hurtling past and opened them again. A green streak of train was visible in the mirror behind my reflection. The reflection that was exactly the same as the last time. The oddest reflection I'd ever seen.

The woman in the mirror was my height. She had the same face as me, oval shaped with cheekbones that my mother had once told me were 'to die for'. Her hair was cut in the same careless style that I'd had for years. But her hair had cinnamon-blonde streaks through the brown. And her oval face didn't look exhausted – in fact it looked as mine had ten years earlier when I was twenty-two – bright, alert and with two sparkling blue eyes peeping from beneath a deliberately untidy fringe. And this reflection's jeans were skin-tight round a firm bum while there wasn't a trace of juice on her snow-white sweatshirt.

The sleepless nights were getting to me, I thought. My brain was frazzled from all the racing around it did every night and having to be constantly alert for Mikey and Lulu during the day. Talking happy rubbish. Now it was apparently so scrambled that I could no longer even see a reflection properly. I was seeing myself the way I used to be. The way I wished I could be again.

I reached out towards the mirror and the reflection did the same. I moved my hand in front of her face and so did she. She was doing all the things a reflection should do but she was doing them looking a million times better than I did. This was creepy. I was clearly hallucinating and I felt frightened. But I wasn't allowed to be frightened. I was the one in charge. I was the parent. I was the one who knew everything, could understand everything, could fix everything. I wanted to cry but I frowned instead.

My reflection smiled. I gasped and covered my mouth with my hands. I was drinking too much coffee, that's what it was. The caffeine was doing something to me. The reflection's hands were covering her mouth too. I took mine away, then reached out towards the mirror and touched it. The glass seemed to shimmer in front of me, as though it was silver liquid. I felt my fingers slide through it and thought, wildly, of Alice in *Through the Looking-Glass*. But that had been a dream, hadn't it? This wasn't a dream. This was really happening. I tried to draw my hand back but suddenly it was in a firm grasp, that was followed by a definite tug and the next thing I knew I was standing in a carbon copy of my bedroom beside the younger, prettier version of myself.

'Well,' I said out loud, 'clearly I must be dreaming even though it feels so real. Or else I've cracked up under the strain.' And I wondered what would happen to Mikey and Lulu if I was found to have lost my marbles completely. Who would look after them then?

'Hi.' My reflection smiled at me.

I'm not doing this, I told myself fiercely. I'm not giving in to a breakdown.

'How are things?' asked my reflection.

I had to get to my mother's and pick up the kids in less than an hour. I didn't have time for breakdowns that featured talking to images of my past. I needed to get a grip on the present again.

'You look tired,' said my reflection.

'Of course I'm bloody tired,' I snapped back at myself. 'I've been awake for three nights in a row because Lulu's cutting teeth. Mikey is going through a rebellious phase and the washing machine broke down on Monday.'

'That's rough,' said my reflection.

'Yes. Well.' I scuffed my toe on the floor. The bedroom wasn't a carbon copy after all. In my actual house the bedroom floor was wood laminate. This was the real thing. And the bed was covered in a pretty white spread with embroidered pink roses cascading over the side.

'But you chose that life, didn't you?' The reflection tossed her streaked hair over her shoulder and smiled at me. 'I remember thinking about it myself. It sounded good. Marriage, kids, the whole caboodle.'

'I might have chosen the start of it,' I said bitterly. 'But did I ask to spend my days with broken washing machines? Did I intend to spend my nights with crying babies? Is that what I chose?'

'Apparently.' My mirror image looked at me quizzically. 'You chose Noel Johnson, two children and a house on the Chesterfield estate. You left me with the job in the insurance company and the shared room with Angela Bellamy.'

I grabbed my own hair by the roots. 'Who are you?' I asked.

'I'm you,' she said. 'I'm Dervla.'

I decided that if I was having a breakdown I might as well play along with it. I might snap out of it more quickly that way. I didn't know anything about hallucinations and how they were caused but I guessed that eventually you came back to earth. All I had to do was wait.

'How is Angela?' I asked conversationally.

'Fine,' said the other Dervla. 'She's going out with Joe Magellan.'

'Joe Magellan? The guy from Operations?'

She nodded. 'He's Deputy Head of Operations now,' she said. 'A rising star in the company. Well, a risen star really. I doubt very much he'll progress any further. But he's doubled his salary and his bonus in the last couple of years.'

'Lucky Angela.' I tried to keep a certain bitterness out of my voice. I'd fancied Joe Magellan myself for a while. But he was way out of my league with his toned and tanned body and his come-to-bed eyes. I looked at the other girl. The other me. Had she fancied Joe Magellan too?

'Angela's not so lucky,' Dervla continued. 'He's going to dump her for a girl in the IT department.'

'How d'you know?'

'I met him for a drink.' She smiled. 'He's a bit of a player, is Joe.'

'He tried it on with you? Even though he's going to dump Angela for a girl in IT?'

'Of course he didn't try it on!' Dervla sounded shocked. 'I'm his boss.'

'You are?' I looked at my alter ego in amazement. 'But I never wanted to stay in Associated Insurance. I had other plans. I did other things.'

'You didn't want to stay,' Dervla reminded me calmly. 'But I did. And I'm Head of Operations, which is why I know that Joe won't get any further.'

'Oh.' I stared at her. She had the look of someone who could be head of a department, which, as far as I remembered, had about thirty staff. She had an air of self-confidence about her that I'd never had. That I'd never have in a million years.

'You're very cool about it,' I told her, trying to keep the envy out of my voice.

'You learn to be cool,' Dervla told me. 'In the cut-throat world of business you learn all sorts of things you didn't think you needed to know. Not that most of us really need to know them anyway. Sometimes I get bored with it all. The posturing. The pretending. The interminable meetings.' She yawned. 'What's it all for?'

I looked at my reflection warily. 'Is that what this is about?' I asked. 'I'm having a hallucination about how much better things really are than I imagine? Are you some kind of inner me who's going to tell the outer me that my life is fuller and better and more wonderful now than it ever would have been if I hadn't married Noel and had two kids? Are you going to say how important my role is now? Are you going to tell me that things would have been worse if he hadn't been so damned stupid as to die! To be dead at thirty-five. To have left me on my own.' My voice cracked. I hadn't said that word in a long time. Dead. It sounded so terrible when it was about Noel. It sounded final and I didn't want it to be final. Sometimes I still believed that he'd come home again even though I knew he never would. I'd known that since the funeral five months ago. But describing him as 'dead' still sounded so wrong. Dead was for other people, not for someone as young and as alive as Noel had been. Not for the man I had married so that we could spend our whole lives together. He hadn't had a life.

'Nope.' The other Dervla shook her head. 'You're right about part of it. This is an alternate reality. You know, a split in the fabric of space, time and all that sort of thing. The mirror is a portal. You can step in and out.'

'Oh for heaven's sake!' I looked at her in exasperation. 'That's all very well in *Star Trek* but not in real life.'

'My life is as real as yours!' My reflection sounded annoyed. 'Just because it's different doesn't make it less real.'

Clearly I had flipped completely. I didn't know what to do. I was good at things like teething babies, and children, with recycling concerns and screwing fake-mahogany mirrors onto bedroom walls, but I hadn't a clue about alternate realities. In fact, I doubted very much that alternate realities existed. The simplest solution is usually the right one. And the simplest answer in this case was that I was in the middle of an interesting breakdown and that my kids would be waiting a long time for me to come and collect them. I knew I should care about that because they'd so recently lost their father but, right then, I didn't. If I was mad I was mad. They'd learn to get over it. I would simply embrace the insanity.

'So what do you do?' I looked around the alternate-reality bedroom. As well as the pretty bedspread there were pots of silk flowers in the corners and a huge Monet print on the wall. There was also a shoe rack containing about forty pairs of perfectly maintained footwear – shoes used to be a passion of mine but right now I was down to trainers and flip-flops.

'What do you mean?'

'What do you do when you're not being Head of Operations and telling Joe Magellan where to get off?' I said.

'Head of Operations is a very important job,' Dervla reminded me. 'If you remember, you aspired to it yourself for a while.'

'I thought it might be nice,' I said. 'But I met Noel instead.'

'And I kept on doing the insurance exams,' said Dervla.

'Bloody hell!' I'd given up those exams. They were too boring for words.

'I went to Grenada for my summer holidays,' she said.

I'd gone to Galway with the kids for a week. It had rained the whole time. To be fair, we'd stayed in a hotel with a swimming pool and a kids club so Mikey had had a fantastic time. But Lulu had been cranky and fretful. She was still cranky and fretful, the complete opposite of Mikey as a baby. I wondered was it my fault.

'I drive a 1.8 Alfa.'

I drove a Fiesta but I preferred taking the train. I was a hopeless driver and got flustered in traffic.

'I'm a member of a really good gym.'

I snorted. It explained the fact that she looked ten years younger than me, I supposed. I bet she was in one of those gyms that had a spa attached where women could book in for facials and body wraps to keep them busy because they didn't have two kids under the age of six.

'I didn't marry Noel, obviously. I didn't marry anyone.'

'And you're better off?'

'Sometimes,' said the reflected Dervla.

'I married Noel, I had the kids. I lost Noel, I lost my life,' I told her.

'You're loved.'

'I'm put upon.'

'You're needed.'

'So are you.'

'Not by anyone who matters.'

'So it is one of these – "I should be happy with my life because I have two lovely children, even though I'm knackered all the time, stony broke and at the edge of reason".'

'Oh, come on!' The Dervla reflection sounded tetchy. 'I'm doing my best.'

'So am I.'

The two of us sat on the edge of the king-sized bed.

'I'm not seeing anyone at the moment,' said my reflection. 'I don't have the time.'

'I'll never have the time to see anyone again,' I told her bleakly. 'And I don't think I'll ever want to.'

'But one day?'

'I doubt it.'

'You're really negative, aren't you?'

'Yes.'

'Do you want this life?' she asked me.

I stared at her.

'We could swap. Who'd know?'

'Everyone.'

'I'm you,' said Dervla. 'Of course they wouldn't.'

I twirled the ends of my hair between my fingers. What if it was true, I wondered. What if somehow it really was an alternate reality and I could step out of the pain and the misery that was my life since Noel had died, and I could take over the life I'd given up instead? We'd agreed that I'd give up work if I had a child because Noel was very much into the idea of full-time motherhood and, to be perfectly honest, I was as well. I'd seen too many of my friends work themselves into a guilty frazzle every day to persuade themselves that any woman really could have it all. It was impossible. So our agreement was that I'd give up work and then do something part-time when Mikey (and any brothers or sisters that might come along) began school. And I never regretted it for one second. I saw other women struggling to look after their kids and their jobs and I was glad that I wasn't one of them. I loved being with Mikey. And when Lulu was born I was relieved in a way, because otherwise I would've felt obliged to go back to work since Mikey had started school by then.

Very occasionally I would feel a bit resentful about the lifestyle aspect we missed out on, as quite a few of our friends had lots of money because they had two whacking great salaries coming into the house. But I knew that I had a lot more than them where it mattered most. Sometimes I wondered what it would be like to have stayed in the insurance business but I dismissed that thought very quickly. I was so bloody smug with my kids, my husband and my belief that I had something that no one else had. And then it disappeared.

Unbelievably, some people said that at least Noel had died and that I'd only have good memories of him. Some said that it was better than finding out that he'd been having an affair or something and having to get a divorce and struggling with the mess that left behind. It was as though his dying was a noble thing to do. Maybe it was. But all I felt was totally gutted. Because part of me was gone for ever and I'd never had the opportunity to let my feelings for him change in any way. I never said it to those friends of mine but at times I thought that it would have been easier if he had had an affair and left me. At least then I could've been bitter and hurt and not have to go through the awful, awful grief that had absorbed me for the past five months. I wouldn't feel as though I was only half-living. I'd have had anger to keep me going.

'Let me show you the house,' said Dervla, who had been watching me out of the corner of her eye. I'd seen her observing me but I didn't care. 'Come on.'

It was the same house. But the kitchen units didn't have sticky handprints or scuff marks on them. There weren't any crayon drawings on the wallpaper. The sofa was cream leather, which I knew would be destroyed in five seconds by Mikey and Lulu. It was gorgeous, of course, but totally impractical.

The garden was lovely. No brightly coloured plastic tractors or slides or paddling pools. Just a neat lawn bordered by bedding plants and a small rockery in the corner beside a wooden bench. I sat on the bench in the warmth of the sun. It was beautiful here. Quiet, peaceful and beautiful. It might be nice to live here.

'What about the children?' I looked at my reflection.

'I'd look after them.'

'No,' I said. 'I mean now. I'm here and they're some-where else. What if anything happens to them?'

'Nothing will happen.'

'How do you know?'

'It won't. I'd be concerned for the children.' My reflection's voice was soft. Wheedling even.

'But you wouldn't love them,' I told her.

'They're my children too,' she said simply.

I wanted to stay here. If I was here then I wouldn't have to face everything on the other side of the mirror. I wouldn't have to care any more. The only person I'd have to worry about was myself. It would be nice just to worry about myself for a while. To have long, luxurious baths without having to keep listening for the sound of Mikey attacking Lulu. To be able to leave things down and not worry that tiny hands could reach them and turn them into weapons of mass destruction. To go out. Oh God, I so, so wanted to go out. With a man. Any man. And get drunk. And have sex. I could really do with having some decent sex again.

'Could we swap back?' I asked.

'I guess so. Once the mirrors are in proper alignment.'

'What do you mean?'

'They have to be exactly right. Today was the first time they were. It's easy to knock them off. Brushing against one, whatever.'

'How do you know all this?' I asked her suspiciously. 'You're only an insurance clerk like me.'

'I've done it before,' she said. 'I think there must be something in me that makes my mirrors main portals.'

'There's more of us?' Well, I thought, at least if I'm cracking up I'm doing it in style.

'There's an infinite number of alternate realities,' Dervla told me. 'Yours and mine are only two.'

'So you've already switched with a different me?'

She shrugged and didn't reply. I wondered what the third Dervla was like. Whether her life was so different that my alter ego had wanted it as badly as I wanted hers. I frowned again as I thought of something else. Even if we switched she'd look a million times better than me. The kids would look at her and think she was a stranger. And the people in the insurance company would look at me and wonder what the hell had happened.

'Do you keep yours exactly aligned all the time?' I asked.

'It's always aligned with somewhere,' she said. 'Not always with your location, of course.'

'But if we swapped . . . I could keep it aligned, couldn't I?'

'Of course.' My reflection grinned. 'But I have to keep my mirror in the right place too.'

'It sounds far too technical for me.' I sighed. 'I was never very good at this sort of stuff.'

'You are, you know. You just don't give yourself the chance. Here, in this reality, you do.'

I chewed my lip. 'So you're offering me the chance of

being the person that I wanted to be yet you're trying to make me feel that I shouldn't take it because you're also pointing out the good things I've got. At least, as you see them.'

'I'm not trying to make you feel anything of the sort. I want to swap.'

'So why don't I just agree?' I demanded. 'Why do I have any doubts, if your life – my life here – is so much better?'

'I don't know.'

'Do I have to agree?' I asked. 'Can't you do it if I don't agree?'

'Let's go back inside,' she said.

We walked through her pristine kitchen, up her stairs and into the equally pristine bedroom.

'I could make a dive at the mirror and leave you behind,' she told me. 'So, no, you don't have to agree.'

'Was that what you did before?' I asked.

'No.' She shook her head. 'The last Dervla wanted to switch with me.'

'Why?'

'She was unhappy.'

'But she had the life you're offering me.'

'I know.'

I was getting a headache.

'Would you?'

'What?'

'Just jump through without me?'

'I'm thinking about it,' she said.

'I want to spend more time here,' I told her. 'It's peaceful.' I rubbed my eyes. 'I have time to think.' I looked at her again. 'Am I happy here?'

'Sometimes,' said the other Dervla. 'Am I?'

'What?'

'In your reality – am I happy? Do I like the kids? I was so terrified of that life, you know. And I thought that being with Noel would stifle me. I thought I would get bored with him.'

'I didn't get bored with Noel,' I told her.

'I should have known I wouldn't get bored with him. He was a good man.'

'I miss him.'

'I don't, obviously. Not in the way you do.'

'Is he alive here?' I turned to her in sudden hope. 'Is he? Can I see him?'

The other Dervla shook her head. 'He died. Brain tumour. Like your Noel.'

'So much for the alternate reality.' The disappointment gripped me like a vice. I realised suddenly how much I wanted to see him again. To have the opportunity to tell him how much I loved him one more time. To feel the touch of his warm skin once more instead of the marble coldness of his dead body. I'd been shocked when I kissed him and realised how cold he was. I knew that bodies grew cold but I never thought that they would be icy.

'He died and I never got to love him or be with him or

239

have his children.' There was real regret in Dervla's voice and tears in her eyes.

I bit my lip. 'But it doesn't matter to you, does it? Because you have a life without him. It didn't destroy you when he died.'

'It didn't destroy you either. And you have the kids.'

'It's destroyed me enough,' I told her. 'And the kids – oh, I love them, of course. But everyone says that they should be a comfort. And sometimes they're just a bloody reminder.'

'So swap,' said my reflection.

Part of me wanted to agree. Part of me was ready to agree. 'If I swapped, what would I do?'

'Live my life. Go to work. Go to meetings. Be in charge of things.'

'Am I going out with anyone?'

'Not currently,' she told me. 'But you had a sensational relationship with a guy in the Bank of Ireland until very recently.'

'We split up?'

She nodded. 'It was a commitment thing.'

I frowned. 'What sort of commitment do you want?'

'I want the family,' she said. 'I want to love people for different reasons.' She smiled at me. 'I would love the children and be a good mother to them and they'd never know that you were here and that I was in any way different.'

'You think?' I looked at her gleaming hair and flawless skin again.

'I know,' she said.

I thought about going into the insurance company every morning. Of going to all those meetings. Of trying to find someone new. I didn't really like the thought of trying to find someone new. And then I realised that it didn't matter what world I was in, I didn't have anyone special any more. If I wanted to have a man in my life (and it wasn't something that was currently very high on my agenda) I'd have to get out there again anyway. Wouldn't it be easier to do that here, in a world where I was someone important, rather than back in my dreary reality?

'I'm not sure,' I said uncertainly. 'I like the idea of a day, but not being able to switch back . . .'

'I might leave the mirror aligned,' Dervla told me. 'I mightn't be any good at the motherhood thing and I might want to get back in a hurry.'

I laughed. 'Probably after the first time that Lulu keeps you awake.'

'Lulu? You called our daughter Lulu?'

'I know.' I looked contrite. 'It was Noel's idea. He always liked it. We actually called her Louise because I said Lulu would look really stupid on her birth certificate, but she's always been Lulu.'

'I suppose I could live with that,' said Dervla. 'I always thought I'd call my daughter something more timeless. Ciara or Rachel maybe.'

'Well, her name is Lulu,' I said.

'And the other child?'

241

'Mikey.'

'Not just Mike?'

'He likes Mikey.'

'That's not so bad.' She grinned at me. 'I can do Mikey.'

I smiled at her.

'So,' she said. 'Are you ready to swap? Because we can't stay here for ever.'

'Well, I know,' I said. 'But maybe we could talk a bit more. You could tell me what it's like . . .'

'No,' she said. 'This whole alternate reality thing only works when one of us is somewhere else. If the two of us try to stay here together for much longer then – voomph!'

'Voomph?'

'*Star Trek* scenario,' she said. 'Our matter will cancel each other out. There'll be a mini-explosion and both of us will cease to exist in either reality.'

'I see.' I did see although I wasn't really clued in about the matter/anti-matter thing. Noel had been. He loved sci-fi. This Dervla might have had an even better relationship with him than I had. Maybe that's why she was sorry she hadn't.

'So, do you want to swap?' she asked with urgency in her voice.

Another train, an alternate reality train, sped by the house. I saw it reflected in the mirror again. I'd brought Mikey and Lulu to my mother's on the train because Mikey loved it so much. He wanted to be a train driver

242

when he grew up. I didn't care what he was once he was happy.

'I can't swap,' I told Dervla. 'I'm sorry.'

'Why?' She sounded frustrated.

'Because – well, oh hell!'

She looked at me in annoyance.

'I'm going to say it, aren't I? That I don't want to change my life. That I love my kids. That I can't change.'

Dervla looked disappointed.

'I know I'm unhappy now but I suppose I'll get over it,' I said. 'And I really think I should get over it at home with the people who mean the most to me.'

'Your choice,' said Dervla, but there was definite anger in her voice. I wondered what it was about her perfect life that she didn't like, why she really wanted to change.

We stood in front of the mirror. I felt her move beside me and, suddenly afraid that she'd make a rush to go through, I pushed my hand towards the glass and jumped.

I landed on the bedroom floor. I stood up and looked at the mirror again. Dervla stared back at me. I realised that she could still come through. The mirrors were still aligned. I reached out and touched the mahogany rim. It moved slightly. The reflection shimmered for a moment and then settled again. The girl staring back at me was the one I'd lived with for the past five months. Dervla with the mousy hair and the dusty jeans and the juice-stained sweatshirt.

I opened the wardrobe, took out a clean pair of jeans

and a black top. Tomorrow, I told myself, I'll make an appointment and get my hair done. A few highlights would be nice. Hers looked good on her. They'd be good on me too. I didn't have to look the way I felt. Not all the time.

Then I turned my back on my reflection, picked up my bag and went to collect my children.

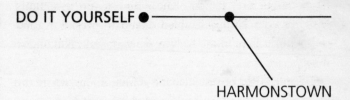

DO IT YOURSELF

HARMONSTOWN

I didn't think that the furniture store would deliver the sideboard on Christmas Eve. But they did, knocking at the door in the afternoon when I was up to my armpits in flour because I'd decided at the last minute to renew the tradition I'd once had of making mince pies, even though I didn't really feel like it.

'You'll have a busy evening,' said the delivery man as he opened the door of the van. I thought he was talking about baking but he wasn't. He slid four large boxes out of the van, 'Sign here.'

I looked at the flat boxes.

'Isn't it assembled?' I asked.

He laughed. 'You're joking.'

'But . . .' I looked helplessly at him.

'The instructions are inside,' he told me.

'How much to assemble it?' I asked.

He shook his head. 'We don't do assembly. Only delivery.' Then he smiled. 'It's not that hard.'

I closed the door and looked at the flat-packs. I'd never done this before. I didn't know how to do this. But I couldn't leave an unassembled sideboard packed in cardboard boxes here in the hallway where it was taking up so much space.

I hauled the boxes into the dining room where I'd intended the Scandinavian-designed piece of furniture to go. I went back into the kitchen, filled the mince pies and popped them into the oven. Then I looked at the boxes again. I took out the instructions. I took out the pieces of wood. The instructions made it look easy. But I doubted them somehow. I spread the page in front of me and tried to match the pictures to the pieces.

I was supposed to have 12 plug-type A but there were only 11. I wasn't sure whether piece Q was the metal joint I was holding in my hand. It was the only single piece but it didn't look like the drawing much and I'd no idea what it could possibly be used for. And I couldn't see how I was expected to hold piece J horizontal to piece K while attaching screw X without either knocking myself out or killing myself altogether. This was ridiculous, I thought, as I wrestled with the unhelpful bits of wood. It was too hard. I couldn't possibly do it. Tears of frustration stung my eyes.

The smell of scorching pastry made me drop piece K onto the floor and hurry back into the kitchen. My mince pies were very well done. I bit my lip. Jerry would have liked very-well-done mince pies. He'd regretted when I stopped making them on the basis that it was easier to buy a couple of dozen from Tesco than do it myself. He'd said that buying them somehow diminished Christmas in his eyes. I told him not to be stupid, that a mince pie was only a mince pie after all. Now I burned my finger on a hot globule of filling which had seeped out of a pie and wiped away another tear. I left the pies cooling on a wire rack and went back into the dining room.

A train hurtled by, passengers standing in the crowded carriages. I could almost feel their festivity, their seasonal camaraderie. They were going home to people they loved, looking forward to the next few days of overeating and television viewing. I envied them fiercely.

I plugged in the Christmas lights. Make things look festive, I thought, even though the room was now a mess and I didn't feel festive. I picked up piece J again and propped it against the wall. That made things easier. I held piece K against it and shoved the screw into hole B. It began to turn. I gritted my teeth and turned it a bit further and then I remembered the electric screwdriver. Jerry used to leave it plugged in all the time. I let myself into the garage and looked around. Eventually I saw it, on the highest shelf, still plugged in. I grabbed it and brought it indoors. Using the electric screwdriver made things much, much easier. I smiled despite myself and read the instructions again. Then I poured myself a glass of wine.

I went back to the garage a little later to look for a substitute plug-type A, which I found in the tool box on the same shelf as the one where he'd kept the electric screwdriver. The grey plastic substitute was a little too long but I cut it down with my kitchen scissors. Then I slid rail D into place. I heard a key in the front door. Tom or Alice, I thought. Both had spent the day in town, shopping. I'd offered to drive them to one of the centres but they'd looked at me pityingly. I remembered that they were teenagers and that they were embarrassed to be seen in my company. I knew that Christmas Day would now be a boring day for them, away from their friends, stuck with me. Stuck with the miserable woman whose husband had left her exactly 355 days ago.

'Yes!' I tapped cover L over screw O and stood back to admire my handiwork. All that was left (after three-and-a-half hours) was to attach legs W and then the sideboard would be complete. Mind you, I wasn't sure how solid the whole thing would be, but it might look the part all the same.

'Where are you, Mum?' It was Tom. I suddenly realised that he would have been one of the passengers on the train, getting off at Harmonstown station.

'In here,' I called.

'What're you – oh my God!' He stood in the doorway, a mince pie in his hand.

'They delivered the sideboard.'

'And you're making it yourself?' He sounded incredulous.

'Yes.'

'But—'

'But what?' I dared him to say that I'd never done this before. And that I was useless at map reading, car maintenance and anything to do with spatial awareness.

'It looks good,' said Tom.

'Thanks.' I grinned at him. 'It's only taken me most of the afternoon.'

He picked up the instructions and looked at them. 'You need screw O to go into the base of the unit,' he told me. 'So's you can attach legs W.'

'I know,' I said calmly. 'But I need to put in plug A first.'

'Did you have all the right bits?' he asked. 'Dad used to say that they never gave you all the right bits.'

I shrugged. 'I had to make an extra plug A,' I told him. 'But it worked OK. D'you want to hand me one now? Those grey things.'

He watched as I pushed it into the gap and then lined up the first leg W.

I heard another key in the door.

'Where are you?' called Alice.

'In here,' we replied.

She'd taken a mince pie from the wire rack too.

'Mum!'

'She's done it herself,' said Tom. 'I arrived home just in time to hand her a plug-type A.'

'It looks great,' said Alice.

'I don't know.' I pushed my fringe out of my eyes.

'Depends on whether it stands up or not when I've finished putting on the legs.'

They watched as I finally screwed the last one into place. Then we righted the sideboard and slid doors S onto rail T.

'Looks OK,' I said diffidently.

'Looks brilliant!' Alice hugged me. 'It's really great, Mum.'

'Thanks,' I said.

Tom walked out of the room. I looked after him anxiously. He returned carrying the mince pies on a plate.

'Anyone for a mince pie?' he asked.

'Don't eat them all tonight,' I begged.

'Why not?' asked Alice. 'They're made to be eaten.'

Tom put the plate in the centre of the sideboard.

'Home-cooking Z. The finishing touch,' he said. 'Way to go, Mum.'

And then they cleared away the cardboard boxes so that we could admire how I did it myself.

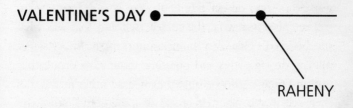

RAHENY

When the four teenage girls clattered noisily onto the train Bronagh experienced a sudden jolt of déjà vu. Perhaps not déjà vu exactly, she thought, as she watched them giggle among themselves; more of a hurtling fifteen years into the past to the time when she, too, wore a school uniform and hung around with friends, laughing at private jokes and wondering what life would be like when she was a grown-up. Of course the friends she hung around with were different to the girls on the train. She'd never been in the cool gang who wore their uniform skirts hitched up as high as possible and had pretty much decided that life as a grown-up would be better than it was now – with more money, more clothes, more friends (especially boyfriends) than they had at present. Bronagh had hung around with the nerdy bunch who always looked uncomfortable in the navy-blue serge, did their homework on the day they were given it, and never knew exactly which label was the right one to wear at any particular time. Bronagh had never been

251

cool, nor had she ever really cared. She thought that those girls who were desperately cool were also desperately in-secure. That was what she told herself and that was what she believed. That they hung around in the short skirts, puffing on cigarettes and boasting about how drunk they got on Friday nights because they had no other measure of their self-worth. She felt proud that she could figure this out and not be intimidated by them. At least, she thought she did. Yet the time when her lack of street-cred really got to her, the only day when it stung like no other day, was the same date as today – Valentine's Day. The day when the cool gangs came into school carrying sackloads of cards from vast arrays of admirers and passed them round each other as ostentatiously as possible so that everyone knew just how many they'd got. And they'd flaunt the same haughty, self-satisfied air as the group of girls who were in the carriage now. The air of girls who were attractive and knew it; who had their pick of boyfriends and knew it; the girls who had it all.

Bronagh had hated Valentine's Day with a passion. She couldn't understand how a day which had the potential to ritually humiliate you was looked forward to by so many people, especially by the girls. It was the day which sorted out the cool girls from the sad ones. It was the day on which she knew that, much as she despised the cool ones, she wished she could flaunt a card too. Because it was the day when her lack of anyone who could possibly be described as a boyfriend was plain for all to see. It didn't matter that the postman hadn't arrived before she left for school, any girl worth her salt had her cards personally delivered the night before by her army of boyfriends and potential boyfriends and secret admirers. Whereas Bronagh knew that none of those existed in her life. And it never really mattered to her except on Valentine's Day. Because nothing counted on Valentine's Day more than the number of cards you'd received.

The cool gang in school was a gang of four. Ayesha, the acknowledged leader, had streaked blonde hair, courtesy of an expensive hairdresser and multiple family holidays to the south of Spain. Her skin was creamy, her eyes bright blue and her lips bee-stung and pink. Whenever she split with a boyfriend there was always another waiting in the wings. Tanya, her closest friend, was also a blonde but without the extra highlights; it didn't really matter, though, she was almost as pretty as Ayesha and had a breathy, child-like voice that irritated Bronagh intensely but which the guys seemed to find totally captivating. Trinny and Jules made up the rest of the gang – Trinny with her burnt-auburn tresses and huge grey eyes who always looked so soulful but had a heart of pure granite, and Jules who was probably the plainest of the lot but whose family were rolling in money and who had her uniforms specially made so that she was one of the only people in school that actually looked elegant wearing it.

Every Valentine's Day the four of them would lug their cards into school and prop the smaller ones on their desks while leaving the huge silk padded ones on the cupboard at the top of the room where everyone could see them. Every year Bronagh wondered how it was that four girls could have their pick of the blokes while she couldn't even find one.

Not that it was important, she'd tell herself. She knew that boyfriends wouldn't be the be-all and end-all of her life. She expected to have a good career and stay single for a while before settling down. But it was a bit worrying that no one seemed the slightest bit interested in her, even if only for a quick snog outside the school gates. She knew that to attract that sort of interest she needed to hang out in places like the rugby club or the cricket club or other local haunts frequented by Ayesha and her pals, but Bronagh wasn't really interested in going to a place where the excitement was all about sneaking in drink and getting legless. She worried that her conformity would leave her stranded on the outskirts of things for the rest of her life but there was nothing she could do about it. She wasn't an outgoing, bubbly, need-to-know kind of girl. So nobody bothered with her very much and she couldn't really blame them.

The last Valentine's Day was the worst. As usual, the gang of four had brought cartloads of cards into school. Bronagh had walked into the classroom to see silk hearts and furry bears and boxes of chocolates festooning the desks. And she'd smiled at her own best friend, Lauren, who generally despised the gang of four as much as she did but who, today, had a guilty grin on her face.

'Hi.' Bronagh dumped her bag on the floor beside her desk. 'How're things?'

'Good,' replied Lauren. 'They're good.'

'See that the place has been turned into a forest of mush again.'

Lauren nodded.

'I mean, it's OK to get the damn cards, but why do they have to flaunt them in our faces every year? And who really wants to get a teddy bear with a red heart in the middle anyway?'

'Well . . .' Lauren still looked guilty. She shrugged and then opened her own bag. She took out a large envelope and smiled lopsidedly at Bronagh. 'I got a card this year.'

'What?' Bronagh looked at her friend in dismay. In all their years at school, when some of the most unlikely girls had turned up with sloppy cards, she'd always been able to depend on Lauren to be cardless too. 'Who's it from?' she demanded.

'I don't know,' admitted Lauren. 'Which kind of makes it more exciting, don't you think?'

Bronagh didn't think so at all. She reckoned it made Lauren's betrayal even worse.

'Let's see.' She reached out for the card and opened it. The writing inside was big and loopy. 'To the one I admire,' she read. 'With lots of love now and forever.' She turned to Lauren and made a face. 'Did you send it to yourself?'

'Bronagh!' Lauren's tone was indignant and her expression hurt. 'Of course I didn't. I'm not that pathetic.'

Bronagh bit her lip. She knew it had been an unfair thing to say. Last year, Mary-Ann Saunders had propped a card on her desk. It was the mushiest sort of card possible, lots and lots of hearts and glitter with a sentimental rhyme that didn't even scan properly. But the writing inside was clearly her own. Everyone had laughed at her behind her back while Jules Gresham had remarked on how much Mary-Ann and her 'secret admirer' had in common. Mary-Ann had flushed red but said nothing. Bronagh glanced around to the back of the room where the girl sat. There was a card on her desk today too. She wondered whether Mary-Ann had faked it again this year. Would Mary-Ann, in fact, always fake it?

'So who's it from?' she asked Lauren. 'I didn't know you were secretly collecting boyfriends.'

'I've no idea,' replied her friend. 'You know there isn't anyone.'

'There must be someone,' said Bronagh.

'Maybe.' Lauren grinned. 'It's kind of exciting to get an anonymous card.'

'Really,' said Bronagh dryly and sat at her desk.

It had never been quite the same between her and Lauren after that. Bronagh knew that she was being silly but she wasn't able to prevent herself from feeling that Lauren had made a move away from her. That the other girl was finding interests outside homework, discussing meaning-of-life issues and despising the gang of four. It turned out that the card had come from the seventeen-year-old guy who lived across the road from Lauren. The family had moved into the house in January and, as he told Lauren when he finally plucked up the courage to speak to her, he'd noticed her immediately but hadn't had the nerve to say anything. Which, Lauren told Bronagh, was rather sweet, didn't she think?

Bronagh didn't think it was sweet. She thought it was pathetic. She thought everything to do with romance and furry bears with padded red hearts in their stomachs was ridiculous and childish and she couldn't quite believe that Lauren had been sucked in by it all.

She studied even harder than before and got nine straight As in her Leaving. She made a statement by not inviting a guy to their graduation dance in a city centre hotel but walked up to accept her school pin from Sister Monica accompanied by Hazel Travers, the only other girl not to have invited anyone either. There was a fairly strong rumour in the school that Hazel Travers liked women more than men but Bronagh didn't care. How often did men reduce women to red-eyed sobbing wretches? How often did they let you down? How often did they mess up your life? Why, she wondered, as she shook the nun's hand, why would anyone be bothered with a bloke in the first place?

After the meal she danced with Lauren's boy-from-across-the-road and thought that he was pleasant but mentally unstimulating. Mainly, though, they danced in groups so it didn't make any difference that she didn't have a partner of her own.

'Why do you hate men?'

She looked in surprise at the guy who'd asked her the question. He'd accompanied Patsey Johnson who was currently dancing with Mary Murray's bloke.

'I don't hate men,' she answered.

'You could have got someone to come with you tonight,' he said. 'But you didn't.'

'I didn't need someone,' she said.

'No, but there's probably plenty of guys who would've liked to be asked.'

'I don't think so,' said Bronagh.

He considered her. 'I didn't think you were a lezzer.'

'Oh, grow up.' She walked away from him and into the Ladies.

Most of the available space in front of the mirrors was taken up by girls touching up their mascara or their lipstick or spraying themselves liberally with a plethora of perfumes.

'I admire you,' Jackie Egan told her, as Bronagh half-heartedly began to re-do her own lipstick. 'You didn't compromise on your beliefs.'

'What beliefs?' Bronagh asked.

'That you prefer women.'

'Oh for heaven's sake!' Bronagh threw her lipstick back into her bag. 'I don't prefer women.'

'So why didn't you ask a bloke?'

Later that night Bronagh asked herself the same question. Maybe she was a closet lesbian, she thought, as she lay in bed. Maybe she simply didn't know it yet. But she honestly didn't think she was. It was just that the whole man thing was so – so overwhelming. That you had to have someone, anyone, just to prove you could do it. Samantha Stevens had asked a guy she'd already broken up with simply so that she'd have a bloke in the photos. Astrid Morgan had chosen one of her older brother's friends. And her own parents – Bronagh pulled the sheets up under her neck at the thought of them – her own parents had been horrified by the idea that she didn't know anyone to ask. Her mother had suggested sons of half-a-dozen friends, all of whom Bronagh had rejected. The dance was the same as Valentine's Day, she told her mother spiritedly, a stupid romantic idealised notion that drove women into total despair because it reinforced the idea that you were no one without a man.

Jean Carter had tried to tell her daughter that it had nothing to do with that at all, that it was meant to be a bit of fun, but Bronagh insisted that it was nothing to do with fun and everything to do with stereotyping and she, for one, wasn't going to be forced into spending an evening with a bloke she didn't know and for whom she couldn't have cared less. And Jean had shrugged and told Bronagh that it was her life, of course, but couldn't she see her way to compromising just a little because she was pretty sure that Ray Campion would like to be asked? But Bronagh was adamant.

She sighed as she tried to sleep. Romance was rubbish, she thought. All it did was make you feel useless.

The train glided into the station and Bronagh snapped back to the present. The four girls were examining each other's cards, reading the rhymes out loud and giggling at the sentiments.

'We're going out for a meal tonight.' The tallest of the girls flicked back her russet curls and replaced the biggest of her cards in her bag.

'Anywhere nice?'

'Somewhere in town,' she said dismissively. 'But decent. He's reserved tables.'

'Maybe he'll ask you to get engaged!' The shortest girl of the four, a pink and white Baby Spice look-alike, opened her blue eyes wide.

'Maybe.'

'Imagine!' Baby looked at her. 'Wouldn't it be thrilling.'

The russet-haired girl just smiled.

Was that the way they still thought, wondered

Bronagh. Surely girls at school these days didn't care so much about getting engaged or married. They wanted to travel the world and have a good time before even thinking of settling down. Didn't they?

'Of course his family's loaded,' remarked Baby Spice. 'You could get married and then divorce him and keep wads of cash.'

'Always an option,' agreed Russet-hair.

Well, thought Bronagh, at least it was more realistic than thinking that you fell in love with someone aged seventeen or eighteen and it would be for ever. That didn't happen any more. It probably never had.

The funny thing was that it had nearly happened when she was eighteen. In the summer, before going to college, she'd gone to France and worked as an au pair for an Irish family who lived outside Paris. Despite the dire predictions of slavery from Lauren and another friend, Margaret, who'd decided to head off to the States and get work in a bar instead, the Irish family were easy to work for and hadn't taken massive advantage of her. And she'd spent the month of August with them in a house in Montpellier, where she'd met a local guy named Henri, who'd seduced her on the banks of the nearby river and told her that he loved her. She'd tried to stay cool and rational about it, reasoning that it was a summer romance for both of them and it didn't really mean anything, but she'd ended up believing that she was the love of Henri's life and so he became the love of hers. She let herself believe that her green eyes were 'emeralds in the most beautiful setting' as he told her. She enjoyed hearing that her dark hair was a 'river of blackness, dark as the night'. She didn't even scoff when he said that if he were to die now that he would choose to die 'drowning in her kisses and the touch of her embrace'. She knew that if any Irish bloke had said these things to her she would have fallen off her feet with laughter but, coming from Henri, it sounded almost reasonable. And seductive. And she fell for it.

Of course it was all complete nonsense. When the Murphys packed up and went back to Paris she sobbed in Henri's arms and he dried her tears and told her not to cry, that he loved her more than life itself and would phone her every day. By the time she went back to Dublin a couple of weeks later he still hadn't called. She would visualise him sitting on the riverbank with another girl, talking about jewels in perfect settings and life-long loves, and she blamed herself for being naïve and stupid and all the things that she never should have been because she had far more sense than that.

The four girls got out at the next station while Bronagh continued on to her stop at Raheny. She'd finished work early today and she was glad to get home and put her feet up before going out again later. She was meeting her boyfriend, Peter, for dinner.

Peter was nothing like Henri. She'd met him exactly a year earlier at Lauren's wedding reception. She'd gone unaccompanied because – despite the fact that she'd had a number of relationships over the past years – there was no one currently in her life. And she wasn't looking. Peter, Lauren's cousin, was meant to have been accompanied by his girlfriend of two years but the week beforehand she'd dumped him and gone off on a trip to the Caribbean to 'discover herself'. Peter was scathing about his former girlfriend. Bronagh was scathing about men in general. They both agreed that the whole idea of romantic love and Cupid's arrow was complete nonsense and that men and women would be better off deciding that they could be good friends who occasionally indulged in a bit of sex. Everything else was a waste of time. They further agreed that getting married on Valentine's Day was the most sick-making thing to do that anyone could ever think of. Bronagh told Peter that she would immediately break off a relationship with any bloke who sent her a Valentine card. Peter replied that the whole thing was simply a ruse by marketing people to give a bit of a spending splurge to February. Utterly wasteful, they told each other, and then sat in companionable silence as they watched Lauren and her new husband, Alan, dance together to the strains of Jennifer Rush's 'The Power of Love'. A song, they agreed, that was scraping the bottom of the soppy-song barrel.

After Lauren and Alan had left (having gone through

the tunnel of love made by the guests) Peter and Bronagh had another drink together. He offered to see her home but she told him that she'd actually booked a room in the hotel because she lived on the opposite side of the city. And he'd shrugged and asked if she wouldn't like to meet up again for a drink sometime. She'd said why not and had given him her number. She hadn't particularly expected to hear from him although deep down she was hoping that he'd call. She'd liked him. More than anyone she'd met in absolutely ages.

He called the next day. She discovered that they still got on with each other. They both had a jaundiced view of the world, one unsullied, she said, by the rose-tinted glasses that so many people seemed to pull on at every available opportunity. Life could be fun, Peter agreed, but basically people were kidding themselves if they thought that it could ever be saccharine loving like the movies. When Peter and Bronagh went to see films they chose adventure ones and both groaned aloud when the sixty-year-old male hero showed his sensitive side to the twenty-year-old leading lady.

'How can Hollywood possibly think that those girls would look twice at liver-spotted old men?' demanded Bronagh one evening.

'For the money,' Peter told her.

'In real-life, yes,' agreed Bronagh. 'But in the movies these aul' fellas are supposed to be ordinary kinds of blokes. Girls wouldn't spare them a thought.'

Peter laughed. 'You're right.'

She smiled up at him. 'I know,' she said. And suddenly he kissed her.

They said to each other afterwards that it was good, honest sex between good, honest friends. And they reckoned that they'd be happy to keep having it. Just as long as neither of them messed up the whole thing by saying things like 'I love you' simply because they felt they should. They assured each other that it wasn't about love. It was never going to be about love.

When she'd told them in the office that she was going to dinner with Peter that night, the other girls had grinned at her and made kissing noises. Bronagh had looked at them in puzzlement and then Gina O'Reilly wiggled her engagement finger and asked Bronagh was it likely that there'd be any news tomorrow. And Bronagh had laughed at her and told her not at all, that Peter was a good friend, nothing more. Gina had pointed out that going to dinner with good friends on Valentine's Day usually meant something more but Bronagh shook her head and said not in their case it didn't. At which Gina had looked disappointed and asked Bronagh why she'd been going out with Peter for so long if she didn't think it was going anywhere. 'Why does it have to go anywhere?' Bronagh had asked. 'We're perfectly happy with where it is right now.'

*

She sat in front of her mirror and dabbed concealer on the spot that had broken out on her nose. She was always astonished whenever a spot appeared on her face, feeling as though she should have got over all that sort of stuff years earlier. But occasionally one made an unwelcome appearance and – like the sight of the girls on the train today – brought her back to her schooldays and her almost-weekly trips to the chemist to buy tubes of Clearasil. At the time when those things had mattered a little more she'd wondered whether or not it was her permanently erupting spotty face that had put blokes off. But when she mused on it to Lauren years later her friend had told her no, it was Bronagh's attitude that was much more effective. Blokes, she told her, had been intimidated by her superiority and her general air of indifference. Bronagh had been rather pleased with that assessment. And happy that it had nothing to do with the spots.

Now she toned down the offending blemish and dabbed her face with light-diffusing foundation. She wasn't sure whether light-diffusing foundation was better than any other sort of foundation but the sales assistant had told her that it worked wonders with slightly older skin. Bronagh had been about to hit the girl over the head when she realised that she was now a woman in her early thirties and to some-one of nineteen or twenty she was an older person. It kind of frightened her to think that, when inside she could easily conjure up the feelings of someone so much younger.

She smoothed on her eye-shadow, dabbed her face

with blusher, slicked her eyelashes with dark mascara and finally applied her lipstick. She was good with make-up, Bronagh knew. She could get her look just right when she put her mind down to it. She smiled as she remembered the heavy make-up Ayesha wore after school, which had seemed so dramatic at the time. She wondered if she had learned to tone it down a little.

Bronagh had decided to get a taxi into town because she'd elected to wear a tight-fitting red dress and matching high-heeled shoes that weren't designed for walking any great distances. She knew that she looked well in the outfit and that it was attractive but not too girly. She wasn't good with flounces and brooches and bits of accessories. Plain suited her but so did strong colours.

The cab was only ten minutes late, which suited Bronagh perfectly although she would've preferred if the driver hadn't insisted on talking about Valentine's Day all the way in to the city. He kept quizzing her about her 'fella' and asking was he likely to do the good thing tonight. Bronagh found it very difficult not to snap at him.

'You're a fine-looking girl,' he told her as she got out of the cab and shivered in the cool February night air. 'Any bloke'd be happy to have you.'

They were the exact words that the guy had said to her on the night of her school graduation dance. Any bloke would be glad. But not her. She wouldn't be happy to have any bloke. She wanted the right one. And she didn't believe that he really existed.

She walked into the restaurant and scanned the tables for a sight of Peter. She smiled as she saw him and pushed her way through the crowded room. Clearly Valentine's Day did wonders for the restaurant trade because there wasn't an empty table in the place.

'I was getting worried,' said Peter as she sat down. 'You're not usually late.'

'Taxi,' she told him diffidently.

He nodded.

'How're you?' she asked. 'What kind of day did you have?'

He made a face. 'Busy.'

Peter worked in a business consultancy firm. As far as Bronagh could tell they were always busy. She smiled sympathetically at him.

'Still,' he said. 'Out and about now and looking forward to a good meal with you.'

She smiled again. She was looking forward to a good meal too. She was starving.

They talked about work and about the new reality TV show that had just started which was gripping the nation but which Bronagh found incredibly sleazy and uninteresting. Peter agreed with her.

'I watched it just to see whether it was worth the hype,' he told her. 'But no, it was awful. Why am I supposed to care about people I wouldn't cross the street to know in normal circumstances?'

Bronagh shrugged helplessly. 'I've no idea. But they

were all riveted to it in the office. They think it's great.'

Peter sighed. 'Is it us?' he asked. 'Are we just out of touch with everything? Have we suddenly become much older than we thought?'

'I don't think so.' Bronagh considered his question carefully. 'I've always felt this way about things. As though everyone else was in on the whole joke that is life except me.'

'I know what you mean,' said Peter. 'But I don't feel that way when I'm with you.'

'Me neither when I'm with you.' Bronagh beamed at him.

'I feel confident with you,' Peter told her. 'I know you're thinking the same way as me.'

'Good,' said Bronagh.

'And sometimes with you I feel as though I can be a bit sillier than usual.'

Bronagh laughed.

'Anyway, silly enough to have ordered dessert when I arrived,' said Peter.

She looked at him in astonishment. 'We never have desserts. And why did you order one before we ordered everything else?'

'I was talking to them while I was waiting for you,' he said. 'And it seemed like a good idea at the time. Not maybe so good now.'

'Oh, go on.' She grinned. 'I feel a bit dare-devilish tonight anyway.'

'Really?' He made a face at her and signalled to the waiter.

The dessert was a dark and white chocolate creation. Bronagh loved chocolate.

'Delicious,' she said after the first mouthful. 'You knew I wouldn't be able to resist.'

'I thought so,' he said.

'This is what I call a nice gesture,' she said. 'Ordering me something you knew I'd like. Not trying to make some ridiculous statement, unlike Ryan Smith in our office.'

'What did he do?' Peter paused with his spoon halfway to his mouth.

'Only proposed to Darinda McLean in the staff canteen at lunchtime,' said Bronagh. 'Darinda was sitting there with all her friends and Ryan comes over to her table, drops down on one knee and professes undying love. What a load of crap. But of course everyone in the canteen is goggle-eyed as he asks Darinda to marry him.'

'And what did she say?'

'What d'you think?' demanded Bronagh. 'She took the – admittedly gorgeous – diamond ring from the box and stuck it on her finger right away!'

Peter laughed although, thought Bronagh, not as much as she would've expected.

'And all the girls in the office were asking me whether or not you were going to do something similar tonight,' she continued. 'I told them that they were off

270

their trollies if they thought you were that tacky.'

'Well, I—'

'The thing is,' she interrupted him, scooping another spoonful of chocolate dessert onto her spoon, 'the grand gesture is all very well but what does it mean?'

'Maybe for some people it means something.' He watched her anxiously.

'You OK?' she asked and popped the dessert into her mouth.

Then she was coughing and spluttering and choking, her face going red and her eyes beginning to bulge. She leaned over the table as she tried to catch her breath but in the back of her mind was the terrible thought that she couldn't and that she might die here in the restaurant in front of everyone.

Peter leapt from his seat and thumped her hard on the back. The offending piece of chocolate dessert was propelled out of her mouth and onto the table.

'Bloody hell,' she gasped. 'What on earth happened?'

Waiters, who'd gathered anxiously around, drifted away again as Bronagh looked at the lump of half-swallowed chocolate.

'Jeez, I'm sorry,' she said. 'I guess that bit wasn't melted.'

'No,' said Peter uncomfortably. 'That bit wasn't supposed to be melted.'

'It must have been,' she told him. 'Everything else was.' She coughed again.

'No,' he repeated.

'What?' She looked at him enquiringly. 'What's the matter?'

'Um . . .'

'Oh, don't!' she cried as he poked at the lump of chocolate. 'I spat that out, Peter. We'll get a waiter to clear it away.'

'I don't think so,' he said miserably.

'Why not?'

'Oh, Bronagh!' He looked at her in despair. 'It's an engagement ring, that's why.'

She stared at him. Then she picked up the piece of chocolate. She realised that it was, in fact, greaseproof paper covered in a mixture of chocolate and sponge. And that there was something hard in the paper. She looked up at Peter again. Then she peeled the paper off the ring.

It shimmered rainbow colours under the lights of the restaurant. It was one of the most beautiful rings she'd ever seen.

'Peter?' She glanced up at him.

'I thought – well, I was just going to ask you but it seemed such a boring thing to do. And I know we don't like the fuss and everything but I thought maybe this once . . . so I got them to do the dessert because I knew it was your favourite.'

She turned the gleaming ring over and over on her palm.

'Look, I've never said I love you and I didn't think I

needed to. I reckoned that if I did the thing with the ring you'd understand.'

'It's a kind of flashy thing to do,' she said slowly.

'Well, I know. I said it's not us and it isn't. Signs on it,' he added mournfully. 'I nearly killed you with it.'

A smile flickered at the corner of her mouth.

'You did rather.'

'So my best shot at asking my girlfriend to marry me almost turned into murder.'

Her smile grew.

'I guess so. Or manslaughter perhaps.'

'Either way,' he said, 'it wasn't what I intended. I should've stuck to the original plan and just said, what about it?'

'But this was a romantic thing,' said Bronagh. She frowned as she looked up at him again. 'We're not romantic.'

'No,' he agreed. 'We're not. But maybe every so often it isn't a bad thing. I mean, we know that the world is basically a crock of shit and that awful things happen all the time. So maybe it's no harm to do something nice, just for each other, now and then. If we care about each other, that is.'

'And you care about me?'

'I've always cared about you,' he said. 'I love you.'

She said nothing. It was all the things she didn't believe in. Showiness. Romance. Making gestures. Making sweeping statements that might not hold up in the cold light of day.

'I'm not actually great at saying this sort of stuff,' said Peter. 'That was one of the things Geraldine, my last girl-friend, complained about. She said I was cold.'

'You're not cold,' said Bronagh.

'She said I didn't care.'

'Of course you do.'

'She said I didn't love her.'

'I should bloody well hope you don't,' said Bronagh, 'when you've just got engaged to me.'

She slid the ring onto her finger and suddenly Peter was beside her and he'd wrapped his arms around her and they were kissing. And all around them in the restaurant, other women were wondering why their boyfriends weren't as romantic as the bloke at the middle table who'd just proposed to his girlfriend in front of a room-ful of strangers and who was kissing her as though he was never going to stop.

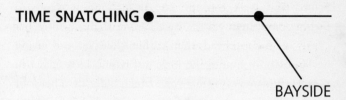

TIME SNATCHING

BAYSIDE

Sometimes Flora thought that she was the ideal candidate for a kidnapping. Not because she was worth snatching – she didn't have any money and it wasn't as though she was any kind of celebrity. But if they ever wanted to do a trial run, she'd be perfect because her life was so measured, so predictable that anyone with a desire to kidnap her could easily work out the best time to snatch her and get away. She knew from the made-for-TV movies that she watched in the evenings that discovering your routine was what it was all about as far as kidnappers were concerned. That if you didn't want to be kidnapped you varied the time you left the house every day, the time you came home, the way you got to work . . . she understood all this but in Flora's case – a poor non-celebrity – varying the routine was quite impossible.

Seven o'clock get up. They'd know that because the light would come on in the bedroom. They wouldn't know what was happening inside the house but they'd be ready for seven forty-five when she'd leave the house with Emma and walk through the neat housing estate to Debbie Murphy's. She'd leave Emma there, kissing her gently on the forehead, then ruffling her hair and giving her an extra hug until the little girl would look at her in exasperation and say – in a voice much older than her four years – 'You're going to be late, you know.' And Emma would be right because then it was a very brisk walk as far as the Dart station and sometimes even a sprint to get there in time for the five past eight train. She never missed it, was always in time to – at worst – hurl herself into a carriage, pressed up against people she didn't know until they arrived at Tara Street and most of them surged out of the train again.

The kidnappers would be able to follow her as she walked along the quays, always at a good pace, a long walk past O'Connell Street bridge, past the Ha'penny Bridge, past Capel Street . . . right the way to the Four Courts. She would arrive at the offices of Lyster, O'Brien, Harris & McKenzie at exactly a quarter to nine and she'd be sitting at her desk in reception five minutes later. Not that it would be easy to kidnap her from the receptionist's desk because it was some construction of a desk, placed slightly higher than the rest of the room and surrounded by the coloured-glass blocks of a counter that separated her from the people who came into the solicitors' office. A small chrome gate stopped them from being able to come behind her desk but nobody ever tried because the whole set-up was far too intimidating. Definitely not worth it as far as potential kidnappers were concerned.

But if they were still watching her, still waiting, they'd learn that she took a fifteen-minute break at eleven o'clock (they wouldn't see her go up to the coffee-room on the first floor and dispense an insipid-tasting cappuccino from the machine in the corner); that she went to lunch at one (walking down to the deli at the corner and bringing a sandwich back to the office because she only had half an hour and it wasn't worth going anywhere) and then, finally, leaving the building at a quarter past five to catch the train from Tara Street that would get her back to Bayside in time to pick up Emma from Debbie's before a quarter past six.

Actually, parents were supposed to pick up their children before six but hardly anybody managed to do that. Every evening harassed mothers (and less frequently harassed fathers) hurried up the neatly cobbled driveway of Care for Your Kids to pick up Francine or Jason or Sorcha or Kevin. It was usually then that Flora realised that nobody would bother kidnapping her because there were surely better pickings to be had from the women who drove the Land Rovers taking up the entire road outside the house or the men who drew up in their company saloons and ignored the double-yellow lines.

It wasn't that the Care for Your Kids crèche and child-care facility was used by extraordinarily rich people, Flora knew. It was just that things had changed over the past few years. People whose second car had once been a clapped-out Fiat Uno were suddenly able to afford something a little bit better. Jeeps and utility vehicles had become very popular with mothers on account of the fact that you could jam them with children and shopping and still have room for yourself. Even if the economic boom that had allowed this to happen had eventually faltered, the signs of it remained. Perhaps some of the SUVs were a couple of years older than they might have been and some of the company saloons weren't the highest spec model that the owner might have expected, but people were getting by all the same.

And so was she. Only she was still doing it by counting out every minute of her day, by knowing that it took five minutes to get organised to leave the office each evening, that it was six minutes to the next bridge. That she didn't have time to buy the evening paper if there, were more than four people in the queue in front of her. That it took exactly seventeen minutes for the train to reach Bayside. That it was four-and-a-half minutes from the station to Debbie Murphy's house. And that she was the one who had to keep it all together because if she didn't turn up there was no one in a company saloon to step into the breach.

She often told herself not to feel sorry for herself. The fact that she was a single parent, the fact that she was the person with the sole responsibility for Emma, was entirely her own fault. And her own decision. Darren Mullen hadn't forced her to sleep with him. Darren Mullen had asked her was she 'using anything'. Darren Mullen had been responsible in his own way. But Darren hadn't wanted to be responsible for a baby that he never dreamed of and a woman that he liked but would never love. Darren was twenty-two when Emma was conceived. Flora was twenty-one.

She'd lied to Darren about contraception because she'd wanted to go to bed with him that night and she hadn't been taking anything since she'd split up with her last boyfriend three months earlier. She'd thought it was good for her to take a break from the pill, because so many people told her stories about how messed up your fertility was afterwards, and she was sure that there was no chance of becoming pregnant. She had, of course, reckoned wrongly. And she didn't blame Darren one bit for not wanting anything to do with her or Emma. To be perfectly honest, she didn't want anything to do with Darren either. He was a gorgeous bloke, no question, but definitely not father material, or husband material, as far as Flora was concerned. She'd told him it was OK not to be involved and he'd looked relieved because theirs had been a two-night stand and Flora Byrne really wasn't his type of girl. But he'd given her €500 when Emma was born. To buy something for her, he'd said. Flora had used the money for a rental deposit on the studio apartment where she now lived. She'd told Emma (who looked at her solemnly with amazing navy-blue eyes) that she'd buy her something lovely from her father later, when they could afford it. And Emma had smiled and got sick all over her.

Next year Emma would be going to school. Next year she'd have to rethink the whole childminding scenario because Debbie only looked after pre-school children. Flora knew that there were childminders who went to the school, picked up the children and brought them back to be looked after, but there wasn't a place like that near her and she had no idea how she was going to manage. It was all very well, she thought, as she smiled up at Karen Richardson who'd arrived to let her go on her morning break, it was all very well people saying that they were supportive of single-parent families. But in reality they weren't. Not in the way that it counted. Not by helping you to manage the day.

She pushed open the door of the small kitchen where the employees of Lyster, O'Brien, Harris & McKenzie took their break. It was empty. She pressed the cappuccino button on the coffee dispenser and took a plain biscuit from the box on the table. Then she sat down and looked through the paper.

John Kavanagh, just out of law school and a very, very junior partner, opened the door and smiled at her. Flora didn't notice him. She was engrossed in an article about autumn fashions. She was gobsmacked by the fact that the writer seemed to think that everyone had €1000 to spend on this season's 'must have' coat. Maybe the kind of person who varied their routine, who had reason to worry about kidnappers, would think nothing of shelling out €1000 on a damn coat but Flora wasn't one of them. And it wasn't even that nice, she decided, as she looked at it critically. The length was just that bit too short to make it elegant. She laughed to herself. As if she even knew what elegant was any more – her wardrobe consisted of T-shirts, jeans and trainers. Except, of course, when she was at work. Then she wore sober navy suits to portray the partners of Lyster, O'Brien, Harris & McKenzie as serious individuals who were always ready to help.

'Interesting stuff?' John sat down beside her.

'Huh?'

'The paper? You were making faces while you read.'

She folded it up, embarrassed. John Kavanagh wouldn't read the light-hearted articles about female fashion. He probably thought that she was laughing sardonically at the latest government promises to do something about over-spending or something equally businesslike.

'Not important.' She looked at her watch. 'I'd better get back.'

'Why?' asked John.

'Because my break is nearly over. And I didn't think junior partners got breaks,' she added sternly. 'I thought you barely had time for cold coffee at your desks.' But though her voice was severe, her brown eyes twinkled at him and he suddenly thought that Flora Byrne was actually quite pretty.

'I'm not supposed to be here,' he admitted. 'But I thought I'd go mad if I didn't get out of that corral for a couple of minutes.'

'Poor you.' She smiled sympathetically. 'Never mind, when you're earning pots of money at some tribunal or another you'll look back on this and be grateful.'

He made a face. 'I don't know about that. There must be easier ways of making money. Kidnapping, for example. Taking you away, Flora Byrne, and demanding a ransom.'

She looked at him in shock. 'You shouldn't even joke about it,' she said.

'Why not?'

'Well – I don't know – you just shouldn't.'

'I'm sorry.' He frowned as he looked at her. 'I didn't mean to upset you.'

'You didn't.' She stood up and walked to the door. 'You were just being silly.'

She sat back at her receptionist's desk and thought about being kidnapped again. She was the silly one, she knew, having crazy thoughts about being watched and followed. Thoughts that had come to her when she first realised that she was pregnant. Thoughts of people watching her and shaking their heads and saying that it was such a shame really because she was quite an intelligent girl and could have done better.

She blinked away a tear. They hadn't been watching her and talking about her really. But she'd always felt that they had. It was all right for women like Liz Hurley and Mel B to be single parents. They had armies of people to help them. They were feted and applauded as they walked down the streets with their lovely babies (who probably wouldn't dare get sick all over them) in their arms, or with their toddler children looking gorgeous in Armani for Kids. They'd even got their damn figures back within a few weeks as well as new escorts on their arms! But real life wasn't like that. In real life people didn't know whether to congratulate you or commiserate with you, and your child was never going to be a designer accessory no matter how much you loved her. In real life it was hard to meet a bloke who didn't care that you had a four-year-old daughter. And in real life it was a matter of running your life so efficiently that you knew with a certainty what you'd be doing at any given minute of the day.

She left the office at exactly a quarter past five. She began walking along the quays again, brisk strides as always.

'Hey, Flora!'

She whirled around at the sound of her name. John Kavanagh hurried up the street. She looked at him quizzically.

'I've been allowed out again,' he said. 'Wondered if you'd like a quick drink?'

She smiled. 'Thanks but I've got to get the train at half-past.'

'One drink?' His tone was persuasive.

'It's nice of you, John, but I can't.'

'Why?'

'I've got to pick up my daughter,' she said. 'I can't be late.'

'You have a kid?' He looked surprised. 'I didn't know.'

'Why should you?' She began walking again.

'What's her name?'

'Emma.'

'How old is she?'

'Four.' Flora glanced at her watch and increased her pace.

'Bloody hell, Flora, slow down – it's not a race.'

She stopped again. 'I have to get the train at half-past because that way I arrive at the childminder's in time. I can't be late. I've been late once already this year. If a parent is late more than once then the child loses its place.'

'You're joking.'

'Wish I was,' said Flora. 'But that's why I can't stop.'

'Fair enough.' John was breathing heavily as he tried to keep up with her. 'Can you arrange for someone else to pick her up some evening?'

She stopped again and turned to look at him. 'No,' she said. 'There's no one. It's only Emma and me. We make it work. She knows I'll be there. I know what time I have to leave, what train I have to catch. It's like clockwork.'

John nodded. 'Guess so. But surely one of the other

parents . . . ?' He frowned suddenly. 'Are you seeing someone, Flora? The dad or anything? I didn't think so but . . .'

She smiled. 'I'm not seeing anyone. Not the dad. Or anyone else.'

'Good,' he said.

'Not that good,' she replied. 'But I don't have time for it at the moment.'

'Rubbish,' said John briskly. 'You have to make the time.'

'I can't.'

'You could if you wanted.'

'Maybe I don't want to, in that case.'

She started walking again, picking up her pace to make up for the lost time.

'Weekends?' suggested John.

'We go to ballet on Saturday mornings,' said Flora. 'My mum's on Saturday afternoon. Swimming on Sunday. And Sunday afternoons are for special treats.'

'Excellent,' said John. 'I could be a special treat.'

'No, you couldn't,' said Flora. 'She doesn't need strange men in her life.'

'I could be *your* special treat,' he said.

Flora laughed. 'I don't need one.'

'Yes, you do,' said John. 'Everyone needs a special treat from time to time.'

'You'd better get back to the office,' she said. 'You've been out for far too long. You'll get fired.'

'No, I won't,' he said. 'I've worked manically all afternoon. And I'll go back later. But not until you agree to either come for a drink with me some evening or let me see you on Sunday afternoon.'

'I don't think you understand,' said Flora. 'I don't want to go for a drink with you. I don't want to see you on Sunday afternoon.'

'Why?' asked John.

'I have Emma to think about,' said Flora.

'And yourself?' He looked at her questioningly. 'If you were thinking about yourself would you go out with me? Or do you just think I'm a complete tosser and you couldn't be bothered?'

She smiled faintly. 'I don't think that, of course.'

'Do you like me?'

'I don't know you.'

'So – get to know me.'

'This is silly.'

They were nearing the station now. Flora took her ticket out of her bag.

'One drink.'

'No,' she said.

'You don't have to do it all on your own,' said John. 'You really don't.'

'Yes, I do.' She turned to him, her ticket in her hand. 'You don't understand, do you?'

'Maybe not,' he admitted. 'Maybe I've no idea what it's like to be you, Flora. But I'm getting the idea. You're a nice person. You love your kid. You'd do anything for her. You're like every mother in the world, I guess. And all I'm asking is that for a couple of hours you give yourself a bit of time.'

'Actually you're asking me to give *you* a bit of time,' she said.

He scrunched up his nose. 'You're right. But . . .' He grinned. 'It'd be a good time for both of us.'

She shook her head. 'I don't think so.'

'OK.' He shrugged in defeat. 'It was worth a try.'

The train was crowded. She stood by the door as it slid out of the station and across the loop-line bridge.

John Kavanagh was the third person to ask her out since Emma had been born. The third person she'd refused. Because she had her self-contained, predictable life working exactly the way she wanted it. She didn't need someone to mess it up and make her feel as though she could be part of a different life again, part of a time when she stayed out late and drank vodka shots and went to bed with people that she didn't love. Besides, she hadn't got a babysitter. Her mum had often offered but she couldn't accept. Emma was her responsibility. No one else's.

She arrived at Care for Your Kids at six minutes past six as usual. Emma was waiting for her, clutching her red bag and her Barbie doll. Conor Foley was standing beside her. Flora smiled at both of them.

'Did you have a good day?' she asked Emma who nodded vigorously.

'Yes,' she said. 'And I played with Conor. He's my boyfriend.'

'Is he?'

'Yes,' said Emma. 'We're best friends too.'

'Are you?' This time Flora looked at Conor.

'Yes,' he said.

Flora wondered whether or not she'd had a best friend who was also her boyfriend at age four.

Debbie Murphy looked at the Kermit the Frog clock on the wall.

'I wonder where your mum is,' she said to Conor just as a maroon Suzuki jeep pulled up outside the house. A tousled-haired woman got out.

'Sorry, sorry, am I late?' she gasped. 'Got held up at a meeting and then got stuck in traffic. You know they're digging a bloody great hole in the middle of the main road – at rush hour? Have they no sense?' She grabbed Conor by the hand and then smiled at Flora. 'I believe these two are best friends. So Conor told me yesterday.'

'Did he?' Flora looked surprised. 'I only discovered today.'

'You must bring her round,' said Conor's mother. 'Let them play together.'

'I'm out at work,' said Flora.

'Oh, me too.' The tousled-haired woman sighed. 'My name's Susan, by the way.'

'Flora.'

'I know your name,' said Susan. 'Conor told me you were the prettiest mother.'

'He did not!' Flora looked at the little boy.

'Yes,' said Susan. 'The prettiest mother by far. And nice.'

'How does he know I'm nice?' asked Flora. 'I never talk to anyone.'

'Maybe that's why.' Susan laughed suddenly. 'You don't give out to them.'

'Maybe.'

'D'you want a lift?' asked Susan. 'You live in the apartments, don't you?'

'Yes,' said Flora. 'But it's fine. We can walk.'

'Don't be daft.' Susan was already opening the door of the jeep. 'Hop in.'

'Are you sure?'

'Of course.'

Flora lifted Emma into the jeep and followed her. 'We should arrange to collect them for each other sometimes,' said Susan as she moved off into the traffic. 'It's hard for me because I'm usually the last to arrive and some of the other mothers aren't comfortable with that.'

'Well . . .'

'Just a thought,' said Susan. 'A blissful one, though. Don't you love the idea of not having to rush some evenings?'

'What about your husband?' asked Flora. 'Can't he do it?'

'If only.' Susan sighed. 'He works in Drogheda. Wouldn't make it home in time in a fit. So it's only me. Sometimes my mum helps out but she has arthritis and it's difficult for her. It'd be really good to have someone else.' She glanced at Flora. 'Obviously, if you don't like the idea, it's no bother but, well, I'm sure there are some evenings when you'd like to work late or have a drink or something?'

'I guess there are.' Flora thought of John Kavanagh. A drink with him would've been fun. It wouldn't have had to lead to anything but it would've been nice to sit in a bar with a man and be herself. Flora Byrne. Ordinary person. Not Emma's mother.

'Think about it,' said Susan. 'We could work out a roster. Flexible, of course.'

'Of course,' said Flora. She smiled at Susan. 'It's a good idea.'

'Excellent.' Susan pulled up outside the apartment block. 'Why don't I give you a lift again tomorrow evening? We could talk about it then.'

'That'd be nice,' said Flora. She got out of the jeep and lifted Emma onto the pavement.

'See you tomorrow!' Susan waved. 'I'm so glad we talked. I've always wanted to meet you. Everyone is full of praise for you – so efficient, they all say. I'm hoping some of it rubs off!'

Flora grinned. Efficient. Her? If only they knew. If only they realised it was all down to timing. She looked at her watch. They were home fifteen minutes early because of Susan's lift. Which would surprise the kidnappers. She laughed suddenly.

'What?' asked Emma. 'What's funny?'

'I was wondering,' said Flora, 'whether you'd like to go for a burger and chips?'

'Now?' Emma stared at her.

'Now,' said Flora.

'But – it's Tuesday,' said Emma. 'We don't go out on Tuesdays.'

'Would you like to?' asked Flora.

Emma nodded.

'Come on then.' Flora took her by the hand. 'Let's tear up the schedule.'

'What schedule?' asked Emma.

'The silly schedule,' replied Flora.

'I didn't know there was one,' said Emma.

'Not any more.' And Flora waved goodbye to the non-existent kidnappers as she brought her daughter for an unexpected treat.

FAITH ●────────────────●

SUTTON

The children play in my garden every day. Of course, I don't want them to play there, but they do anyway, running through the flower beds and breaking my rosebushes. I planted the rosebushes because I thought they might deter them but I know now that it was a vain hope. If anything, it encourages them.

At first, I didn't know that my garden was a sort of communal playground. When I was working, I left the house at eight o'clock every morning to catch the train at Sutton and I was rarely home before six. Most of the children had gone home for their tea by then and if a few diehards ran through the flower beds I would rap on the window until they ran out onto the street again.

I suppose they think I'm a bit of a lunatic, because it's not really as though the garden is anything special – just a lawn spotted with weeds and surrounded by the flower beds containing a mixture of bulbs and seeds I've accumulated over the last few years. And, of course, the rosebushes.

But it's the principle of the thing that gets to me, because I just don't like the children tramping through my property. Most of my friends agree with me; they think that the kids should be hounded out immediately because it's an invasion of privacy. It's not even as if they are friends of my own children.

There's the thing. If they were my kids' friends, it wouldn't really matter so much because mine would play in their gardens too and it would all even out in the end. But it doesn't work like that and so right now I simply feel resentful.

People will say I'm resentful for the wrong reason but they'd be mistaken. I'm not resentful because my own daughter isn't out there with them, running wild, her blonde hair flying in the wind. I'm resentful because Dr Marsh said I'm to have peace and quiet, and how can I have peace and quiet when that gang are screaming their heads off outside my window?

Two of them are from across the road; their names are Beverley and Laura. I don't know where the little red-haired child is from – in other circumstances I'd quite like her, but she's the one who does most damage because she doesn't even notice the thorns on the bushes and breaks the branches regularly. Then there are the boys; James is one, and the other child, who is older than the rest and quite ugly, is called Sebastian.

I'm amused by this fad of calling children by grandiose names and am amazed at how the most unattractive kids seem to have the most superior names. Little Annemarie McGann is easily the prettiest of them all, but her mother often calls her Annie. Sebastian, on the other had, is never called Seb, and Beverley never Bev.

My daughter's name is Sarah. Dennis and I both liked the name, we thought it was feminine and not too gimmicky. Her full name is Sarah Anne Murray, but she's actually down on her birth certificate as Faith.

I'll never forgive Dennis for that. After all the time we spent agonising over names, he went and called her Faith. No question of my feelings on the matter, I'm unconscious, and just because of that priest all our decisions come to nothing.

He said it was proof of our faith in a Higher Being and Dennis agreed. Personally, I think Dennis was afraid of the priest. Most of them are domineering at the best of times, and this was the worst of times.

Everything had been going so smoothly. A touch of morning sickness in the early stages, but I got over that fairly quickly. I suffered a bit with high blood pressure too, which was a little frightening, but they kept it under control. Dennis and I went to the parenting classes and the prenatal classes and just about every class you could think of until the day I was brought in, screaming in pain and horribly aware that it was all going wrong.

Even then I never believed that I would lose Sarah because people don't lose babies nowadays, do they? I had every confidence in the hospital and they were wonderful to me.

But things went more and more wrong and now I can't really remember too much about it. There were bright lights and loud noises but they all seemed to come from miles away. All I wanted then was for the pain to stop because I was afraid of it.

I woke up later and Dennis was holding my hand. He looked terrible. I don't remember asking him anything but he told me that our baby had lived for five minutes and he'd had her baptised by Fr O'Malley and he'd called her Faith.

I tried to tell him that Faith wasn't our baby's name but he wouldn't listen. Why won't men listen when you tell them things? Dennis is simply dreadful like that. He droned on and on about Fr O'Malley and what a comfort he was and he never said anything about our daughter. I tried to ask him but it was hopeless, he just talked about God and another chance and although I knew he was upset I just wanted him to shut up and go home.

We'd decorated the front room as a nursery. Pale-pink walls with pale-blue cartoon characters, just in case Sarah had been Sam. That was the name we'd chosen for a boy. God knows what Dennis would actually have named him.

They were very kind at the hospital but they don't understand, do they? To them it's just another incident and, of course, it must be, but they don't quite see that my life is ruined. After all, I changed my life for the baby, but she isn't here.

I rap on the window and the children look guilty. I wave a finger at them and Sebastian, horrible child, sticks out his tongue. But by the time I open the front door they're running down the street laughing and shouting.

I'm tempted to run after them but I'm not really fit enough. I stand in the garden and enjoy the warmth of the sun on my face. I feel as though a walk would do me good because I'm not really a sedentary person and I'm fed up with sitting around so much.

One of the reasons we bought this house was because it is close to the train station and the schools and shops. Actually, we're a bit too close to the railway line for my liking because sometimes the noise of the trains can be overwhelming, but it's very convenient. For Dennis, of course, not for me. He's the one who goes to work as though nothing has changed. I'm the one who's at home alone. When I go out now it's mainly to the shops. I don't usually bother with the supermarket because it's noisy and crowded; instead I go the local shops a ten-minute walk away.

I pull on my jacket. I need to get milk and perhaps a newspaper. I used to read the papers from cover to cover every day but that was when I was an administration assistant in Forbes & Forbes and reading the paper was a nice break between dealing with irritable customers and the equally irritable partners. I don't really miss Forbes & Forbes. I think I was looking for any excuse to leave.

It's really warm now and I'm beginning to think that

an ice cream would be nice. The first shop is a newsagent and so I decide that I'll treat myself to a 99 cone. It's my favourite.

I don't know why some people have children at all. There is a pram with a little baby outside the shop. Outside! Where anyone could simply walk away with her and with the sun blazing directly onto her delicate little face. Do they have no sense of responsibility?

She's a very pretty baby, with peaches-and-cream skin and soft, blonde hair. About the same age as Sarah, if Sarah had lived. I tickle her under the chin and a little fist grabs my finger.

I feel sorry for Faith, the baby who died. It was a tragedy but these things happen. Some people are lucky, others are not. I'm lucky though, I think, as I carefully release the brake on the pram. My baby is pretty and so healthy. My baby Sarah. But I really must take her home. She's had plenty of fresh air and I don't like to leave her in the sun for too long.

I smile to myself as I push the pram away from the shops, down the street, across the road and into my life.

THE PURPLE COAT

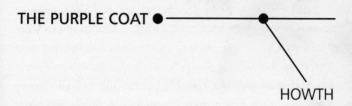

HOWTH

We arrange to meet at Howth. I don't think that we'll bump into anyone we know at Howth. After all, I'm coming from Greystones and she's travelling from Blanchardstown, so it's distant enough. There's a pub beside the train station and that's where we agree on. She tells me that she'll be wearing a red coat and a scarf so that I'll recognise her.

I almost say that a red coat seems a bit frivolous for this meeting but I manage not to make any comment at all. All the same, the red coat has thrown me a little because I've already visualised how she'll look. Small, I think, because I'm not that tall myself. Pale-faced. And I'd previously thought that her coat would be grey or black – whenever I think of her I think of her in shades of grey and black. Except for the scarf which, in my mind's eye, is one of those old-fashioned silk squares, gold and green and patterned with horses, horseshoes, horsewhips and a smattering of pale-green shamrocks (or are they clover?).

I don't know why I imagine her like that but I always do.

But now the red coat has thrown me and I'm having to reconsider my own wardrobe a little. I'd intended to wear black myself, a soft leather coat which I'd bought two years ago but which always looks good. But I can't wear black if she's wearing red. I'd be the one to look dreary then. So in my lunch-hour I rush into Arnott's and blow a ridiculous amount of money on a deep-purple wool coat with a fake-fur trim, which looks seasonal and colourful and brings out the brown in my eyes. I buy new boots and a bag as well. I hadn't intended to buy the boots and the bag, of course. At the last minute, rushing through the cosmetics department, I splash out on a fresh lipstick too. I think I'm going crazy.

When I get home that night I try the new coat and boots along with the blue dress I'd always intended to wear. The dress is figure-hugging and I feel both elegant and comfortable in it. It looks well with the boots. I like the coat too. I reckon that I'll be cool and confident at this meeting because I've prepared myself well for it.

Donal doesn't know. He'll kill me when he finds out. He'll be hurt and angry that I haven't told him and I do understand why he'd feel that way but I haven't been able to talk to him because I don't want anyone else's sympathy right now, not even Donal's. I feel bad about this but there's nothing I can do. I'm going to meet her and I have to do it on my own terms. My own terms means on my own.

It's arranged for the following evening at half-past eight. I could go from work but I need to come home first to get my head together and spend ages on my make-up and clothes. I'm going to look great. I picked this evening because it's Donal's five-a-side football night so he won't be at home wondering what I'm doing.

I get on the Dart. I realise that I'm going to be early but I don't mind about that. When I arrive at Howth I go for a walk along the pier, letting the blustery wind whip my air around my face and redden my cheeks before walking back to the pub. I notice, as I catch a glimpse of myself in the glass, that I now look unkempt, my previously styled look having been blown apart by the weather.

I look around me. Perhaps this wasn't the best place to meet. It's a young pub and being in my thirties I'm dragging up the average age. She's fifty-five so she must look totally out of place. I don't see her and I'm relieved about that because it means I've time to go to the Ladies, comb my hair and re-apply my new lipstick.

But as I walk past one of the tables a woman's voice says 'Louise?' and I turn towards it. She stands up and is, of course, nothing like I imagined. She's not tall but she's taller than me. Her hair is a soft gold colour. Her face is remarkably unlined for someone her age and her red coat is cashmere. The cream scarf, draped loosely around her neck, is also cashmere. She wears tiny ruby earrings and a thin gold chain with a ruby stone. She doesn't look out of place at all.

'Margaret,' I say. I frantically smooth my wayward hair.
'Yes.'

I think of saying, 'Well, nice to have met you,' and simply walking away. I don't want to talk to her. She's the wrong woman as far as I'm concerned.

'Would you like a drink?' Her voice is clear, though quiet. I see that there's a half-finished brandy in front of her. She must have been here early too. If I'd come in when I arrived first, I wouldn't look windswept and messy like I do now. I could've been the one looking serenely elegant with my drink in front of me.

'I'll get my own,' I tell her even as I stand indecisively in front of the table. I'm not sure whether to go to the loo and fix my hair, just sit down and wait for someone to come and serve me, or go to the bar and order a drink. I don't even know what I want to drink.

'I'm going to tidy my hair,' I say finally. As I walk towards the Ladies I order a glass of red wine from the lounge boy who's wiping down the tables.

I look at myself in the mirror. I'm a mess. My eyes watered in the wind earlier and my carefully applied mascara is smudged. It's supposed to be waterproof but I've yet to find a mascara that doesn't leave me with panda eyes. I do my best to wipe the worst of it away. Then I drag my brush through my hair and do my lipstick again. I'm glad I bought the lipstick, it's really rich and creamy and looks fantastic.

Maybe she'll be gone. Maybe seeing me was enough.

She's still there, though, sitting back in the seat looking totally unperturbed. She can't be fifty-five. She looks about forty-five, which isn't much older than me really. I sit on the edge of the seat opposite. She smiles at me. Her eyes are brown too.

'It's great to see you,' she says. 'I'm really pleased you came.'

I can't think of what to say in reply. The lounge boy puts my drink in front of me and she's taken the money out of an elegant silver-grey purse before I even have time to scrabble around in my bag. I'm not going to force the money on her. She can buy me a drink, I suppose. I didn't want anything from her but a drink is probably the least she could do.

She smoothes her golden hair behind her ear. Obviously it's dyed and obviously her natural colour is now stone grey because nobody with brown eyes could have natural hair that colour.

'I'm really pleased you came,' she says again.

I shrug. It's meant to be a dismissive sort of shrug but I have a feeling that it looks uncomfortable and gauche instead. She's making me feel very, very gauche, even in my purple coat, blue dress and sexy boots.

She exhales slowly. 'I wondered, was there anything you wanted to ask me? Or if you'd just like me to tell you about it? Or . . .' Her voice fades as she looks at me.

'I don't suppose there's much to tell.' I shrug again. 'You were pregnant. You weren't married. You gave me away.'

I can see the pain in her face now, etched in the fine lines around her eyes, but her expression is still carefully neutral.

'I had my reasons of course,' she says.

'Everyone does.' I'm doing my best to keep my voice from shaking. 'It was a different time. I'm sure you thought you did the right thing.' I start to feel angry. 'After all, you must have struggled to keep yourself going.' The look I give her expensive coat is pointed. Kind of disdainful, I think.

'I didn't struggle in that sense,' she tells me. 'At least not at first. My parents looked after me, you see.'

Funnily enough, I've never thought about her parents. Certainly not as people in their own right who are genetically connected to me. I've never thought about anyone other than her. I know that other children who discover they're adopted often weave elaborate stories about half-brothers and half-sisters and myriads of other relations but I never have. She's been the only one.

'They probably weren't best pleased,' I say.

'No.' She smiles wryly. 'No. They were furious.'

'I would be too.'

'It's different with daughters,' she says.

She knows that I have two sons. I told her that in the letter I wrote to her, after I discovered who she was. I hadn't wanted to write, not really. Once I found out that she was alive I thought that would be enough. But she was on the register, she was prepared to make contact with me. And I couldn't help myself, I ended up writing to her. It was the strangest letter. Short and to the point.

> *Dear Margaret Killeen,*
> *My name is Louise McIvor. I am your daugh-*
> *ter. I am married with two sons. If you wish*
> *to contact me please e-mail the following*
> *address.*
> *Louise McIvor*

I gave my work e-mail. It was a week before she replied and I'd begun to think that I'd made a mistake in only giving her an e-mail address. After all, I reasoned, she was over fifty. What were the chances of her even knowing how to send an e-mail?

> *Dear Louise,*
> *I am so glad that you contacted me. Please*
> *suggest a suitable time and place if you wish*
> *to meet.*
> *Yours sincerely, Margaret Killeen.*

It wasn't exactly warm. But that was fine. I didn't really want warmth from her. I just wanted to see her. I had, of course, thought of setting up something and simply spying on her, not actually showing up at all. But I didn't think that would be fair and I suppose a part of me felt sorry for her, the small grey-haired woman who had once given up her child because she couldn't afford to keep her. Only, of course, she wasn't a small grey-haired woman and it appeared that keeping me wouldn't have been so difficult.

She picks up the brandy glass and sips the drink. I do the same with my red wine.

'My parents were very strict,' she says eventually. 'Very, very strict. They didn't give me a choice.'

'Everyone has choices,' I tell her. 'Sometimes we just make the wrong ones.'

'I thought I was making the right one.'

'I suppose you all say that.' I know my voice has become a little louder and I make an effort to pitch it lower again. 'I suppose you all say that you thought you were doing the best for the child at the time.'

'Yes,' she says simply. 'Because not to think that . . .' She frowns. 'Not to think that would mean that you didn't care. And of course I cared.'

'But not enough to tell your parents you were keeping me.'

She has no response to that and I'm glad. I reckon I've punctured that self-satisfied glow just a little bit. She doesn't look quite as cool and confident as earlier.

'Tell me about yourself,' she says.

'Nothing much to tell,' I reply. 'My parents are wonderful people. They know that I decided to find out about you. They're very supportive.' I know I sound defiant. I know, too, that my mother, Bette, wasn't exactly thrilled when she heard I wanted to find out about my natural mother. I understood that. I told her that she'd always be my mother as far as I was concerned. But that I had to see the other one.

'I'm glad you were happy,' she says.

'Sometimes happy. Sometimes not. Always loved.'

She flinches.

'I got married when I was twenty-five,' I continue. 'My eldest boy is twelve. My other boy is nine.'

'What are their names?'

I'm not sure I want to tell her their names. 'Tadgh,' I say eventually. 'And Fiachra.'

'Very Irish.'

'Donal teaches Irish,' I tell her. 'He's my husband. Their father.'

'I'm glad,' she says, 'that you have a husband and two children.'

'You?' I ask.

'I was thirty when I got married,' she says. 'There were no more children.'

I stare at her. 'Why?'

'I don't know. We tried. I always thought, you know, a punishment thing maybe.'

'That's ridiculous.'

'I know. But we all think ridiculous things.'

'And your husband?'

'He was disappointed.' She picks up the brandy glass again but puts it down without drinking anything. 'He wanted sons. For the business.'

'What business?'

'A haulage firm.' Her smile is faint. 'Very industrial sort of stuff.'

'He owns it?'

She nods.

'Are you rich?'

She shrugs. Not like mine earlier. Hers is an elegant sort of shrug. No matter what she says now I know that she is rich. It's bred into her. It should be bred into me.

'We're comfortable,' she says.

'I guessed as much.' I look at the red coat again and the cashmere scarf.

'What about you?' she asks.

I laugh. 'I told you, Donal's a teacher. I work in an office. We're not rich. My parents weren't rich either. We were comfortable, but I think it's a different sort of comfortable.'

'Perhaps.'

'Still.' There's an edge to my voice now. 'Money can't buy you everything.'

'No.'

I can't think of anything else to say. There's lots of things I want to say but I know that I won't say them here. I want to say that I dreamed of her every night for months after Bette told me about the adoption. And that I built her up into a tragic figure, someone who'd been an outcast because of her baby, maybe even been sent to a Magdalene laundry. I'd imagined her life as one of misery and poverty and unhappiness and I dreamed that maybe one day I'd find her and forgive her.

She doesn't need my forgiveness. She doesn't need anything at all from me.

'How old were you?' she asks suddenly.

I look at her in puzzlement.

'When they told you. How old were you?'

Eight. Bette sat me down and told me about the day that herself and Hugh chose me. They hadn't actually chosen me, of course, they were given me. But I believed it at the time. Bette told me that it made me even more special which is, I think, the standard form when telling adoptive children that you're not actually their mother. You're even better than their mother. Because you chose them. I felt special when Bette explained it to me and I didn't care about anyone else. Even as I grew older I didn't care because I loved Bette and Hugh. And my older brother, Tommy. He's adopted too but everyone says we're the spitting image of each other. And as a child I was always being told that I looked exactly like Hugh. Actually, I do.

I tell all this to Margaret who listens in silence and fiddles occasionally with the silver bracelet on her right arm.

'I didn't want to,' she says abruptly. 'I really didn't.'

'It's in the past,' I remark. 'I don't care.'

'I do.' Suddenly she's speaking fiercely, her face intent, her eyes black. 'I care. I cared then and I care now and I'm sorry, sorry, sorry that I didn't have the strength to do things differently.'

I'm a little frightened by her. I liked her better when she was cool and detached.

'They would've thrown me out,' she says. 'That's what they said. And that's what they would have done because they believed that I was a sinner. I know it sounds crazy today when nobody cares any more. But it mattered then. I was a sinner and I'd shamed them and they would've thrown me out and I just couldn't see how I'd ever look after you because I was too young and too silly.'

This time she drained the brandy glass. I ordered two more drinks.

'I kept wanting you back. Even after I signed the papers I wanted you back. So they brought me to England with them and we lived there for ten years and I was supposed to forget about you.'

'And did you?' I keep my voice as light as possible.

'Of course not,' she says even more fiercely. 'How could I? I kept asking them what had happened to you but they pretended it had never happened at all. They wouldn't let me talk about you.'

'It really doesn't matter,' I tell her.

'So I came back to Ireland and I tried to find out for myself but of course I couldn't.'

If it was me I know I'd be crying by now. I want to cry but she doesn't, even though I sense that she's having to work at keeping it all together. If she'd cry things would be a bit easier.

'Then I met Ken and we married and I do love him

very much but we didn't have any children.'

'I'm sorry.'

'And I know it's not a punishment but it's hard to be rational about it sometimes.'

'Does Ken know?' I ask.

'Yes.' She bites the inside of her lip. 'I told him when you contacted me first.'

'How did he take it?'

'Not particularly well.'

I realise that she understates everything. 'Not particularly well' probably means that he blew a fuse. Who could blame him? Poor man.

'Look, all I want you to know is that I didn't do it lightly,' she says, her voice quite even again. 'I agonised over it. I still do. It's not something you actually get over.'

'I know all that,' I reply. 'I always thought you agonised.'

'Thank you.'

'But I always thought it was because you were poor.' I look at her with difficulty. 'I never believed there could be other reasons.'

'I think about you every day.'

She's trying to keep up the confident appearance but she doesn't look as chilly as the woman of earlier. I can't help wondering if I've inherited that youthful skin. It'd be nice to know. I really can't believe that she gave birth to me. I grew up with women like Bette all around me, women who looked like mothers, slightly plump, always

311

cheerful, generally harassed. Of course it wasn't really like that, it's just how I remember it. Bette is five years older than Margaret but they're poles apart. Bette's hair is snow white and she doesn't have a discernible waist any more. She goes to line dancing and art classes though, and once a month goes out with a gang of 'the girls'. Bette is fun. This woman, my mother, would never be fun.

Neither of us have touched the drinks I bought.

'Perhaps I should go now,' she says eventually.

I nod briefly. 'If you want.'

'The first time is the hardest,' she tells me. 'That's what everyone says. But if we meet again—'

'I don't know,' I interrupt.

'It's up to you.' She stands up and begins to button the red coat. It's really lovely. 'E-mail me.'

'Is it your home address?' I ask.

She nods.

'Glad to see you're technology-literate.' Bloody hell, I think, that sounds so patronising.

'Oh, I still work in Ken's office,' she says. 'Only mornings now. I do the phones, secretarial type of stuff, you know. Keeps me occupied. So I'm totally clued in about e-mail and text messages and all that sort of thing.' She smiles suddenly and all at once I see a resemblance. Not to me. But to Fiachra, my younger son. He smiles in exactly the same way. It chokes me up a bit but she doesn't notice. She's still smiling. She looks so much better when she smiles.

'I'll be in touch,' I say.

'Will you?'

'Yes.'

I know I will. I didn't want to open this box but now that I have I can't just walk away.

'I'm glad you contacted me,' she says.

'I don't know how I feel about it.' It's probably the most honest thing I've said to her.

She smiles again. 'I've had longer to think about it than you.'

'I guess so.'

She leans awkwardly towards me and pecks me on the cheek without putting her arms around me or anything like that. She smells of soap and Elizabeth Arden.

'Can I ask you one thing?'

I nod. 'Whatever you like.'

'Where did you get the purple coat?' she asks. 'I've been admiring it all the time. It's wonderful on you.'

THE CURTAIN FITTER ●———————●

MALAHIDE

The great thing about not having to go to work every day, thought Maddie as she gazed out of the bedroom window at the steady rush of people hurrying down the road towards the train station, was not being a commuter any more. She'd always hated the crush to get on the train or the bus, pushing against hordes of people who always seemed to be bigger than her or have bonier elbows and take up even more room than her so that she ended up squashed against a window or pressed up against somebody's armpit. She'd looked forward to the time when she could give it all up to be a full-time mother even though sometimes she wondered if it was an impossible dream. Of course, wanting to be a full-time mother had only happened after she met and married Conal. Until then she wasn't sure that she was cut out for motherhood at all.

But it had happened, even though it had all taken longer than she might have expected, and now she liked her life – even though sometimes she felt that her vocabulary had contracted to a half a dozen words or phrases. They were (in no particular order): no; yes; do what I tell you; because I say so; not now; and, put that down. It seemed to her that she'd be able to function pretty well if they were the only things that she was allowed to say because they covered most of the eventualities that occurred in a day of looking after Kathryn and Nerissa. Yet whenever she found herself annoyed or irritated at home she remembered what it had been like before and she immediately felt both guilty and ungrateful.

From the moment she became pregnant with Kathryn she'd dreamed about leaving Telemart, the distribution company where she worked, so that she could stay with the baby. But it hadn't happened until after the birth of her second daughter, Nerissa, because the mortgage on their house had taken up such a huge chunk of both their salaries that it was essential for her to keep working. It was only Conal's promotion that had made leaving work a reasonable proposition and she'd been so glad the night he came home and told her that she'd actually cried.

Those last few months of working at Telemart had been a complete nightmare as she tried to fit in an inflexible schedule with the demands of motherhood. It was extraordinary, Maddie felt, how often Nerissa would throw up just as she was about to go out the door, or how Kathryn would go to bed like an absolute angel on a Friday night when none of them had to be up at the crack of dawn the next day, but how she'd refuse to go to bed and somehow manage to keep them awake all night during the week. She thought that it was because the girls were looking for attention. She was very clued in to the whole idea of attention-seeking children because she'd been one herself.

But even if she could understand them, it was still a waking nightmare for much of the time. She hadn't realised just how exhausting it could be and she wondered how it was that some of the people in the office didn't seem to mind staying up all night with a crying baby and being at their desks at nine o'clock the following morning (or seven-thirty, if you were unlucky enough to be on the early shift). It was a complete mystery to her. She asked Sylvia McCormack, the mother of three sons, how she managed it, and Sylvia always laughed and said that working in Telemart was a total breeze compared to bringing up those kids and that she came into the office for a rest. When Maddie pointed out that she couldn't possibly be rested if she'd been awake all night, Sylvia simply shrugged and said that you got over that part of it eventually and that Richard was pretty good about getting up whenever one of them cried.

Conal was good about it too but Maddie always felt as though she were letting herself down if she wasn't the one to wake up at the first sound, even though sometimes she was totally worn out. Whenever Conal told her that he didn't mind being woken up at three in the morning she smiled and said it wasn't important – he might not mind, she thought, but she did.

But for ages, because of their finances, she worried whether or not she'd ever give up work at all. Or, as she put it to her friends, whether she'd manage to give up working outside the home. It might be a politically correct kind of distinction, she felt, but there was no way you could say that looking after two children under the age of five was anything but hard labour, even if was something you wanted to do. Nevertheless, working outside the home was still a distinction that most people made and, if she was honest with herself, it was a distinction that Maddie made too. She knew a lot about mothers working outside the home. It was the way she had been brought up.

Her mother had been a PA to the managing director of a manufacturing company and had stayed working for all of Maddie's childhood. She grew up in a house where both parents left at the same time every day, her father driving to the plant in Swords where he worked and her mother dropping her off at school on her way into town. She was used to being looked after by Mrs Kerin down the road (the mother of her second-best friend, Lydia) until her own mother got home. It was simply the way things were as far as she was concerned but she couldn't help thinking that Mrs Kerin, who stayed at home all day and who baked cakes and had coffee mornings with the other mothers on the street, somehow had a nicer time than Deirdre Duchovny who talked about memos and meetings when she got home in the evenings and whose cake-making abilities were restricted to a hard, dry fruit square at Christmas. Maddie often wished that their own house smelled of apple tarts and soda bread like the Kerins' did and she also wished she had brothers, sisters, a dog and a cat, like Lydia. (Being allowed to jump up and down on the double bed would've been nice too – although it wasn't strictly allowed in the Kerins', Lydia's mother occasionally turned a blind eye to their trampolining activities.)

Maddie's mother had always emphasised how important it was to have something for yourself, something that nobody else could interfere with. She told Maddie that it was essential not to be dependent on anyone. Maddie never quite understood why, because Deirdre depended very much on Maddie's father to do things round the house and to pick up his only child on the occasions where Deirdre herself was delayed at work. Deirdre kept tomes by Germaine Greer and Marilyn French beside her bed and had been on the train that had gone from Dublin to Belfast over a quarter of a century earlier so that women could bring condoms into the Republic. She kept a newspaper photo of the gang of them on the station platform, waving their condoms and cheering wildly. Maddie's mother was an independent woman even if she did try to make sure that Maddie's father ate healthy foods and took enough exercise.

Maddie sometimes thought that Deirdre had continued to work simply to make a statement and she (very
occasionally) resented being part of that statement. She
hated it whenever Deirdre would remark to a friend that
it was easy to combine working with motherhood and
that it hadn't done Maddie any harm – wasn't she the
most well-adjusted child on the street? And hadn't she
come top of the class yet again for her English reading?

Deirdre had nagged Maddie to go to college and have
a marvellous career but Maddie hadn't been in the slightest bit interested. She told Deirdre that she just wanted a
job, enough to earn money to buy clothes and jewellery
and have her hair done every week. The first company she
went to offered her a position as a receptionist and she
loved it. The reason she loved it was because she enjoyed
answering the phone, she enjoyed dealing with customers'
queries and she enjoyed being friendly and helpful. Her
mother nagged at her to aspire to something higher.
Eventually, and in her own time, Maddie moved on to
another, bigger company and then to Telemart who
employed over 500 people and where she was a manager.
Deirdre was relieved when Maddie was made a manager.
It sounded important.

Maddie liked the people she worked with and invited
thirty of them to her wedding. They threw a baby-shower
for her when she announced she was pregnant and then
brought her out a few months after Kathryn was born,
dragging her around Temple Bar in a T-shirt that had

Learner Mum emblazoned across it. Right then she was glad she was part of the Telemart crew even though she was wondering whether or not Conal had taken the right bottle of milk out of the fridge and whether he'd heat it to the correct temperature.

It was the constant worrying about what was going on with her child that made it so difficult for Maddie to concentrate at work after Kathryn was born. She wondered how Deirdre had coped – had she simply managed to put her completely out of her mind while she was taking dictation or whatever it was for her boss at the manufacturing company? Had she ever worried about Maddie in the same way that Maddie worried about Kathryn? Or had Deirdre complete faith in Mrs Kerin's abilities to weather any crisis? The questions tormented Maddie though they weren't ones she'd ever ask her mother. But she did wonder why Deirdre had decided to have a baby at all given that there seemed to be so many more important things in her life.

When the day of her departure finally came round, Maddie told everyone that she'd really, really loved working with them but that she was taking on a much bigger challenge now. And they'd laughed and applauded her and told her to keep in touch before hurrying to the pub for a few drinks. Maddie stayed until ten in the evening and went home. As she put her key in the lock she suddenly had a sense of place and belonging, stronger than she'd ever felt before.

321

It was weird not having to battle with Conal for the bathroom in the morning. It was strange to realise that she could walk around all day in a scruffy pair of loungers if she wanted. It was particularly odd to know that she didn't have to leave the house at all unless she felt like it. She loved the lack of commuting, the ability to read a newspaper at odd hours of the day, the whole nurturing thing. She couldn't understand why women thought it was important to do something else when the job she was doing was the most important one in the whole world. And she resented all the time that she'd had to spend away from Kathryn while she was working in Telemart. Because, she reasoned, it wasn't possible to be Superwoman no matter what the books and the magazine articles might tell you. Even if, from time to time, you thought that being Superwoman might be fun. Actually fewer and fewer magazines told her that these days; now it was all about downsizing and quality of life and focusing on the things that really mattered to you.

Like your husband and your children.

Conal was one of the commuters Maddie watched that morning. He walked briskly down the pathway and across the road towards the station, not looking back as he'd done in the first months she'd been at home to see her standing at the window with Nerissa in her arms waving him goodbye. She knew those kind of things don't happen for ever. Life isn't like that. You can't kiss your husband every morning in the same way as you did that first morning together. You get into a rhythm of doing things that doesn't allow time for kissing and waving and smelling the roses. Sometimes you just have to get on with life and worry about the roses later.

Maddie turned from the window and looked at the scene of devastation that was her daughters' bedroom. There were rag dolls, Barbie dolls, Teletubbies, Bob the Builders . . . she felt as though every toy that had ever been made ended up on the floor of Kathryn and Nerissa Doyle's bedroom. How was it that her children had so many things? Especially so many things that they didn't seem to need. Or want. Maddie picked up a selection of abandoned Barbies and miscellaneous toys and threw them into the big wooden chest at the end of Kathryn's bed.

She needed to tidy up this room because the fitter was coming today to put up the new blue and yellow curtains she'd ordered a couple of weeks ago. She'd planned to get new curtains for ages because the old ones, the first ones that had been put up after Kathryn moved into the room, had been mauled by her sticky little fingers so often that they were eventually beyond cleaning.

Walking along the little row of shops near the station one afternoon she'd seen the perfect material in the window of a shop, which proclaimed itself to be the Top Curtain Supplier in Ireland. Maddie had laughed at that. She found it funny that a tiny shop in the suburban town would have the nerve to call itself the Top Curtain

Supplier in Ireland but she supposed they might as well aim high. And they did have the ideal material in the window. So, with Kathryn pulling out of her hand and Nerissa sleeping in her buggy, she'd pushed open the door and gone in.

The Top Curtain Supplier in Ireland didn't even have enough room for her to turn the buggy around. It was tiny, crammed full of fabric books and samples of work. Maddie told the woman behind the counter what she wanted and the woman arranged for someone to go out and measure the windows; probably Robbie, she told Maddie, her son.

Robbie called around later that afternoon thus impressing Maddie with the Top Curtain Supplier's efficiency. He was a well-built man with broad shoulders, cropped hair and twinkling blue eyes. She'd leaned against the wall as he measured the windows in less than five minutes. She'd wanted to think of something to say to him, anything at all, to keep him in the room for a little longer. Because he was easily the sexiest man she'd ever seen in her life. As she stood and watched him she was horrified to realise that in her mind she was imagining his beefy body without the navy-blue overalls emblazoned with the Top Curtain Suppliers in Ireland logo on the pocket. And she was wondering what it would be like to make love to him right here and now, the kids downstairs glued to *The Teletubbies*. The image was so strong that she nearly groaned out loud and she had to leave the room in case he could see the desire in her eyes.

He was gone ten minutes later with a promise that the curtains would be ready in a couple of weeks. And she was in shock. Because she couldn't believe that she'd just had an erotic fantasy about a man who fitted curtains for a living. It was the storyline of tacky porn movies – bored housewife, bloke with a hammer action drill . . . she closed her eyes and tried to replace the mental picture of Robbie with a picture of Conal instead. But the only image of Conal that she could conjure up was last night's memory of him sprawled in the armchair in front of the TV, his mouth slightly open as he slept. It wasn't his fault, of course. He was exhausted.

The bank where he worked was installing a new computer system and Conal was on the team that was working on the installation. So he was busy all the time and his conversation had become brief and perfunctory. He'd kiss her when he came in (sometimes), he'd swing Kathryn into the air and play with her until his dinner was ready, he'd tickle Nerissa under the chin and then he'd fall asleep in front of the TV. Maddie understood why he was so tired but she didn't think that falling asleep in front of the TV was what should be happening when you were in your thirties; to her it was the preserve of the older generation. Only it seemed that Conal had become the older generation all of a sudden and surely she wasn't so far behind. Her entire life had shrunk to dealing with

Kathryn and Nerissa, and feeding Conal – it wasn't really meant to be that way, was it? Even though it was what she wanted.

The curtain fitter wasn't coming until the afternoon. She was astonished at how nervous she was about it. She knew that she wouldn't be able to stay in the house all day so, because the weather was fine, she decided to bring the girls for a walk along the marina, which she knew Kathryn loved. Later her daughter could run around the green as Maddie sat on one of the wooden benches and glanced through the paper while, with a bit of luck, Nerissa had a nap.

But when it came to reading the paper she realised that her hands were trembling and all she could think about was the curtain fitter's visit. If he only knew, she thought, that she was shaking with anticipation at simply seeing him. She'd given him no indication of interest on his previous visit, he couldn't know that she'd thought about nothing else in the past few weeks. Even last Saturday night – her and Conal's designated love-making night – she'd thought of Robbie, the curtain fitter, as she'd lain beneath her husband while all sorts of crude double entendres about poles and fittings flitted through her mind so that she was both turned on and amused by it. And then, as Conal lay asleep beside her, she felt very guilty. After all, her husband was killing himself so that they could have the kind of lifestyle she thought she wanted. He was doing his best for her to live the dream that she'd always wanted to live. He believed in it too. It wasn't his fault he was so busy, nor was it his fault that he didn't have a body like Robbie's. She'd never gone for that hunky, beefy type before. She liked the way Conal looked. She'd always been more into mind than matter. At least, that was what she thought.

And maybe that was the problem. Sure, she had to deal with about 100 things at once now that she was at home all day with the children. Without doubt she had to use diplomatic skills she never knew she possessed, creative accounting to buy what they wanted when they wanted, decorating abilities beyond anything she'd ever dreamed of. But none of those things made her think outside of herself. None of those things were about other people. Everything she did was centred on her home and her family and, she was horrified to admit to herself, it might not be enough any more. She'd only realised this after her erotic fantasies about the curtain fitter. Until then she'd been happy with her life. OK, there were days when it wasn't as exciting and fulfilling as she'd expected, but on those days she always reminded herself of how rude some customers could be, or how aggressive the Telemart sales targets were, or how bloody awful it was on the half eight train to town. And then she'd remind herself that her time was her own and that she didn't have to live her life according to anyone else's rules.

(Except perhaps Kathryn and Nerissa's.) And she'd feel a little bit guilty that she'd had those feelings when she knew that it was what she'd always wanted. Of course whenever she'd imagined being a stay-at-home mother, she'd envisaged a serene and happy person walking hand-in-hand with her children along a sandy beach, her voile dress wafting gently in the breeze; in real life it was usually track-suit and trainers and shouting at Kathryn to stay away from weird items that had been washed onto the shore. In her mind's eye her kitchen was an updated version of Mrs Kerin's – warm and aromatic and the hub of her home. In fact the kitchen was small and dark and most of the time was completely hidden by baskets of washing or ironing. She hadn't quite realised that there was so much mundane stuff to do. And no matter how hard she tried, she could never quite believe that cleaning the house from top to bottom was fun. But she wanted to be a family person. That was her ambition. Nothing else had ever even snagged her interest.

She hadn't got involved in anything that went on in the town. She wasn't part of the amateur dramatic society (well, she couldn't act for peanuts anyway), nor the singing group (ditto singing); she wasn't interested in salsa dancing or flower arranging (how many people actually did flower arrangements any more?), or any of the other groups that frequently advertised for members by sticking up notices in the shop windows. She was an ex-working mother who was now with her children all the time and who'd really enjoyed it at the start but was now beginning to get edgy. And the reason she was getting edgy was because she was afraid that she was turning into the same kind of boring person that her mother had warned her about. Only she'd never believed that Mrs Kerin was boring. She'd never believed there was anything wrong with devoting your life to your family. Yet she had a horrible feeling that somehow she was managing to get it as wrong as she always thought her own mother had warned her about, even though she was trying so hard to get it exactly right.

Now all she had to talk about was Kathryn's latest escapade or Nerissa's latest attempt at a coherent word. She told herself that all these things were worthwhile, that they were the things you remembered on your deathbed, not whether or not you managed to solve the problem of a silly Telemart client, but she was uneasy about it all the same. And she couldn't help feeling that Deirdre, who had died from a short battle with cancer before the birth of her second granddaughter, was looking down at her, shaking her head and wondering if everything she'd ever taught her was simply going to waste. And was she turning into one of those sex-starved bored housewives who regarded every man who walked by as fair game?

'Kathryn!' she called out to the little girl who was about to disappear into a clump of purple-tipped hebe bushes. 'No. Stop. Come back here immediately.'

'I've lost my ball.' Kathryn looked defiantly at her. 'It's gone into the bush.'

'That was silly, wasn't it,' returned Maddie. 'You can't go in after it. You'll destroy the plant.'

'But I want my ball.' Kathryn's lip wobbled.

'You've lots of balls at home,' said Maddie.

'But that's my favourite.'

'You should have thought of that before you threw it there.' Maddie knew that her tone was abrupt but she couldn't help herself.

'I hate you,' said Kathryn.

Maddie said nothing but grabbed her by the hand and began the walk home.

They had tuna sandwiches for lunch. Kathryn's rage at the loss of her ball was tempered by the glass of Coke that Maddie allowed her to have instead of the milk that she was normally made to drink. She was also cheered by Maddie's permission to watch her favourite *Rug Rats* video. The *Rug Rats* was for Nerissa too. It was currently the toddler's favourite. Of course Maddie had entertained notions about videos and DVDs being occasional treats in the home rather than everyday things to do but it hadn't worked out like that. Although the children loved playing with her (she was a whizz at building tall Lego towers) they would then insist on watching their favourite TV programme. And Maddie usually didn't have the energy to stop them.

She left them in front of the TV while she tidied up their room. She wondered why it was important to her that it was as neat as possible and why it mattered that the curtain fitter would think that she was a good mother who could also keep a tidy home. For God's sake, she thought despairingly, it's not as though he'll even notice what my house is like. It's not like he'll even notice me. It's not as though I matter to anyone any more.

She rubbed her forehead. That was a ridiculous thing to think. She mattered to Kathryn and Nerissa, didn't she? She had a responsibility for both of their lives. That was important stuff, wasn't it? Much more important than her old job where she would have arrived home in a rush and not cared what anything looked like. So why was it, she wondered, that she felt so damned unimportant now?

She'd just finished hoovering the carpet (which, she told herself, was incredibly silly since the fitter would undoubtedly drill holes in the wall which would necessitate her hoovering it again anyway) when the van pulled into the drive.

'He's here!' cried Kathryn, who was acutely tuned to any changes in household routine and who had jumped up at the sound of the van's engine. 'The curtain man is here!'

'OK, OK,' said Maddie as she came down the stairs. 'There's no need to get hysterical about it.'

She arrived at the door just as the bell rang, thinking how pathetic it was to have changed into a Wonderbra.

'Hi,' she said, as she opened the door.

The girl standing in the porch was around the same height as Maddie but she looked taller because of the cut

331

of the blue overalls she was wearing. Maddie stared at her. The girl tipped back her baseball cap so that the peak was no longer hiding her blue eyes. 'Top Curtain Suppliers in Ireland?'

'Yes,' said Maddie. 'Where's Robbie?'

'On another job,' said the girl cheerfully. 'I'm Michelle.'

'You're doing the curtains?' said Kathryn. 'Mum said a man was doing the curtains.'

'Not today.' Michelle beamed. 'It's me.'

'But you're a girl,' said Kathryn.

'Oh dear.' Michelle grinned at her. 'Haven't you got a curtain-fitter Barbie?'

'No,' said Kathryn. 'But I have a ballerina one.'

'And I bet she's lovely,' said Michelle. She looked at Maddie. 'Are you ready for me? Will I bring in the stuff?'

'Yes,' said Maddie.

Maddie carried the curtain fabric up the stairs, followed by Michelle with the poles and the drill, and then Kathryn, helping Nerissa climb the stairs on her hands and knees. Maddie couldn't believe how desolated she felt. And she thought, glumly, that she was being punished for having changed out of her overwashed Dunnes Stores bra into the Wonderbra.

'Nice room,' said Michelle as she looked around.

'It's ours,' said Kathryn. 'Me and Nerissa.'

'Pretty name,' said Michelle. '*Merchant of Venice*?'

'Huh?' Maddie looked at her.

'Nerissa. Wasn't she Jessica's handmaid in *The Merchant of Venice*?'

'Oh. Yes.'

'Great play.' Michelle took a steel tape measure from her pocket and began measuring the window. 'I loved that bit about the pound of flesh. Bloodthirsty, wasn't it?'

'Um . . . I guess so.'

'I'd better get my stepladder,' said Michelle. 'Otherwise I won't be able to do this properly.'

She went out of the bedroom and down the stairs.

Maddie watched through the window as she took a steel stepladder from the van and brought it into the house. She felt cheated. She'd waited two weeks to see Robbie again, two weeks in which her fantasies about him had become more and more explicit, and now she was being fobbed off by a girl wearing a red baseball cap. Maddie hated baseball caps.

'These are great curtains,' Michelle told her, as she slid a bit into the drill and climbed the ladder. 'Really fantastic colours.'

'They're blue and yellow.' Maddie was getting tired of the girl's relentless cheerfulness.

'Yeah, but such vibrant blues and yellows.' Michelle switched on the drill and placed it over a mark in the wall.

Maddie cleared her throat. 'Where's Robbie?' she asked diffidently.

'Got stuck on a job in Clontarf,' said Michelle. 'So I came along instead.'

'I liked Robbie,' said Kathryn. 'He told me I was a fine thing.'

'That's my brother,' said Michelle.

'He's your brother?' Maddie was shocked.

'Yes.' Michelle grinned. 'Family business.'

Now that she'd mentioned it, Maddie could see a similarity between Michelle and Robbie. Mostly around their laughing eyes.

'So you've both become curtain fitters.'

Michelle smiled. 'I make them as well. Robbie also works in a courier company.'

Maddie thought about Robbie astride a motorbike and swallowed hard. Then she grimaced. Robbie was a courier and a curtain fitter. Michelle was a seamstress and a curtain fitter. Maddie was a stay-at-home mother. Was she the only person in the world who couldn't do two jobs any more? Why did being a stay-at-home mother now seem so utterly useless?

'Can I help?' Kathryn looked up at Michelle hopefully.

'Sure. Just be ready to hand me that metal piece there when I ask for it.'

Kathryn took the bracket that Michelle had pointed to and held it carefully in the palm of her hand.

'I suppose you've been doing this all your life?' asked Maddie.

'Nope. Last six months.' Michelle made another mark on the wall. 'But don't worry, I know what I'm doing.'

'This is a boy's job,' said Kathryn.

'I don't think so.' Michelle chuckled.

'But your brother is a boy,' persisted Kathryn.

'So?'

'So why are you doing it now?'

'Why not?' asked Michelle.

'I haven't brought her up like this.' Maddie got up from the bed where she'd been sitting. 'I believe in equal opportunities. My mother worked for years. I only gave up because there were two of them.'

Michelle turned to look at her in surprise. 'What are you talking about?'

'Her views,' said Maddie. 'Stereotypical. Curtain fitting being a man's job. She knows anyone can do anything.'

'But you said it would be a man,' protested Kathryn. 'I know girls can do anything but you said it would be a man. You said it would be a really nice man with a really nice bum.'

'Kathryn!' Maddie looked at her daughter in horror while Michelle laughed.

'I said that he was well-built,' she told Michelle. 'He is.'

'I know.' Michelle screwed the bracket into the wall.

'I didn't specifically mention his bum.'

'You did,' said Kathryn. 'You said he had a nice bum when he left.'

Maddie flushed. She'd made the remark, jokingly, to diffuse the tension that had built up in her as she watched him work. She hadn't realised that Kathryn was listening. Which was stupid because Kathryn listened to everything.

'Anyway, my brother does have a nice bum,' agreed Michelle.

'So have you,' said Kathryn.

'Thank you.'

Maddie couldn't speak. She left Kathryn and Nerissa in the bedroom and went downstairs to get a drink of water. She was lucky that Kathryn hadn't said anything to Conal about Robbie's bum. Although if she had, Maddie knew that she would have been able to make a joke about it to Conal. He wouldn't have realised that she meant anything by it. But this girl, Michelle, had looked knowingly at her as Kathryn's words had echoed round the room and Maddie felt as though her whole secret fantasy had been laid bare in front of her.

But she was being silly, surely. She was being silly because in her head she'd blown the whole thing up so much and because it had become important to her even though it wasn't really important at all. Like everything. She rinsed the glass under the sink. It seemed to her, suddenly, that she wasn't able to tell what mattered or what didn't with any degree of conviction.

She went upstairs again. Michelle was sliding the hooks onto the curtains with experienced fingers while Kathryn sat cross-legged on the floor and watched. Nerissa was ignoring them, playing with pieces of Duplo, absorbed in her own world. Nerissa was the more self-contained of the two, Maddie thought. Nerissa would be the daughter who kept secrets.

'OK then.' Michelle stood up and began to hook the curtains onto the tracks. 'Let's see how this looks.'

'Brilliant!' said Kathryn.

'Great,' said Maddie.

Michelle nodded. 'Excellent.' She began to tidy away her things.

'Why curtain fitting?' asked Maddie suddenly.

Michelle shrugged. 'I like it. I've always liked the sewing part of it but that's finicky kind of work. This is different. I like doing the two.' She smiled. 'It's satisfying. And the variety is important.'

'I guess so.'

'Oh, yes,' said Michelle. 'Absolutely.'

Maddie looked at her as she slung her stepladder over her shoulder.

They followed her downstairs. Kathryn helped her put her toolbox in the van.

'Well, thanks,' said Maddie.

'You're welcome.'

'It was a great job.'

Michelle smiled. 'I'm not as quick as my brother yet. I'm good but he's really good. And it is a skill, you know.'

'I can see that,' said Maddie. 'I'm hopeless and it takes my husband hours to do anything like putting up a shelf.'

'I'd be hopeless at the motherhood thing,' said Michelle.

'Anyone can do it.'

'Not properly,' said Michelle. 'Anyone can have them but not everyone can bring them up.'

'Maybe.'

Michelle closed the back door of the van. Now that everything was put away Kathryn and Nerissa went back into the house, out of the chill easterly breeze that had begun to blow.

'I switched jobs with Robbie,' said Michelle as she opened the driver's door.

'What?'

'Me and Robbie. We switched jobs. I was supposed to do Clontarf.'

'Why?' Maddie tried to keep the anger and disappointment out of her voice.

'He fancied you,' said Michelle.

Maddie stared at her.

'He told me that he fancied you but that you had two kids and he didn't think it would be a good idea to call on you again because he wanted to kiss you the last time.'

'You're joking.'

Michelle shrugged. 'No.'

Maddie felt a warm glow envelop her. The curtain fitter had fancied her.

'He was nice, your brother.'

'With his nice bum.'

Maddie flushed and Michelle laughed. 'He's always been good-looking, Robbie,' she said. 'He works out in the gym. Bit obsessive about it, though. He's a brawn man, not a brain man.'

'Is there anything wrong with that?' asked Maddie.

'Nope. But he wouldn't suit you. Not long term.'

'How do you know?'

'Come on.' Michelle grinned. 'It's one thing thinking about having an affair, it's another thing actually having one.'

'Who said anything about an affair?' demanded Maddie.

'Robbie is good at recognising it,' said his sister. 'You wouldn't believe the number of women . . . that's why I do lots of fittings now.'

'He sends you instead if he thinks that a woman fancies him?'

Michelle nodded. 'There are times when he says he'd like to give it a go. But then he thinks about his wife and kid and reckons better not.'

'He's married?'

'Yes,' said Michelle. 'And he does his best to keep out of temptation. According to him, though, there's a lot of it out there.'

'And he thought I was temptation?'

'Yes,' said Michelle.

Maddie still felt a glow of pleasure. So what if this Robbie bloke was apparently propositioned all the time and turned it down because he was a man who was apparently devoted to his own family and wasn't going to risk a bit on the side. Which was kind of nice if somewhat difficult to believe any more.

'So was he expecting me to jump on him or was he just afraid he'd jump on me?' asked Maddie eventually.

'Mutual jumping, that's what he was afraid of,' said Michelle.

Maddie laughed shortly. 'Does it really happen so often?'

'It can if you want it to.' She got into the van. 'I'd better go. I've another call to make.'

'Another woman that Robbie was afraid to see again?'

'No.' This time Michelle's grin was broad. 'A bloke who's just moved into one of those new apartments near the estuary. Young, free, single . . . bet he won't be able to resist me.' She winked at Maddie as she put the van into gear and edged out of the driveway.

Maddie walked back to the house. She still wasn't certain about the outcome of the day. She couldn't help but be flattered that Robbie had apparently found her attractive although she was uneasy that her own interest in him had been so transparent. Nevertheless it was nice to know that someone thought that she was capable of jumping on him and that he was equally capable of jumping on her. There hadn't been much jumping with Conal lately. It was too predictable to be considered jumping on each other.

The girls were watching *Rug Rats* again. She went into the kitchen and filled the kettle. She loved her family, she

really did. She loved being there for them, solving prob-
lems for them, knowing that they could always depend on
her. But she needed to have something else. Something
for her. Something that nobody else could interfere with.
And maybe if she had that then she'd have more to give
to the others too.

She wondered whether she'd be any good at curtain
fitting.